PRAISE FOR THE APPALACHIAN MOUNTAIN MYSTERIES

"**GREAT !! BOOK** Lynda McDaniel can write. Reads like a literary piece." —Wooley, Amazon Vine Voice Reviewer.

"**FIVE STARS!** Lynda McDaniel has that wonderfully appealing way of weaving a story, much in the manner of Fannie Flagg. The tale immediately drew me into the town, the intriguing mystery, and the people. A real treat to read and made me anticipate meeting the characters in yet another installment." —Deb, Amazon Hall of Fame Top 100 Reviewer

"**The most satisfying mystery I've read in ages.**" — Joan Nienhuis, book blogger

"**The story has a wonderful balance of drama, mystery, and suspense** that easily left me wanting more. What made the story that much more appealing is that it is more than a just a cozy mystery, as the author interweaves Della's personal journey of self-discovery and sense of community she finds along the way in the small Appalachian town." —Kathleen Higgins-Anderson, Jersey Girl Book Reviews

"**Marvelous read!** A compelling story told through two remarkable narrators [who] possess the same hopes and dreams for a new life. They describe their home life in such great detail that you like you have

been transported to a small mountain town and are fortunate enough to catch a stunning glimpse into living and working in the deep woods." —Yvette Klobuchar, author of *Brides Unveiled*

"Thoroughly enjoyable and intriguing with descriptive powers and beautiful mountain scenery. Intense family and friend dynamics with character vulnerabilities and complex relationships that steal the reader's heart and make this mystery a must-read." — Pam Franklin, international bestselling author

"*A Life for a Life* is one of the most satisfying books I've read this year. Everything about the book delighted me. *A Life for a Life* has also been compared to *To Kill a Mockingbird.* Both are character-driven and back a strong message of forgiveness, redemption and acceptance." —Ana Manwaring, writer, blogger

"McDaniel's mystery novel delivers a pair of unforgettable crime-solving characters. Using her keen knowledge of the charm (and less than charming features) of life in the North Carolina mountains, she lured me into her story and kept me there. I hope Della, Abit, and the gang will be back!" —Virginia McCullough, award-winning author of *Amber Light*

Your free book is "Waiting for You."

Want to spend more time with Abit Bradshaw and Della Kincaid in Laurel Falls, N.C.? Get your free copy of my prequel novelette, *Waiting for You.*

I've pulled back the curtain on their lives before they met in Laurel Falls—between 1981 and 1984. You'll discover how Abit lost hope of ever having a meaningful life and why Della had to leave Washington, D.C.

Haven't started the series yet? *Waiting for You* will get you started in style.

Get your free copy of *Waiting for You* here:
www.lyndamcdanielbooks.com/free

Murder Ballad Blues

A Mystery Novel

Lynda McDaniel

This novel is a work of fiction. Any references to real
people, events, establishments, organizations, or locales are intended only
to give the fiction a sense of reality and are used fictitiously. All others are
products of the author's imagination.

Published in 2020 by Lynda McDaniel Books

ISBN: 978-1-7346371-2-0

Printed in the United States of America

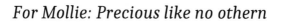

For Mollie: Precious like no othern

Autumn 2005
Harlan County, Kentucky

Prologue: Abit

He was gaining on me, but I couldn't run any faster. The sun had dipped below the mountains, casting dark shadows across my path. As I made my way through the dense forest, I struggled to push bramble and brush outta my way, which only made it easier for him to catch up.

The birds must've been singing, but I couldn't hear a one. Not the hum of insects or the song of frogs. It'd rained the night before, enough to awaken their music, but I didn't catch a single note. Just the beat of blood pounding against my eardrums as I ran for my life.

I knew who was behind me, and I knew he meant me harm. With each breath I thought about my wife, Fiona; our young'un, Conor; and our dog, Mollie, precious like no othern. Thinking of them helped keep me going.

I had no idea where I was headed, just racing through the hills of Harlan County, Kentucky. Years ago, I'd come this way when Fiona and I'd first met. I felt a wave of sadness wash over me that such a happy place now had a taint to it. Or worse. I might die here. Then again, maybe that was exactly the kinda place you wanted when you were facing the end.

Crazy thoughts like that kept pecking at me, like turkey buzzards on carrion.

I grew up in woods like these, though I never spent much time in them. As a boy in Laurel Falls over in North Carolina, I mostly sat round feeling sorry for myself, watching TV, or hanging out in my chair, the one I leaned against the front of Coburn's General Store.

I shook my head, trying to chase away such thoughts. This was no time to worry over my past. I needed to pray I'd have a future.

I caught a break when I rounded a curve and saw the path branch up ahead, one fork sloping downhill in a way that let me slip outta sight before he could see which way I'd taken. Footprints already marked the soft, damp ground, so mine wouldn't stand out.

Just after the turn, the path grew thicker with brush. But that was fine by me. Instead of picking up my pace (a notion my legs were screaming against), I could slow down and hide. I crawled in a rhododendron thicket and tried to quiet my breath. Hard to do while struggling for air, but my only hope was to disappear in the tangle of branches and leaves. A sickly sweet smell from the rhododendron leaves made me queasy, or was that just fear messing with my stomach? I took a deep breath and held it. And listened.

Earlier, back at the barn, I'd done a good job of sneaking up on him. I'd heard a woman scream and ran toward her, careful-like so he wouldn't see me. I had no doubt she was about to become his next victim.

As I snuck alongside the barn, I looked through a knot hole and saw he held a small woman in a chokehold, a gun to her head. And I could hear her crying and offering him money. But by then I knew he wasn't after material reward.

I inched toward the barn door and peered round the opening. He turned toward me. I heard the gun go off, and I ran. My legs ached, my chest cried for mercy, but neither were life threatening—not like the man chasing me. The man the FBI and I were after.

Yeah, you heard me right. Me and the FBI. Abit Bradshaw helping the FBI find a vicious killer of mountain folks. I prayed he didn't add me to his list first.

Spring 2005, Laurel Falls, N.C.
Seven months earlier

Chapter 1: Abit

"I wish they'd hurry up and catch that murderer."

I'd been studying a sad story in the *Mountain Weekly* about a killing when Fiona snuck up behind me and started talking while reading over my shoulder. I flashed back to a time a man on the Metro train in D.C. caught me reading thataway when I was up visiting my friend Della Kincaid. He started shaking his newspaper in my face, shouting at me to cut it out. Of course I'd never do that to Fiona.

"Honey, don't worry about it," I said. "He's not round here. This took place over in Randolph County."

"Well, that's still awfully close for some nutter to be wandering round. Who knows where he's hiding out after drowning that poor woman? Everyone working the night shift at the hospital is on edge."

I tried to console her, telling her life would soon settle down again. Back then, I never dreamed that sort of thing would mess with our lives the way it did.

That evening we headed out to one of our music gigs. Our bluegrass band, the Rollin' Ramblers, had a growing following, which meant we were traveling farther to larger towns and bigger audiences. The band had changed a lot lately; Fiona and I were the only original members left. She still played fiddle and sang vocals, and I sang backup, but I no longer played ole Bessie, my bass fiddle. I'd grown partial to the mandolin Fiona'd given me, the one that'd been passed down through her family in Ireland. I sold Bessie to Rhonda Ross, who replaced me just fine. We'd also added Owen Kent on guitar and Marshall White on banjo. And of course Conor. Somehow, even with all those changes, we had the same sound, maybe better.

Fiona, Conor, Mollie, and I barely fit in her Ford wagon, but we made it. The rest of the members all piled into Owen's van, which was big enough to carry Bessie and the other instruments. We all used to travel in what had oncet been the Rollin' Store bus, but it'd gotten too old to repair. And to be honest, we didn't really need a bus. Back then, we were just playing at being bluegrass rock stars.

As we rode along, I noticed Fiona wasn't saying much, just looking out her window. Then it hit me. We were heading east, toward a venue not all that far from Randleman, where the murder had taken place. That was still a good forty mile southeast of where we were playing, but I knew how her mind worked.

She'd never talk about it with Conor in the backseat, but he was messing round with Mollie, so I took a chance. I put my hand on hers and asked real quiet-like so he couldn't hear, "Are you still worrying about the murder?"

At first Fiona acted like she hadn't heard me, but then she gave a little nod. I told her all the same things I'd said earlier, about him not coming near us.

"Oh, Rabbit, let's not talk about it now."

Rabbit. That's what she called me when she was feeling softer toward me. Back on the first day I saw her, I was so dumbstruck when she asked my name, I said, "Er, Abit." It wasn't just because of her pretty red hair and green eyes. I was fumbling for the right name to tell her: either my nickname, Abit, or my real name, Vester Junior. I hated Daddy's name, and I'd gotten used to being called Abit, even though it wasn't a nice name, either. I came by it when Daddy told everyone, "He's a bit slow," and over time that shortened to Abit. That made him feel better, letting the world know he knew he had a retard (his word). Turned out a lot of my slowness had to do with how people treated me—and how I saw myself.

But I had to hand it to that gal. Oncet we got set up on stage, Fiona didn't bring her worries with her. She played her fiddle and sang with all her heart. And Conor? He may have been only 8 year old, but he brought the house down sawing on his pint-sized fiddle when we played "New River Train." Mollie worked the crowd, too, getting more petting than we could give her in a week.

We got home round eleven, and I put Conor to bed. That evening, the little fella was all keyed up, so I read him a story. It still blew my mind, the idea of *me* reading to anyone, even a young'un. I'd had a time of it in school, lagging so far behind that Daddy yanked me out when I was only 12. When I turned 16, I got a second chance at The Hicks—the Hickson School of American Studies—thanks to Alex Covington, Della's ex-husband and now-boyfriend, or whatever you call it at their age. That was where I'd learned mountain music and woodworking, two things that saved my life.

When I finished the story, I set the book down on his nightstand. Conor's eyes were closed, and I tried not to disturb him. I reached to turn out his cowboy-on-a-horse lamp, the one I'd found last year when I was cleaning out Mama's old house.

"Daddy," Conor said, giving me a start, "tell me a story."

"I just did, son."

"No, *tell* me one. About when you were my age."

A bad feeling washed over me, close to being sick to my stomach. My boy didn't need to hear any of *those* tales. I'd never told him one; I just let him think his grandparents were as fine as a little boy needed to believe. But now I regretted being so careful. Maybe I'd cut off too much of my life, working so hard to make his different. Surely there was *something* I could share.

He was looking at me funny when Annie Totherow popped into my head. I was older than Conor when I first met her, but that wouldn't matter. I started wondering what'd happened to her—it'd been years since I'd thought of Annie—and I hoped things had turned out good for her.

"Daddy!"

"Okay, okay," I said, chuckling, "here goes."

I wove a tale of happiness on the playground and having fun at Annie's family home when I went to buy honey, which her daddy was famous for throughout the county and beyond. I cleaned up my childhood good enough for a Hallmark card. It wasn't a lie—those really were good times. Conor just didn't need to know what went on in between. By the time I was running outta ideas, I looked over and his eyes were shut tight. Damned if he didn't have a little smile on his face.

I stopped by our bedroom to kiss Fiona goodnight before heading to my woodshop in the barn. I needed to finish a coupla dining-table orders (something I always seemed to put off, for some reason), but I also needed some thinking time. I'd put up a good front to Fiona about the murder, not wanting her to know it'd unsettled me too. I knew bad people lived amongst us or could slip in tomorrow. Della and I'd worked on some nasty crimes done by people we'd thought were real nice. Those were the kind that threw you. Scoundrels and con artists putting on a show of being loving parents, social workers, shopkeepers—then doing the meanest things right in your own hometown.

It was long after one o'clock before I'd smoothed out enough rough wood and raw feelings to think about getting some sleep.

Summer 2005, Laurel Falls, N.C.

Chapter 2: Della

My day started deceptively like every other—coffee, shower, breakfast before heading down the steps to my store, Coburn's General Store.

I'd gotten a reputation for complaining about the store, but really, that was no more than the usual grumblings about any workaday job. I was actually quite fond of the old place (established 1910, or so the sign over the door said).

When I'd bought it in 1984 from Abit Bradshaw's father, the store and apartment above it were in shambles. All these years later, I still marveled at the transformation. Everything I'd ever learned, crafted, or enjoyed doing showed up somewhere in the renovated spaces. I had the kitchen I'd always wanted with a window framing an ocean of mountain peaks stretching toward the distant horizon. The sunsets still dazzled me.

And I still got a kick out of ordering new items for the store shelves. Some sold well, others were losers, but even the worst-case scenario wasn't bad—I got to eat my mistakes, literally. Over the years, I'd had to find new suppliers when they quit, gave up, or moved on. Even a year later, customers still complained about missing the preserves and pickles from my old friend Cleva Hall.

At 88, Cleva was long retired from being a school principal and recently retired from the hard work of putting food by. "Why would I go to all that trouble anymore?" she'd asked the last time I tried to order jams and piccalilli, her mood uncharacteristically dark that day.

For the most part, though, she was the happy, true friend I'd valued for more than twenty years. I didn't see her as much since she'd moved to Boone to live with her favorite niece, but we made a point of having lunch together a couple of times a month. And I enjoyed getting over to the "big city" of Boone.

I closed my apartment door and headed downstairs, trying not to spill my coffee. As I reached the bottom step, I saw something in my Jeep that wasn't there the evening before. Through the windshield I could see a man asleep in the backseat. We didn't lock up much in Laurel Falls. Oh sure, I secured the store every evening, but cars and homes seemed safe enough without the encumbrance of keys.

It was way too early for a confrontation of any kind. I figured whoever it was would wake up and leave of his own accord once the sun turned the Jeep into a sauna. When I turned toward the front door, though, something caught my eye. An apricot-colored waistcoat, which at that moment began rising to a sitting position.

"Hello, hello, hello," said Nigel Steadman, rubbing his eyes like a toddler. "I didn't want to disturb you when I got in so late last night. You know how those trains and buses to Timbuktu are."

"Yes, I do know all about that. What I don't know is why you were on one. And wait a minute. There aren't any buses to Laurel Falls that time of night."

"I did have to resort to a bit of hitchhiking," Nigel said, faking a chuckle. He looked forlorn as he brushed imaginary lint off his shirt in a vain effort to neaten his appearance.

"Well, I'm glad you got here safely, but why were you sleeping in my car? You should have come up and stretched out on the couch. You know I leave the door unlocked—and you're always welcome."

Nigel and I went way back to my crime reporter days in D.C. A British subject, he came to America to ply his trade—forgery, something he was extremely good at. I'd interviewed him when I was working on a story about the shady dealings of some other criminals, and he'd provided invaluable, hard-to-find background. I earned kudos for that series, and I'd been grateful to Nigel ever since. In the process, something clicked between us, and we'd stayed in touch.

"I'm sure you're right, my dear, but I didn't want to be a bother." As he extricated himself from the Jeep, he tugged on his waistcoat and tried to press the wrinkles out of his suit. He ran his fingers through his silvery hair, but he still looked bedraggled.

"Never mind all that," I said as I grabbed him into a hug. "Good to see you, for whatever reason."

When he broke the embrace, we both stood there, self-consciously at a loss for words. I was still in shock. I'd never seen Nigel quite so nonplussed—and unkempt. He had the beginnings of a beard, and he'd lost his usual sartorial splendor somewhere en route. "Now I know *how* you got here, but that doesn't explain *why* you're here."

Before I finished that thought, I *knew*. Nigel, who'd turned over a new leaf when the feds offered him the choice of jail or working for the Treasury Department, had turned that leaf over again.

And he knew I knew. He looked anywhere but at me—at his dusty wingtips, the missing button on his waistcoat, even the mailbox out front of the store. Eventually I cleared my throat and plowed ahead. "Come on, Nigel, I don't think it was my winning personality that made you hop on a train to Laurel Falls."

As his hands scoured his stubbly face, he looked so unsettled, I changed my tack. "Hold on. Let's go upstairs and get you some breakfast and a shower. When you're ready, come down to the store, and we'll talk." He nodded and started for the steps. "Wait a minute. Where's your suitcase?"

"Er, I didn't have time to pack."

Chapter 3: Abit

"Rabbit, there's a man coming up the drive."

Fiona was funny about strangers arriving unannounced at our farm. She was as friendly a person as I'd ever met, but she was a protective mama bear when it came to her family, especially when Conor was home. I swear if the postman came up to the house every day, instead of leaving our mail in our box down at the road, she'd still call out, "Rabbit, there's a man coming up the drive."

I wasn't worried. This guy looked old and kinda stooped over. We had our share of folks coming round, needing a place to settle for an evening or two. I'd've let them stay in our guestroom, the one I'd built at the west end of our barn; sometimes Fiona and Conor and I went out there just for fun, like we were on vacation. But Fiona said she didn't want the drifters to get too comfortable. Instead, I'd found an old bed frame left in the barn by the last owners and put an inexpensive but new mattress on it. That plus a few blankets and a pillow served them better than most.

When I was growing up, our barn had what was called hobo signs marked on it, the way they did when Daddy was a boy, letting fellow travelers know if it was a good place or a mean one. Kinda like AAA does now for motels. It was my hope we'd get good signs, if travelers still did that kinda thing.

We were seeing more drifters. It'd always been tough making a living in these parts, but now folks all over the country were feeling the pinch of hard times. I had trouble understanding that, given how rich our country was, but that seemed to be the way of the world. All these so-called Christians talking about pulling themselves up by their bootstraps, when they knew good and well they'd had plenty of help along the way. I had to wonder what they were daydreaming about every Sunday when the preacher read from the Bible how Jesus wanted us to help those in need. Mama made me go to her church, and while I never took to their notions of no dancing, no music, no being different, now and again something would strike me deep down and stick with me.

I figured Christianity was a fine plan, if only people would *practice* it. Like trying to look out for one anothern, especially the little children and those who didn't have much. I worked at living thataway, though I failed plenty of times, like when I'd get pissed at somebody for nothing that really mattered or forget to do what I'd promised Conor. But my life was better for trying.

I went to greet the old man, and Conor came running outta the house to follow me. I watched over my shoulder for Fiona. She'd've called him back in if she'd seen us, but I figured the boy needed to be round different kinds of people. Besides, we'd never had a lick of trouble from the drifters. Maybe because of an evening Fiona always packed an aluminum pie tin full of chicken and beans and cornbread and sent me out with it.

"Can I help you?" I asked, Conor hanging on to my overalls.

"Anywhere a man could bed down?" he asked, his voice gravely and tired.

"We do, for a night or two. Let me show you." We went to the back of the barn, and he seemed pleased at the humble setup.

"Hi," Conor said, looking round my leg.

The man's face broke into a big smile, and he wiggled his fingers at Conor, who wiggled his back. I realized then the man was younger than I'd thought from a distance. I mentioned we'd rustle up some supper for him, and I swear his bloodshot eyes got wet. We excused ourselves 'til suppertime.

He ended up staying two nights. On the third morning, I headed out before breakfast to ask him to move on, but he was already gone, the bedding folded neatly. I noticed something atop the pile of blankets. A harmonica. At first I thought he'd accidentally left it behind, but then I knew it was for Conor. His way of saying thanks.

I didn't show it to Fiona 'til I'd scrubbed it good. She'd've had me soak it in bleach or boiling water. (Not really—she was a fine musician and wouldn't do that to an instrument.) When she came in asking me what I was doing, I held up the harmonica and told her about the man leaving it for Conor. She smiled. I knew she was thinking the same as me, that someone with practically nothing had given our boy a gift, a kindness not to be overlooked.

By the time I finally got over to my woodshop, the morning was shot. I started banging round, trying to hurry things. Deadlines always made me nervous, at least when they got close.

"Chill, man."

That would be Shiloh, aka Bob Greene, a man (more like a growed-up boy) who helped me three days a week in the shop. We'd met at The Hicks, where he learned to make the finest dovetail joints and finish furniture with a patience I didn't have. More recently, he'd perfected three-way miter joints that made our furniture prettier than ever.

We'd worked together five or six year, and he had this uncanny way of knowing what was going through my head—though at that moment I hoped he couldn't pick up on me thinking what a jerk he could be sometimes. All ashram this and guru that. Over the years, I'd come to realize he was Mr. Enlightenment as long as it had nothing to do with *his* life.

I carried on like that, railing in my head about everything I could think of that wasn't going right: Shiloh, money, and murder at the top of the list. Then I saw Mollie in the corner of my eye. She liked to hang out with me in my shop and somehow never got underfoot, though she did catch her share of sawdust. Late in the day, when we'd head for the house, she'd comb her wiry black-and-white fur—that shaking all over dogs do—and a cloud of dust would rise up and blow away in the breeze. Just looking at our calm, trusting dog made all my petty thoughts fly off, not unlike that sawdust.

Besides, I felt lucky I'd found a way to earn a living I loved, and Shiloh helped make that happen. Money was tight sometimes, but we managed. Not sure why he got under my skin so that day, except maybe his patchouli was on extra thick. Or maybe it was all the commotion about that murder. Whatever, I had a case of the grumps, and Shiloh was right. I did need to chill.

A little later, when we were talking over how best to inset a piece of marquetry in a sideboard, the phone rang. For oncet it was good news.

Chapter 4: Della

I called Abit to tell him his old buddy was back in town. Then I brought out the percolator and sat down in a rocker across from Nigel. We drank our coffee in silence, until he felt ready to explain what was going on. "I believe I told you the Treasury Department made me retire a few months ago," he offered as an opener.

"Yeah, you did, and I figured it was about time. I knew lots of folks who had to retire well before the age you are now."

"Ah, yes, don't remind me. I am well past mandated retirement, but they'd kept me on because, well, I'm so good at what I do." He paused, then added, "Now don't give me that raised-eyebrow look. I'm not bragging, it's true."

"I know it's true—but it's also true those talents got you in a load of trouble in the past. What's the story this time?"

"I'm getting to that." Nigel got up, brushing crumbs from his rumpled suit, though he'd managed to iron it upstairs and look somewhat presentable after a hot shower and close shave. He walked to the back and helped himself to more coffee. He drank tea in the afternoons, but for his elevenses he preferred coffee. When he sat back down, he continued. "Some bureaucrat declared I was too old to work there. As if crime—and outsmarting it—knows time."

"Okay, but I haven't heard anything that would necessitate your skipping town in the middle of the night."

"It wasn't the middle of the night. You know that train schedule better than I. I got *here*, Timbuktu, in the middle of the night." I nodded, conceding that volley, then gestured for him to go on. "So back to D.C. You know me. I'm not used to sitting around doing nothing, and I was feeling, well, all sixes and sevens."

"That has a financial ring to it."

He managed a wan smile. "Yes, I felt restless, and of course that led to itchy fingers. That's the only reason. I don't need the money. I was just bored."

"Oh, Nigel. What have you gotten yourself into?" Years ago I'd made a vow to stop sticking my nose in other people's business. I'd had varying degrees of success with that, but in this case, Nigel had dumped this unholy mess in my lap.

His face flushed. "A bit of bother, I'm afraid. Seems the man I was doing forgery for wasn't some hapless bloke, but rather a gangster of what I've only recently learned is considerable ill repute. RICO, if you catch my drift. And to make matters worse, the feds think *I'm* the man RICO paid me to forge the signatures of. Oh, it's all very complicated, and quite unforeseeable, but needless to say, I couldn't stay in D.C. And I had nowhere else to go. My daughter and her children moved to New York recently, but that turned into a blessing. Thank heavens they're not close by in case RICO or the feds come looking and ..."

"Oh great," I interrupted. "So instead they follow you down here to *us*!"

"Now, now, of course not, my dear. The feds aren't looking for Nigel Steadman—they don't realize it's a forgery because I did such a good job signing for Rodney Highsmith." He looked so pleased with his abilities, I felt like growling at him. He hurried ahead with a somewhat plausible explanation. "They're looking for Highsmith, and no one—RICO, Highsmith, the feds—have any idea where *I* am. This is the last place any of them would look. And I'm good about covering my tracks. I forged a few documents so this boyo I know could take a long trip to Mexico—as Highsmith. It's just a red herring, but it will throw them off track for some precious weeks. He's still down there on a beach somewhere with enough money to travel before returning home to his real life as Michael Monahan."

I wasn't consoled. "One crime begets three or four. Isn't this how you got caught before?"

"Let's not get into all that past history."

"What other kind is there?"

He looked flummoxed. "I'm sorry, my dear. What is your question?" He turned his hand flamboyantly like Pavarotti singing *La donna è mobile*.

"There's only one kind of history, Nigel. Past. Which is what your penchant for forgery should have been. Quit stalling—and don't you dare wave your hand at me again, dismissing me as though I were just being silly. I wish I were."

Just then the bell over the door rang.

Chapter 5: Nigel

Luckily, some customers came in and saved me from Della's grilling. She let it go, at least for a time, and introduced me as her friend from Washington, D.C. We all nodded and smiled at each other in that polite, if somewhat awkward, social custom in the States. Rather a sweet gesture on Della's part, as though I were a visiting dignitary from the nation's capital. Unfortunately, I knew there wasn't a speck of dignity about what brought me to Laurel Falls.

An older woman grabbed my arm rather brusquely and walked me over to the cheese counter. "What is your favorite English cheese, Mr. Steadman?" she asked. I quickly determined that Della didn't stock Stilton, and since I didn't want to diminish her offerings, I lied and said Wensleydale, which sat foremost in the case. It's a fine cheese, just not my personal favorite. But that woman wasn't really cheese shopping, was she?

Within minutes another customer butted in to ask me about tea and scones and everything British with the urgency of someone expecting the Queen to arrive any minute for tea. I'd lived in America almost as long as ole Blighty, but I played along. Anything to avoid Della's probing, reporterly questions.

A third woman (Della later informed me she was one of the posh second-home customers) cornered me about

England, inquiring where she should visit on her trip later that summer. She actually drew herself so close to me, I worried she might lay a hit and miss*on me.

After that flurry of customers, I managed to avoid telling Della anything more about my troubles for the rest of the day. I assumed it would all come out in the days ahead.

It did. Just not the way anyone wanted.

* Cockney rhyming slang for *kiss*. See glossary in the back for more words and definitions.

Chapter 6: Abit

We had anothern.

This killing came a coupla months after the first one, only this time the victim was a man, killed with an ax. I dreaded Fiona finding out where it happened—only thirty mile west of here in Kona, N.C. She'd say it was a dark cloud of menace drifting dangerously close to our home.

And sure enough, she was beside herself after a long drive home from the hospital, no doubt fear riding shotgun the whole way. Not that Fiona was a flibbertigibbet. Far from it. But like I'd said, she was a mama bear about her family, and our well-being moved her deeper than most.

Fiona had one of those cell phones, though half the time she couldn't get a signal. They said the mountains made it harder, and so did metal roofs. We had plenty of both. I got it why *she* needed one, but *I* didn't want to go dragging the outside world into my life all hours of the day. Besides, I was usually at home or in my shop, so what was the point? If, for instance, there was an emergency with Conor while I'd gone into town, anyone trying to reach me knew to check with Della.

What really got me was when people walked in the woods and jabbered on those things. They'd often travelled long distances to get up here, away from it all, and yet they'd walk right by a stand of Jack-in-the-pulpits or a blooming thicket of laurel while talking to someone who, more than likely, they needed a break from, which was why they were up here in the first place. Or they walked round town talking on them, nearly getting run over by Elbert Totherow's delivery truck. (That almost happened a week ago.) No, I planned to stick to the phone I had at home and live my life wherever I happened to be at that moment.

I heard Fiona carrying on about how the killer was now going after men, too, so it was long past time for me to have a cell phone. "Why, Shug?" I asked. "So I can shine the flashlight in the killer's eyes? Or bash him in the nose with it?"

"Oh, Rabbit, don't be such a pillock. So you can call for help. If not for your own sorry arse, at least for Conor's sake."

"But think about it. By the time the law got way out here, I'd be long dead."

That set her off crying, and I could see how my comment wasn't helpful. I told her I was sorry about a million times and slipped off to make her a cup of tea. As she sipped it, she said I'd made a crackin' good one, so I knew she wasn't too mad at me.

I'd hoped that would smooth over everything, and she'd forget all about that phone. But the next day, she was upset all over again when she got home from work. (I couldn't help but picture patients getting jabbed harder with a needle or squeezed tighter with the blood pressure cuff when those nurses came back from a break where they'd talked nonstop about the murders.)

"Shug, something bad is happening somewhere all the time," I said, thinking that would console her. "People get laid off work, their mama and daddy die, their dogs get sick. There isn't a day that goes by without sorrow tagging along. We can't go borrowing trouble that's not on our doorstep."

"But this *is* on our doorstep!" I heard her foot stamp under the dining table.

Not really, but I didn't know what else to say, so I just listened. And to be honest, when she started repeating herself, my mind kept traveling out to the barn where orders were waiting.

"You're not listening to me, but I'm serious. This is something that could come home to roost. I had a shiver."

Now *that* caught my attention. Fiona had some Irish gypsy in her. Whether she felt shivers or geese walking over graves, she knew things before they happened. She was a good Catholic, but she'd held on to her pagan ancestry too.

We carried on like that for a while, and I kept trying to downplay the murders. That wasn't to say they didn't worry me. I felt uneasy too, not only about the sorrow they brought but as if something I needed to know had been laid out before me, yet just outta reach.

Chapter 7: Abit

The next Saturday after Fiona left for work, I figured it was a good time to take Conor and Mollie to Coburn's. Earlier that week I'd had some orders that'd slipped past their promise date, and much as I'd wanted to see my old friend Nigel, I'd needed to finish them before heading into town.

We all piled into my truck, and when we pulled up at Coburn's, Conor ran into the store ahead of me. Della always made a fuss over him and gave him some kinda treat his mama didn't usually let him have. That day it was a cookie I wouldn't't've minded eating myself, but she didn't offer me one. (Then again, I reckon she didn't feel the need to offer; she'd always given me anything I'd asked for.)

I looked round for Nigel. When I spotted him standing near the register with a flock of women surrounding him, I had to work hard at not laughing.

Oh sure, his silvery hair still looked dapper, what Della called his Fred Astaire look. And I could hear that he still spoke in that magical, proper way. What got me tickled was how he was dressed in a baggy flannel shirt, jeans rolled up at the hem, and a striped apron.

I managed to keep a straight face until I saw Della looking at me, her eyebrow raised that way she does. I had to step outside to get myself together; I didn't want Nigel seeing me laughing at him. Fortunately, he hadn't noticed me, what with all the women fluttering round. When I came back in, I whispered to Della, "What happened to his waistcoat? I've never seen him without it."

"Oh, he wore it, all right. And wore it. And wore it. I finally scrounged up some of Alex's old clothes and forced him to wear them. His suit was starting to smell, in part because he'd been living in it for days. And, as you may recall, the Brits don't favor deodorant all that much."

"Well, that just makes him fit in round here." I'd tried to make her smile, but she was too worked up. "So why doesn't he just change his clothes?"

"He doesn't have any. He came in a hurry." I was about to ask why when she went on. "When he got a look at himself dressed like that," she said, pointing at his hillbilly outfit, "he tried to put his suit back on, but I wouldn't let him. So go easy on him, okay?"

"Not a problem, now that I'm over the shock. I just need to wait for my turn with him." I nodded toward some woman making a fuss about the English marmalade Della stocked. "Do they buy anything, or do they just coo over him?"

"Oh, sales are up, which is a good thing, and he actually helps a lot."

I knew Della could use an extra hand ever since Mary Lou married the sheriff, which, for some reason, meant she wasn't working at Coburn's.

"As you can see, he's popular with the women," Della said, blowing her bangs up as she let out a big sigh. You didn't need to be the smartest guy in the room to sense there was more to the story. I asked. "Oh, it's just close quarters upstairs," she explained, smiling kinda sad-like. "I love the guy, but with Alex coming down …"

"Maybe I can help," I said, an idea popping into my head.

"Oh, that would be great, Abit!"

I wasn't sure what she was on about since I hadn't told her yet what I had in mind. "You mentioning Alex made me remember how he bought me all those clothes back when I was a kid. I'll never forget that. It was the start of the new me. And in a way, this is a new Nigel. Down in the hills, without his wardrobe, and where it sounds like he plans to stay a while. What I'm trying to say is I want to take him clothes shopping."

"I do remember that day," Della said, smiling. "I didn't even recognize you at first. But this isn't about the start of a new Nigel—it's more like a return to the old Nigel. And I doubt he'd go along with buying anything from the local dry goods store. He's used to custom tailoring."

"Well, I planned to buy them for him."

Della got one of her looks. "I'd rather you did something else."

Just then Nigel called out, "Hello, hello, hello!" The women had gotten what they wanted (from the looks of things, it wasn't just food), and Nigel wandered over. I gave him a big bear hug, something that always flustered him. I reckon the men in England hadn't learned the abiding pleasure of throwing their arms round someone they hadn't seen in a while.

We talked about all the family things, though mostly about mine: *How's your wife, Fiona? Fine. And your little boy, Conor? He's out back; you won't believe how big he's gotten. And your woodworking? Keeping me and Shiloh busy.*

Then I asked about his daughter and grandkids. No way was I gonna wade into his business matters. From the little Della had told me, it didn't sound good.

As these things had a way of doing, the recent murders came up. Della didn't seem that worried. After all those years living in D.C. chasing crime stories, I reckon it would take one happening right in Laurel Falls to get her riled. All she said was she was sorry for the families left behind. Nigel nodded.

When we'd finished catching up, Nigel asked Della if he could take a break. I looked at my watch, and sure enough, just like at home with Fiona, Nigel needed his teatime. "I'll just pop up the pears for a Rosie."

I musta looked lost (I was) because Della piped up, "He's going upstairs for a cup of tea."

"How'd you know that?"

"What else? I wrote a story on Cockney rhyming slang years ago, and it so fascinated me, I've never forgotten some of the more colorful words." Della watched Nigel close the front door after him, and then looked at me kinda funny.

"What?" I asked.

"I need a favor."

"Anything."

"I want Nigel to stay in your guestroom." I musta looked funny right back at her, because she added, "You said *anything*."

"Look I love the guy, too, but …" She'd caught me off guard. I got it when she explained that after a week together in her small apartment, she was tired of having a houseguest. Not so much Nigel—anybody. Alex was the only exception, and he was heading down from his home in D.C. in a few days oncet he finished writing some story about the president trying to take away Social Security. Della and I had talked that over, especially because folks round here had been in a dither. They counted on that check more than others might. Lots of them had worked long hours at the t-shirt factory and had that money taken out of their pockets each week. It seemed mean-spirited to have it taken away twicet.

Anyways, Della was right to ask. We did have space in our guestroom in the barn. Shiloh had been staying there, paying a small amount of rent, but he'd moved out recently, or rather *in* with his latest girlfriend.

"I don't think Nigel will be any trouble," she went on. "He's started to relax, feeling safe in our remote outpost, as he calls it. I hate to mention that he needs to move on, and I keep putting it off. But if you offered for him to stay at your farm, that would feel different. He'd love it. And he's got plenty of money, so you could charge him rent."

Later after supper, when I told Fiona about Nigel, she insisted he stay rent free as long as he liked. She reminded me that without him and his story about second chances (and some strong nudges while I was visiting Della in D.C.), we might never've gotten back together after she'd left me for anothern—which meant we wouldn't have Conor. She knew that would win me over. Besides, I figured she wanted a fellow tea drinker round.

Turned out, she got that and a whole lot more.

Chapter 8: Abit

I started looking at our summer from Conor's view, and I didn't like what I saw. Oh sure, the little tyke made the most of any given day. He read books and worked on a model airplane I'd bought him last time I went into town. He and Mollie played endless games of tug of war, and he loved going over to "Uncle" Nigel's room for elevenses on mornings Nigel had off.

And we were enjoying our best summer of music gigs, which kept him busy practicing his fiddle and harmonica. But both Fiona and I had been awful busy with work, and I knew he'd overheard us talking about the murders. I wanted to do something extra nice for him.

I went down the drive to get our mail, and I was leafing through one of those free circulars when something jumped off the page at me. That evening, holding up the ad from the paper, I told Conor and Fiona I wanted us to go to Lake Winnepesaukah over near Chattanooga. I expected them to ask what in the world that was, but Conor jumped up and hugged me round my legs. I looked at Fiona.

"He had a little friend from school visit there," she said, ruffling his hair. "He came home begging to go, and with all the uproar about, you know, Randleman and Kona, I forgot to mention it."

I told them I'd been wanting to go since I'd heard about it at The Hicks, which made Conor start dancing round, I guess from the delight of sharing this hankering with his daddy. One of the boys at The Hicks lived in Chattanooga and went every year, sometimes more than oncet a summer.

We all went to bed looking forward to the trip, not realizing how it would change everything.

The sun wasn't up yet when we left that Saturday. The night before, Fiona packed a lunch, and I got her wagon ready for the road. The next morning, Conor was sound asleep when I carried him in the dark to the car and settled him in the backseat.

It was a good four-hour drive, but we made it fun with stories, songs, and apples dipped in peanut butter, which Conor got all over his face. Just before Chattanooga, we stopped at a roadside table and ate some of Fiona's fine fried chicken (you'd've thought she was reared right here in the mountains instead of Clifden, Ireland) along with my coleslaw. I'd even learned to bake biscuits, which were a little tough, but with enough butter and Mrs. Ledford's strawberry jam, they tasted just fine.

When we finally reached Lake Winnie, as they'd started calling it, we laughed as Conor raced first to a beautiful white wood rollercoaster then over to the antique carrousel and old-timey Ferris wheel. I saw from the look on his face he couldn't figure out why we hadn't done this sooner. To be honest, I couldn't either.

We watched as our boy steered his first-ever ride—an airplane going round in a big circle one foot offa the ground—with the firmness of purpose of a 747 pilot. I had to turn away when my eyes filled up, afraid Fiona would notice. I thought I heard her scoff at me, but when I looked over, she was trying to cover her own tears with a fake cough.

Oncet he'd ridden all the little-kid rides, he talked me and Fiona into going on the rollercoaster. We all squeezed into one car and wedged Conor in the middle for safety, if there was such a thing on a rollercoaster. We rode it twicet and then the Ferris wheel. I'd never been to a park like this in my thirty-some year, and it was possible I was having even more fun than Conor.

Until I rode The Scrambler. Fiona took one look at me after that ride and offered to take Conor on a few more while things settled down for me. I walked over to the lake in the middle of the park, filled with some kinda huge fish. I was watching them glide round when a security guard sauntered over.

"Biggest damn carp I've ever seen," he said as a three-footer swam by. He stood about six foot three like me, though he was bigger round the middle. You could tell he liked wearing a security guard uniform, and to be fair, he looked smart in it. When he took off his cap to wipe his brow, I could see his white hair cut short, military-style.

I reckon he was bored and wanted to shoot the breeze. I mean, other than a little roughhousing, what did he need to secure in an amusement park?

We talked for a while, the way men back home did over a Dr. Pepper on a hot summer day. We exchanged names—his was Leonard. He looked puzzled when I told him mine, but I just kept talking; I'm not the first person in the world with a peculiar name. When he asked where I was from and I told him, his eyes got big. "Oh, over where all them murders are happening."

When I said, "Just two," he looked at me like I was Jack the Ripper. I guess it did sound hard-hearted, as though two weren't two too many. I didn't know how to explain myself, so I just asked, "How'd you hear about them?"

"News like that travels fast," he said, straightening his uniform and putting his cap back on. He bowed out his chest before saying, "You know, we had a spell of it over in this part of the state about five years ago. Sounded a good bit like what you're going through." I nodded the way people do when they want the talker to go on. "A young woman from somewhere around Knoxville got beaten to death with a piece of stove wood, and some other girl got killed; I believe she was suffocated. We never caught the guy."

I'd been staring at those crazy fish while he talked, not focusing on every word 'til he said "we" and "caught." When I looked up, Leonard told me he still worked on the police force back then—just moonlighted at the park on the weekends until he retired from the force last year. "But the lead detectives on the case never made much headway. A real shame. As you can imagine, the families were—are—torn up. Now what was the second girl's name? She was from Chattanooga, and I should know her name." He hemmed and hawed a while and finally added, "Oh, yeah, Mimi Allen."

And just like that, I got that feeling again that something important had been said, but I couldn't put my finger on it. Fiona had her shivers, but my signs weren't as clear.

I was glad when I saw Fiona and Conor heading our way. I introduced them, and Leonard tipped his cap and gave a Lake Winnie deputy's badge to Conor. Fiona pinned it on his t-shirt, and it just killed me how tickled that boy was with his simple gift.

On the trip home, as we wound through the mountains, I kept thinking about a different trip—the one through Virginia, back in 1989 when I was chasing those con artists who'd fleeced me and The Hicks. And when I met Fiona. I loved that story so much that even though I knew Fiona had lived it and Conor had heard it a dozen times, I started telling it again.

"Daddy, I've heard that one before," Conor said, but like any good storyteller, that didn't stop me. I saw Fiona wink at Conor as I took us through Virginia and up into Kentucky and back. Seemed to help get us home faster. Conor fell asleep before we got to Murphy, which gave me a chance to tell Fiona what Leonard had said about the killings five year ago. I told her about the funny feeling I had too.

"I don't like any of this," was all she'd say. She reached back and covered Conor with her jacket.

Oncet home, after we tucked Conor into his bed, Fiona and I weren't far behind.

Chapter 9: Abit

A bad dream splintered my sleep.

I usually didn't remember dreams, but this one was clear as a drive-in movie. Some guy—I couldn't see his face—came to one of our gigs and started dancing with women at the show. As we played different songs, one by one the women began to disappear, vanishing from his arms. When he grabbed Fiona, I woke up in a panic.

"Rabbit, what is it?" Fiona mumbled, her head buried in her pillow. I knew I couldn't tell her about it, what with all her superstitions, so I just made out like the dream had already left me. "Well, I'm sure it's because of these damned murders," she said as she burrowed deeper under the covers.

"Don't worry, Shug. It was just about our music." That much was true, and she seemed to accept it.

I had a devil of a time getting back to sleep. I kept thinking about what Leonard had said, and it stirred something inside me about the music playing in the dream. I tried to remember which tunes, but they were just out of reach. At a guess, I'd've said they were ballads. After a while, I slipped back to sleep and mercifully didn't dream, at least that I recalled.

The next morning, Fiona asked me again about my dream. While I got the coffee started, I told her some of what I could remember, sticking to the ballad parts. When she went on about how we were spending too much time thinking—and dreaming—about the murders, I wanted to ask why, then, was she bringing them up again, but I didn't want to start our day off wrong.

Conor came wandering into the kitchen, still sleepy and looking for his breakfast. Fiona grabbed him and hugged him 'til he squirmed. "Conor, darlin', breakfast will be ready in a little while. Why don't you go out to the living room and play with Mollie?" He gave her an odd look, but turned round and did what she asked. Then she whispered, "These goings-on are scaring me. I know we can't ignore them, but I don't want *you* getting involved."

"Well, which is it?" I asked, keeping my voice low, though I'd bet you a dollar Conor was listening just beyond the doorway. "Do you want to spend time thinking about this, maybe doing something about it, or do you want to ignore it?"

"I just know how you and Della get yourselves involved in these kinds of things, and I worry about you putting yourself in danger."

"I don't much like it myself, but when something important makes itself known, do you just turn and run because it's not convenient? How well do you think I'd sleep if I did nothing and this killer kept on and on?"

"Rabbit, that's what the sheriff is for."

"Most of the time, but I'm working on something they'd never think of. Not even one of those fancy profilers you see on TV. I believe music, *our* music, is somehow key to what's going on, and that's likely not anywhere on their radar. I don't know exactly how it all plays out yet, but I'm working on it. Then I'll go to the sheriff."

Fiona went real quiet-like. I knew her well enough to know she wasn't finished. "What? What are you thinking now?"

"Your father complex."

"I'll admit Daddy was plenty complex, but ..."

"No, honey, it's a psychological term. It means you're still trying to please Vester, something that's never gonna happen, even if he were still alive."

"That's the stupidest thing I ever heard." I knew she'd been taking some psychology courses through work, and I'd worried when she signed up that she'd bring all that home. And she had, standing there sounding all high and mighty. "I *don't* want Daddy back in my life."

"He's not *back* in your life because he's never *left*."

Now that stung. I didn't like people thinking they knew what was going on inside me. Then she came over and hugged me. "Will you pay attention to when you're doing something just to please him, wherever he may be looking down from? Ask yourself if it's what *you* want or are you trying to win his favor, albeit through a different authority figure?"

She had me there. I didn't understand all that she'd just said, but if that complex started with having a father who beat you down to nothing, mostly with his words but sometimes his fists, then I was its poster child. In a flash I saw Daddy standing there, lording over me. But he wasn't alone—I saw Sheriff Brower, the one before our current sheriff, Aaron Horne, along with my school principal, Mr. Donnelly; the gym teacher, Tony Leland, and some I couldn't quite make out. I was starting to see her point, but I told her I needed to think on it.

"I hope you will, Abit. And be careful. I see what comes into the ER, and there are enough crazies out there to go round—and round. You know, it could be more than one person. What if a couple of blokes are killing people?"

"Oh, I know it's one man doing all this."

"Oh, yeah, and how's that?"

"I just do. You aren't the only one who knows things."

Ever since Lake Winnie, I'd had a strong sense those Tennessee murders were tied to ours. I didn't want to worry Fiona, so I told her I was still looking into what Leonard had told us. That part was true. "Besides," I added, thinking I'd thought of the perfect way to end the conversation, "there's too big a gap in time between those Tennessee killings and ours."

"Not if the killer were in jail or a mental hospital," Fiona said, getting right back into it all. "He could've been put away all this time and just got out a few months ago."

She finished her coffee and got up to make Conor an egg-in-a-hole. That was a kind of kiddie food she grew up with, but truth be known I loved it too. I felt like a fool when she made me beg her to make me one, but I did it. Then I grabbed her and kissed her.

When I let go, she got down to frying the egg in a hole cut outta the middle of a piece of buttered bread. Some recipes say toss out the hole, but Fiona's too tight for that. She browned it separate and served it with marmalade.

She called Conor in and added, "Maybe during one of my breaks I could do a little work on the computer." (We didn't have one at home.) "I'll let you know what I find out."

Chapter 10: Abit

"I don't believe I've ever seen jeans and a flannel shirt look quite so, well, tailored."

Mr. Tate, owner of Tate's Dry Goods, was admiring how good Nigel looked in his new duds. I had to agree. Those clothes of Alex's didn't fit him worth a lick, but when he got his proper size, you'd've sworn he'd had them made custom.

And he knew it. It didn't take much prodding to get Nigel to model everything he was trying on. Seemed as though oncet he was over the blow of wearing flannel shirts and denim pants instead of silk suits and velvet waistcoats, he really got into it.

While he was hamming it up, making us double over laughing as he twirled and pointed one toe forward with his hands on his hips like some fashion model on TV, I noticed one of the sales clerks taking an awful lot of notice. (Of course how could you *not* with the show Nigel was putting on?) I hadn't ever seen this guy round, but then again, I didn't get out much anymore. I had a lot of furniture orders—plus a family to spend time with.

But he had a weaselly way about him. A thin mustache that I'd swear looked drawed on. Longish hair with Brylcreem running through it, looking more greasy than groomed. Short and stocky—but strong. Not somebody I'd want to mess with. I noticed he kept staring even after Nigel quit joking round. Then again, he was probably just bored with refolding shirts people messed up and left for him to tidy.

When Nigel went up to pay for all the clothes and underwears (he refused to let me pay since he was living in our guestroom rent-free), Mr. Tate brought up the murders. They were on everyone's mind, trailing through their lives wherever they went. Nigel and I made the right noises and nods and headed home. It was teatime.

As we came through the front door, I saw that Fiona had laid out her best china from Ireland. She was excited to have an almost-fellow countryman over for tea. (The English and Irish, I'd come to hear a good bit about, have done terrible things to one another, but she saw Nigel as closer to kin than anyone else nearby.) She even shared some wheatmeal biscuits from the private stash her father sent now and again. Nigel likely didn't realize what an honor that was. Conor got some from time to time, but I rarely got offered any, though I'd've probably told her to give them to our boy.

We sat round drinking our tea, and thank heavens no one mentioned anything about why Nigel was down here. No need to know the details. He was our friend, and that was enough. And like Fiona'd said, we might never've got back together if he hadn't encouraged me to call her. I looked over at little Conor eating a biscuit, getting chocolate all over his face and hands, and I reckoned I owed Nigel the world.

"Now if you need anything, anything at all, Nigel, just ask Abit." Fiona was showing Nigel his guest "cottage." That was what she called it even though it was just a nice room at one end of a barn. I figured calling it that made her feel a little like she was back home.

She was good at being hospitable (especially when she could send folks my way for anything they needed). And she'd put some nice things out there for him—an electric kettle, teapot, cozy, Irish tea, more biscuits, fresh bread, jam, this and that.

We'd bought a new mattress for the maple bedstead I'd made for the room, and Fiona'd put a fine old quilted coverlet on it. (Conor and Mollie started bouncing on the bed, and I had to get after them.) There was a small chest of drawers, a hotplate, and a little fridge I'd found at the dump that worked just fine. I'd placed a pretty little table and chairs I'd made under the window. I'd always liked taking my meals near a window, and this one had a flower box outside filled with pink and white flowers Fiona'd planted earlier in the spring.

We didn't really know how long Nigel wanted to stay, but I was excited about having my old friend close by. We'd worked it out so I'd take him in to the store four days a week, and I'd drive him round for any errands he needed to run. He'd never learned to drive (which some days sounded like a good idea).

We left Nigel to settle into his new home, and I went back to work. Those orders weren't gonna make themselves.

Things went along fine for a while. Then a few days later, as I was closing up my shop for the evening, damned if I didn't see that weaselly store clerk heading down our drive.

Chapter 11: Nigel

The sun poured in the window of my new abode. I liked the way Abit had positioned the window so the morning rays streamed on to the breakfast table. That and a good cuppa made the day start in the finest fashion. Too bad the rest of the day failed to live up to its dawn.

My regular shift at Coburn's went just fine. When Abit picked me up to head home, I brought along a few things for an easy supper: a hunk of farmhouse Cheddar, half a baguette, an apple. It was all I wanted after Della had shared scrumptious chicken piccata leftovers for our midday meal.

As I settled into a lovely rocker I'm sure Abit had made, I poured a glass of port from a bottle Della insisted I bring to the cottage. Very kind of her—she'd called it a barn-stall-warming present. Indeed, my room may have had such a humble beginning, but it was charming now with many of the comforts of home. (And though I'd never tell Della, it was good to get out of her cramped quarters.)

While I was still staying at Della's, we'd had one of our little dust-ups. She was worried, I believe, that I was enjoying working in her store too much. "You're not cut out to be a cheesemonger," she'd said, waving her hand toward that counter. "You're a man of the world. Besides, I don't want to come to rely on you only to have you head off to, to, er, Timbuktu."

"I thought I was already in Timbuktu," I said with a smile. "And you know, I wouldn't mind staying a while. It all seems rather pleasant." I forced a chuckle as I sipped my tea, but I didn't fool her.

"You know what I mean, Nigel."

She was right. I wasn't a cheesemonger at heart. I enjoyed the store, but I knew eventually I'd grow weary of the day-in/day-out monotony. That evening I was particularly glad to be away from the store, sipping port and relaxing to the rhythm of the rocker. The day had had its drama, like that monster child who'd stuck her hand in a large apothecary jar of chutney and squeezed it as though she were making mud pies—then marched round the store getting sticky goo all over Della's nice displays.

A knock on the door interrupted my recollection. It was just a light tap, so I thought it might be the little nipper, Conor. When I opened the door, I was startled by a smarmy-looking bloke who barged his way in.

"Howdy, Gramps."

His temerity was so astonishing, I couldn't even mumble a hello. What in the world did this blighter want?

"We're so glad you came to our little mountain town."

At that point, I wasn't so sure I was, especially when he began pacing around my room as though he owned it.

"Look, all you have to do is sign a few things for us to make some good money," he said as his index finger smoothed the pencil-thin (and revolting, in my opinion) mustache hovering above his upper lip.

"I don't know what you're on about. And whatever it is, I don't want—or need—your bloody money."

The cretin (I still didn't know his name) started laughing. "Don't pull that bullshit with me, Steadman. I know all about you—or at least what Google coughed up for me. Have you tried that yet? Amazing what it can find about someone in seconds. A lot better and faster than that stupid 'Ask Jeeves,' which I thought must be something slipshod from your homeland, given the name and all, but turns out I asked Jeeves, and 'he' is from kooky Berkeley. Go figure. That's the crazy world we're living in. And 'he' didn't know shit. But Google did."

I had no idea what he was talking about and told him so.

"Oh, never mind all that—the point is, I know about your past. You're a master forger, and when I saw you at Tate's, I knew something was off. I'm smart that way. And you gave off all the signs. Like when I watched you getting a whole new hillbilly wardrobe. That's when I started putting two plus two together and got a lot more than four."

"Whatever do you mean? What signs?" I was stalling, but it was all I could think to say.

"That you're on the lam. You know, on the run. I mean, who shows up here talking all British proper-like with no change of clothes? And nowhere to live except in that goober's barn?"

His slight of Abit tore right through me. Abit had had his troubles getting through school, but he'd worked hard to find his rightful place in the world—more than this bloody bastard could ever hope to accomplish. I believe if I'd had a gun, I would have shot him through the heart. No question about it. I was grateful all I had was a glass of port, which I threw in his eyes.

While he fumbled round trying to get the sting out, I was able to push him out the door. Abit had forged (that word again! I can't get away from it!) a lovely iron latch that was sturdy enough to hold the door against his rantings and ravings.

"Get the hell out of here, you scoundrel," I shouted through the heavy wooden door. "And don't come back!"

I pressed myself against the door and listened. For a time, all I could hear was my heart, knocking considerably louder than the cretin had. Eventually, though, I could discern a rattly old muffler as he drove away. I inched over to the rocker and sat heavily. Its gentle rhythm once again restored my calm as I rubbed my hands along the arm rests, which Abit had sanded and polished to a silky finish. I poured myself another port.

I should be ashamed to admit it, but I used to love the forger's life. It had its ups and downs, of course, but I was fortunate and enjoyed many more of the former. And when I was up, I was positively skyrocketing. Plenty of money, never a dull moment. I made a point of ripping off only rich people, which, as I saw it, made me a sort of modern-day Robin Hood. My wife, however, was no Maid Marian and threw me out of the house when she realized what I'd been up to. That would have been when the coppers came and carted me off to the nick. Before that, she thought I was a stockbroker!

But times had changed. I had changed. My tenure at the U.S. Treasury Department had been exciting—catching the bad guys and all that. If they hadn't let me go, I would never have gotten itchy fingers again. But I was like a junkie; I needed a fix.

And what a fix I was in.

Chapter 12: Della

My favorite customer, Myrtle Ledford, was telling me about her husband, Roy, when the bell over the door jangled. I looked up and saw a most peculiar man sporting a pencil mustache and a fedora. Nothing like my usual customers. He closed the door behind him and searched furtively with beady eyes. Then he spotted what he came for, and it wasn't piccalilli.

Nigel had just come from the backroom, where we'd been cutting a large wheel of Parmesan into wedges. The odd little man met him at the cheese counter. Nigel blanched, and I knew Fedora spelled trouble.

Nigel jerked his head toward the back in a most un-Nigel-like way, as though he'd been watching too many film noir. But of course he hadn't been *watching* them— he'd been *living* them during those years before we'd met. Now I could only stand by as he reclaimed his old way of life.

"What is it honey?" Myrtle asked, her voice warbly from a botched medical treatment over in Murphy.

I shuddered. "Oh, just one of those twists that life throws at you when you think everything is going swimmingly."

She chuckled at my old-fashioned word. "Well, be grateful you've had a stretch of swimmingly. Can't say I remember one."

Myrtle's hardscrabble life included too many heartaches to recount. They'd dealt with lifelong poverty, the death of a child, and a lengthy separation when Roy, her husband, went "up the river for moonshine." Myrtle uprooted herself to follow him to a small apartment near the Ohio federal penitentiary. Now Roy was in the hospital following his second heart attack, and Myrtle had stopped by to pick up a few of his favorites. As she hoisted her bag of groceries, I tossed in some Scottish oatmeal cookies I knew he liked.

"On the house. And please tell Roy I look forward to seeing him back at the store."

"More like on the bench out front," Myrtle said with mock irritation. Yes, Roy was of that generation of men who let the womenfolk do all the shopping and cleaning and birthing and, well, you name it. He and an ever-changing gaggle of men sat out front on the beautiful bench Abit had crafted, carving along the back the silhouettes of men who'd sat with him all those years ago. Before Roy got sick, he held court out there, jawing while Myrtle shopped. But she seemed to love him dearly, and I hoped they would still have times together that *did* go swimmingly.

When she left, I walked to the back. Nigel stood outside, alone, smoking a cigarette and looking for all the world like he wished he were somewhere else. I'd never seen him smoke before.

I joined him and asked to bum one. "I've quit," I added.

"Me, too," he said. We laughed.

He lit my cigarette, and I drew on it deeply. "Who was that funny looking guy with the fedora?"

"Oh, just some bloke I shared a drink with."

"What's his name?"

"Er, uh, one of those double names so popular in these parts. I believe he said Johnny Ray."

I knew he was stalling. "Making friends, eh? Though he doesn't seem like your type."

"Well, you know how it is, not too many of my type, as you put it, round here."

"Plenty with your heritage, but you're right. I'm glad you're settling in and meeting some people." As he started to say something, I interrupted. "Hey wait a minute, where'd you get a drink?" I knew our county didn't have much to offer in that department. They let stores like mine sell wine and beer, but bars around here were scarcer than a big paycheck.

"Oh, there are ways. And places."

I let that go. "So how long do you plan to lay low in Timbuktu?"

"Oh, who knows? You're not trying to get rid of me, are you? I'm rather enjoying myself, and I believe sales are up since a dashing bloke from the Old Country started selling cheeses and wines—and lagers."

He was right. Now that Nigel was ensconced at Abit's, I could truly appreciate having him around—just when I needed help.

We'd finished chiseling that Parmesan into small pieces by the time Abit came to take Nigel home. He walked in with questions of his own. "Who was that guy with the lousy muffler, Nigel? It sounded like a tractor pull from inside the house." He was smiling so I knew he was just giving Nigel a hard time.

"That would likely have been Johnny Ray, right?" I added, piling on.

Nigel frowned. I did too. I knew trouble begets trouble, and we had no shortage of that in Laurel Falls.

Chapter 13: Abit

"Both girls were killed five years ago. One lived near Knoxville but was visiting an aunt in Chattanooga; the other one lived in Chattanooga."

Fiona was telling me what she'd found on the computer during one of her breaks. Nothing much beyond what Leonard had shared, but I listened carefully. When she started in on the girl from Knoxville, I got anothern of those funny feelings. At that moment, I chalked it up to the chilling stories of both those girls being killed by some lunatic.

"The first one was beaten to death with a stick, but the other one—the one the guard said was Mimi Allen—was found out in the woods by a hiker. She'd been tied up …" Her voice wavered, and she took a deep breath. "and seemed to have been suffocated. Oh, Rabbit, this is sickening; I don't believe I can help with this anymore."

I'd never asked her to get involved, but I knew *I* couldn't stop. Not yet. Then Fiona added, "One more thing. I had trouble finding any news on the second girl. I searched for murders of a Mimi Allen in the past ten years, and nothing came up. Then I did a search on just Allen, and I found it."

"Man! I can't believe you could do all that and still find time to stick people with needles and thermometers."

She wiggled her fingers toward me. "I'm good at lots of things, Abit, me boy." We both kinda laughed, though not with much mirth, given what we'd been talking about. "Seems Mimi was just a childhood nickname. The article said her real name was Barbara."

I dropped the plate I was carrying to the supper table.

Fiona's face went as white as holly wood. "Oh, Rabbit. What an eejit I am. I was so busy at work, I just printed this out without thinking. 'Barbara Allen.' You're right. These killings *are* connected to our music."

"And 'Knoxville Girl.' We've been calling her 'the girl from Knoxville,' but she was the *Knoxville girl,* and she was killed with a stick of wood, which is how I believe she died in the murder ballad." I stopped for a minute to get my thinking straight; all kinds of ideas were pouring into my head. "And Barbara Allen in the song died of grief. Seems to me grieving feels like you're suffocating, which would be as close as a killer could make it."

My heart started racing something fierce. Our music *was* tied in, and if we could dig deeper, it could lead us to the killer. But just as quick I realized we'd only uncovered possible clues about *Leonard's* murders. Nothing linked them to ours. That was still a long shot.

But I knew who could help us figure that out.

Chapter 14: Nigel

Friday evening Abit and his family invited me to join them at one of their musical events—a gig, I believe he called it—and we all trundled off together to somewhere named Seven Devils. England has many quaint names for its towns—Great Snoring and Nether Wallop came to mind—but I believe North Carolina has us beaten with the likes of Seven Devils, not to mention Shacktown and Shatley Springs.

Our destination was an old school repurposed as a music hall. Scores of people huddled near the stage area, and more kept filing in throughout the show. I felt what could only be called familial delight as the crowd cheered its approval when Fiona sang a new song Abit had composed. One that, I noticed, necessitated his stepping in quite close to her when he joined her for the chorus. A lovely sight, indeed.

Playing mandolin and fiddle, respectively, Abit and Fiona were obviously the stars of the show. But when Conor came out on stage (he was such a young boy, Fiona'd explained, he performed only a few songs), the cheers and claps grew louder yet, and all eyes turned to the little tyke. He could fiddle with the best of them, and when he and his mother sang "Keep on the Sunny Side of Life," even my crusty old heart skipped a beat.

Abit had mentioned they had a new banjo player, Marshall White, and I must say, the chap played well. (Speaking of colorful names, Abit said White had replaced Tater Matthews, who'd left for California.) White played what Abit called a break during "Flint Hill Special," and I was surprised I didn't see smoke coming off his picks.

The evening was a grand respite from my troubles. When we returned to their homestead, Abit and I shared a lager in my room once Fiona and Conor turned in for the night. It was my first time chatting alone with Abit since his fateful trip to Churchill Arms in D.C. I couldn't help but marvel at the fine young man sitting across from me. A far cry from the wide-eyed, high-water-trouser boy I'd first met two decades ago. When he left round midnight, I felt a sense of contentment I hadn't known in ages.

The next day—Saturday, Della's busiest day at the store— I was waiting on Clare Someone-or-Other, one of the women Della said hadn't come in more than a time or two before I'd arrived. I had to admit these women were making this old git feel a wee bit younger. As she was dithering over which cheese to buy, the front door bell jingled. I looked over.

"Oh, Mr. Steadman, am I boring you?" Clare asked, followed by a coy titter. Actually she was, but that wasn't what had diverted my attention.

"Not at all, Clare. But I do need to take care of something rather urgent. Now that you know more about them, can you decide on your own whether you want farmhouse Cheddar or Caerphilly?" I was glad she didn't pick up on my gritted-teeth delivery; she assured me she'd be right there when I finished with my matter.

Thank heavens Della was upstairs on her lunch break; she'd have been ever so mum and dad to see that scoundrel back in her store. I guided Johnny Ray Meeks by the elbow into the back, then outside behind the store. He started in telling me how I was part of his plan—forging documents for the sale of mountain land. After he explained the scheme to me, it seemed rather simple, which was good. Like the American expression KISS—keep it simple, stupid—the best plans are the least complex. But it was also amateurish, which deeply concerned me because cocksure idiots like Meeks and the like almost always got caught.

"I told you. I'm not going to do any of this for your slipshod enterprise," I said, getting right up into his face. "You're a bunch of bloody plonkers, and you don't own me." I believe I even pushed a finger against his chest.

"Go on, Gramps. Shout away. But I *do* own you." Then he shoved me! "You gotta do this. Unless, like I said before, you want me to contact the FBI, D.C. police, and anyone else who'll listen. You don't cooperate, I'll tell 'em right where to find Steady-hand Steadman. Besides, it's easy money. You should be thanking me, not giving me shit."

"You won't need to call them. They're going to catch you because of your sloppy ways. And if you do call them, I'll squeal on *you*, matey. Ever thought of it that way? When you turn me in, I'll turn you in." I definitely pushed my finger against his chest that time.

"Watch it, Steadman. You're underestimating how big this operation is. You're thinking it's just me and a couple of rubes, right? Well, think again. And don't forget we know where your goober friend lives—with his adorable little boy and lovely wife. You wouldn't want anything to happen to them, would you?"

"You are despicable," I spat with all the indignation I could muster. Which wasn't much considering how hard my back was against the wall, both physically and metaphorically. "I won't do it. And I don't want or need your filthy lucre."

"Nothing filthy about it, Gramps. It's getting nicely laundered, thanks to you."

Just then Della appeared at the backdoor. The look on her face made Medusa appear grandmotherly. "You are not welcome in this store, Mr. Meeks," she said in a frighteningly calm voice. "Don't ever let me see you here again."

"Okay, Gramps. I see you've got your girlfriend to protect you. But we're not done."

He turned to leave and shoved a thick brown envelope at me. What could I do but take it?

After that, we went back into the store without saying a word. (Mercifully, Clare had left.) I busied myself scraping cheeses, the way Della'd taught me. I was amazed to learn how much that helped to preserve them. As it turned out, they were living, breathing things that needed grooming, just like the rest of us.

After a while, I heard Della clear her throat. "Anything you want to tell me?" I felt like telling her to mind her own business, but then I realized she *was*. This was Meeks' second time to corner me at Coburn's, and she couldn't have crooks like him hanging round her store. I just shook my head.

In the long silence that followed, I could almost hear the wheels turning in her head. Eventually, her curiosity got the better of her. "Anything I can do to help?" This time I just ignored her. "Well, don't let the so-called simple life around here fool you," she added. "Your friend is likely involved in a whole lot more than you might think."

I just waved her off. "As you well know, I've been in crime's major league longer than I care to remember. This is more like tee-ball my grandsons used to play. I can take care of myself."

"Maybe, maybe not."

"He's just a penny-ante crook," I mumbled as I restocked the marmalade department. It had taken quite a hit lately.

And that's how we left it. Until all hell broke loose.

Chapter 15: Abit

"Who passed this up to the stage?"

My hand was shaking as I read what was written in red lipstick on a napkin. TOM DULA. "Where did it come from?"

Fiona musta heard something in my voice because she came over and gave it a look. "It's just a request, Rabbit," she said, patting my back.

But that was only half of it. I knew it was referring to a murder ballad, and "Tom Dooley" was one we'd never played. It'd been done to death, as it were, especially back in the day of the Kingston Trio, Doc Watson, and the like. Some popular songs you play because people expect them, but others just need to have a rest. What really troubled me was most folks didn't know the guy's name was Dula, not Dooley. Whoever wrote this was up on murder ballads.

I hadn't yet gotten the nerve to call on Wallis Harding, who knew more about murder ballads than anyone round. I wasn't accustomed to people believing in me or my ideas, so I'd held back, afraid he'd laugh at me. Not that Mr. Harding seemed like that type, but you could never tell.

We'd met when he came to The Hicks to talk about mountain music and folklore. That's how I knew he lived not far from Laurel Falls. So naturally, after Leonard's tales about the deaths of the Knoxville girl and Barbara Allen, I wanted to talk with him. I hoped he'd share our belief that those two names coming up and the mention of "Tom Dula" within a couple of weeks of one anothern was too much of a coincidence.

The day before that gig I'd found my notes from The Hicks. Fiona and I recalled only the simplest versions of the stories behind those ballads, and as much as I'd dreaded reading up on such hateful crimes, I knew I needed to before taking my ideas public.

In "Knoxville Girl" a man meets a girl and starts courting her. And then who knows why, they go for a walk, and he starts beating her with a stick. He really goes at it and she dies. For the life of me, I couldn't figure out why that story inspired somebody to write a lovely waltz-like ballad with such gruesome lyrics. And then years later inspire someone to kill a poor girl from Knoxville the same way.

As for "Barbara Allen," man, that song is so mournful, it sounds spooky. Whenever Fiona sang it at home, I'd get chills every time. (The Rollin' Ramblers would never perform something that dreary.) Seemed some man on his deathbed sent for Barbara, and when she arrived, he told her he was in love with her. Typical of mountain ways, she held a grudge because he'd slighted her oncet. When he dies, that's when she goes off and dies of grief because she really did love him. At least that's one version; there are a slew of different ones out there.

The band members were looking at me funny, wondering why I'd freaked out so over that napkin. But they didn't know what all I'd found out about our recent murders. And they didn't seem to think murder ballads were as ugly as Fiona and I did. Maybe because they didn't have kids, or they'd seen so many TV shows with serial killers they were numb to the notion. Or like most people do, they thought that kinda violence would never come close to home.

Whatever, Fiona and I were in agreement about not playing those ballads when Conor was round. I crumpled the napkin and threw it away.

Later, while we were playing a slower song, "Lonesome Moonlight Waltz," I glanced down at my plucking hand and lost a beat when I saw what I thought was blood on my fingers. Then I remembered that damn lipstick. Fiona gave me a look, but I shook my head and got back on track.

Even so, I spent the rest of the evening peering into the crowd whenever I could, trying to imagine who'd sent us that request.

Chapter 16: Abit

Just as I was stepping off our front porch to head into town, I noticed a black Mercedes parked in the drive. At first, I couldn't imagine how the Merc had gotten outta the barn where I'd parked it. After a moment, I realized it was a lot newer model than the one Alex had given me back when I was a kid, though the body hadn't changed all that much.

And, of course, Mollie never met (or barked at) a stranger. She danced round the car, trying to get the attention of the man and woman inside.

I walked over and the woman rolled down her window. I introduced myself. They did the same, then told me where they lived. I knew from the address they were second-homers.

"We saw a sideboard we really liked at the Maury's," she offered. "We wanted to see about getting one for ourselves."

That's how it went. All those folks who moved up from big cities hung out together. I reckon that was only natural, but it seemed a shame they weren't interested in getting to know something about our ways too.

I opened the shop, and we filed in. It was real clear they weren't dog people; Mollie tried hard to convert them for a minute or two, but when I told her to settle down, she took to her shop bed. As I wrote up the order, the wife walked round and looked at pieces in various stages.

"You're so lucky," she said. "I don't have a creative bone in my body."

"Now that just can't be right," I said.

She looked startled. "What do you mean?"

"Well, you probably do all kinds of creative things you take for granted, but they're worthy of praise and consideration."

I gathered from the looks on both their faces that I'd offended them. I hadn't meant to, but I hated hearing people tear themselves down. What a waste to limp along with half-assed attempts and make-do efforts (like I'd done for so many year). I wished everyone believed they *could* try their hand at something new, even if their first attempts weren't all that great. The atmosphere at The Hicks was like that. Even those con artists who ripped off the school were awfully creative.

No one said much after that. We just exchanged money for the promise of a sideboard.

I drove into town and pulled up in front of Coburn's. It still felt funny parking there, instead of running down the steps to say howdy. I'd grown up in the house on the hill above the store, but now a writer lived there. She'd moved up from Atlanta, and Della said she'd fixed it up real nice, though she mostly kept to herself. I hoped she'd added some insulation. In wintertime, the butter of a morning was softer from the refrigerator than if it'd sat on the breakfast table all night.

I'd timed my visit for lunchtime, telling myself Della would be freer to talk with Nigel watching the store. But who was I kidding? I was partial to her cooking, and she knew it.

Oncet we finished a big bowl of chicken stew she'd warmed up—along with some apple pie from a new baker (we both agreed was a keeper), I laid out my thinking about how the murder ballads were some kind of clue, especially for the ones earlier in Tennessee. When I was done, Della nodded, but I could tell she was holding something back.

"What?" I asked.

"Well, you *could* be right." I knew there was a big *but* coming. She'd been a good, maybe great, reporter in D.C., and she'd mentioned over the years how she always gathered as much information as possible before writing anything.

She sipped some coffee and thought a moment before going on. "If I were reporting on this story about the murders happening today, I couldn't include the Tennessee murders. They have no real ties to what's happening now. I'll admit those two seem connected to your music, but what about the two from here? Do they share any similarities with murder ballads?"

"I don't know. I just have this sense …"

"Well …," she said, stretching out the word and twirling her fork midair as if to say, *how can you find out?*

"There is one guy I can ask—Wallis Harding. Have you met him?" She shook her head. Figured. He wasn't the kind to come to her store, even if he was driving by and needed a quart of milk. "He's a mountain music expert. Self-taught but he really knows his stuff. But before I go and get him all involved, I was wondering …" She motioned for me to get to the point. "… do you think that creepy Johnny Ray Meeks has something to do with all this? I don't recall seeing him round here 'til just about when these murders started."

"I don't suppose we can rule anyone out," she said, pinching some pie crumbs with her finger, "but he doesn't seem like a killer. And according to Nigel, he's lived here for some time, probably under your radar. No, I think your best bet is this Harding character."

Chapter 17: Nigel

I'd underestimated Johnny Ray Meeks, a most unfortunate presumption. I'd thought he was just a small-time con artist, someone who'd only pick on unsuspecting locals, luring them into his web until they were too entangled to get out.

Like me.

A couple of weeks after Meeks cornered me at Coburn's, Della's fears were confirmed: Meeks *was* the frontman for sizable (and ever so shady) real estate deals. Back in my heyday, I'd discovered how hard it was to trace such transactions, in part because government regulations were quite lax in the U.S. and the U.K. It required little planning or expertise to launder large sums of money that way.

After delivering several rounds of forgeries to Meeks, I came to understand how their scheme worked. I forged documents so they could buy property under false names or names of dead people (most unsavory!). My work allowed them to file the right documents "legitimately"—only they were buying shacks and steep, untillable land for hundreds of thousands of dollars more than their worth. Large sums of money could then be deposited legally, so to speak, and thereby laundered. Subsequent sales of those same properties put "clean" money right back in their pockets.

I reckoned the dirty money came from all the marijuana grown in the area. Or moonshine. Or worse. I felt sick to my stomach thinking about what crimes they were profiting from thanks to my handiwork. What had I brought into my life? And into Della's and Abit's? They felt as much like family as my daughter and grandsons.

I was getting soft—I *wanted* to get soft—but I needed to start thinking more like the old Nigel Steadman.

All this talk about laundering reminded me I was about to run out of clean clothing. Abit had run a load for me last week, but I didn't want to impose on the boy more than necessary. I'd noticed the laundromat in Laurel Falls, just a short walk from Coburn's, so the next morning when Abit drove me to town, I carried along a couple of pillowslips filled with wash.

"Planning on skipping out on us?" Della asked when she saw my bulging baggage.

"Not at all, my dear. I thought I'd head down to the laundromat on my break."

"Well, look out for Blanche Scoggins. She's got a million signs up about what not to do, and she doesn't like men. Or women. Or children. You might recall she disowned her own child. Of course, she was a criminal, but still …"

When I opened her front door, Blanche Scoggins looked up, frowning. "Hello, hello, hello, Ms. Scoggins," I said with false cheer. "I'm Nigel Steadman. Pleasure to make your acquaintance."

"I know who you are," she grunted, a scowl now creasing her forehead.

"Ah, and I know who *you* are," I replied with a knowing smile.

She maintained her severe facial expression and didn't say a dicky bird. Then to my surprise she suddenly burst out laughing. A right old cackle. "Well, I reckon you do, what with that Kincaid woman bending your ear. Don't believe everything you hear." She began tidying her hair, which she'd pulled back in a rather severe bun. A few gray strands had fallen out, and she slipped them behind her ear. "Let me help you with that," she added, scurrying over to start sorting my laundry.

I felt ever so humiliated to have her fussing over my personal clothing, but at least all my smalls were new. Nothing to be ashamed of, I supposed, but nonetheless I could feel my face start to color.

"Oh, don't be embarrassed. I've seen more things than you can imagine," she said, elbowing me as she talked. "Like them thongs the girls are all wearing now? They get wrapped around the agitator, and I have to cut them loose. And the men who don't ..."

"Er, thank you. I get the picture."

"Ha! A gentleman in our midst. Well, I'll be damned." She slapped me on the back and finished sorting my clothes, adding some detergent from behind the counter. "No charge," she said and actually winked at me! But when it came time to feed the washer, she was all business, holding out her hand for coins. I couldn't get them out of my trouser pocket fast enough.

"It'll be thirty minutes 'til they're done. Why don't you join me for a bite of lunch? Tell me all about yourself."

Over some rather nice ham biscuits and sliced tomatoes, Blanche listened to my stories (some of which were actually true) with the intent of fans watching England in the World Cup. By that time, I was beginning to wonder if this woman really was Blanche Scoggins; perhaps it was her day off.

When I returned to the store empty-handed, Della didn't waste a moment before starting in. "Did she confiscate your clothes because you broke one of her rules?"

"Er, no. Actually, I had a rather pleasant experience, all things considered. I'm not sure why you've had such a difficult time with her. Quite a nice lady."

"Are you sure this was Blanche? Kinda tall, long gray hair in a bun?" I nodded. Della got a glint in her eye. "Oh, I see," she said, her eyebrow going up. "She's sweet on the elderly English gentleman. Not surprising. But where are your clothes?"

My clothes were still in the dryer; Blanche promised to deliver them on her way home. She explained she lived just down the road from Abit in Hanging Dog. (Ha! Another remarkable hamlet name.) "Professionally folded and wrapped—no extra charge!" she'd called out as I left, smiling and waving. To Della I said, "She's delivering them when she heads home. Apparently she lives …"

"Oh, I know where she lives," Della interrupted, "and you'd better have Abit there when she stops by. Otherwise she might want to spend the night." Della started laughing, and for the second time that day I felt my face flush.

As it turned out, Abit *was* at my room when Blanche drove up. I scurried out and thanked her profusely while Abit just stood in the doorway. She scowled at him (I'd begun to see that was a favorite expression of hers) but pleasantly bid me a good evening.

When I walked back with the bundle in my arms, Abit was grinning from ear to ear. "Well, well, well. Good thing I was here to scare her off."

"Not you, too!" I grumbled. Next time I *would* impose on him for the use of the washer.

The following evening, Abit stopped by my room to ask if I would mind Conor on Tuesday, my day off from the store. He needed to make some furniture deliveries and Fiona was scheduled to work.

So it was just me and the nipper on the farm that day. And Mollie, of course, who seemed to love every occasion—new people, a romp in the woods, a lazy afternoon with her family.

Conor was an easy child to be with, and why wouldn't he be with Abit and Fiona as parents? When I saw children reared that way, I couldn't help but muse how my life—and really, that of most anyone I knew—might have turned out differently if we hadn't had to work through the effects of drunken, dispirited parents.

Anyway, Conor loved my idea of baking scones. I used to be quite a good baker in my day, when I had a family that enjoyed eating my confections. Living alone above Firehook Bakery in D.C. had spoiled me, and I hadn't baked in years. Out here in the hinterland, though, I found myself missing a good scone. (Della's baker tried, but in my opinion, she kept missing the mark, turning out something more like American muffins.) Conor helped mix the ingredients, and before long, he had as much flour on his hands and shirt as the board we were cutting them out on.

"Could we make some that look like stars and Christmas trees?" Conor asked. He went over to a cupboard and began pulling out a bag of biscuit cutters. It wasn't even close to that season, but hey, why not?

"Well, those cutters will squash the dough," I said, "but there's no reason we can't use a knife to the same effect."

Turned out I hadn't lost my touch. The rose beautifully and came out of the oven golden, and if I did say so myself, delectable. The trees and stars lost a bit of their shape, but then who besides the very young hadn't?

I suggested we take tea in my room. I recalled, even after all these decades, how much fun it was to be in someone else's abode. Conor clapped his hands and grabbed a basket to help me carry all the tea accoutrements. I already had a brown teapot in my room along with a tin of tea and an electric kettle, so we just took the scones, jam, butter, knives, plates, serviettes—oh, honestly, tea could be such a bother!

Conor was working on his second scone (one star, one tree) and Mollie on her third (Conor *insisted* I cut some smaller bone-shaped scones) when I heard the knock on the door. A knock that had become all too familiar. I knew our lovely tea party was over before I opened the door.

Chapter 18: Abit

We hadn't had any more killings, and life had drifted back closer to normal. Fiona lost her jitters, and I had new furniture orders to keep me busy.

But thoughts of murder trailed after me wherever I went. In my shop, I heard those ballads in every hum of the saw or whir of the drill. Finally, when we had a lull in music gigs—I'd stopped worrying people didn't like our music anymore; things like that just happened—I got myself dressed and ready to call on Wallis Harding.

I drove a fair piece past Beaverdam and turned down a road that was too rutted for my truck. I parked and hiked in to Mr. Harding's cabin. You might think log buildings all look the same, but I grew up with them and could see what made each one different. Maybe a wraparound porch or some dormer windows or pretty flower boxes. Harding's had a weathervane on top with different stringed instruments pointing north, south, east, west. The center of the vane was a bass fiddle. I wanted one.

I was relieved to see Wallis' pickup parked next to his cabin. There was no calling him on the telephone because he didn't have one, so it was my good luck he was home. I noticed a late model four-wheel-drive SUV next to the truck, which meant he had company. I hoped he'd have time for me.

Before I got to his porch, I called out, "Mr. Harding? It's me, Abit Bradshaw." You couldn't be too careful when showing up unexpected.

I saw his front door open before I saw anyone in the doorway. Wallis wasn't much taller than five feet something, and in the dim light of his tree-shaded porch, I almost missed him. (Later on, he told me he'd been tormented by a nickname as bad as mine—Pee-wee Harding.) He sported a stubbly beard, and his longish hair rose out like a white halo round his head. "I know you, boy. You play a mean bass fiddle."

How 'bout that? He knew me for what I *could* do. "I'm proud you recall that, Mr. Harding. May I talk with you about something?"

"Well, I could spare you a few minutes. My son, Keaton, and I were planning to go mushroom hunting. Perfect time after that FREAKIN big rain we just had."

My heart sank, and I reckon my face showed it because next thing I knew he was holding the screen door open for me. "Come on in. How 'bout a cup of coffee? I've got enough time to get started with whatever brought you all the way out here, and you're welcome to come back."

"Thanks, Mr. Harding."

"Call me Wallis, please. We don't hold to formal conventions here."

I stepped inside the cabin, which was a lot neater than I'd expected. He had one main room—kitchen, dining, living room—with a bedroom on each side. As I walked toward the kitchen area, I saw Keaton standing by the stove. He nodded at me, and I returned the gesture. No introductions necessary. He was dressed real preppy-like, at least that was how Alex had described clothes like that.

The only messy area was where Wallis musta done his work. Papers and books piled all round a couple of card tables he'd set up. That gave me hope some answers lay in that corner.

Wallis looked smart in a new flannel shirt and ironed jeans. I couldn't imagine him bent over an ironing board, but stranger things happened round here. I kept staring at his tangled white hair. That plus the way his wire-rimmed glasses magnified his eyes gave him the look of a wild man.

Which made it all the more amazing how well-regarded Wallis was for his mountain music knowhow. His family had lived here a long time, or as Wallis put it, they were "born, bred, and buttered right cheer." He learned about our music from his mama, who'd passed it down from her daddy. They were all fiddlers, and I'd seen Wallis play a time or two, years ago at The Hicks. Now, though, he mostly spent his days in that dark little corner, studying old books and papers so he could write books and articles of his own. I reckon you'd call him a hermit, but the way I saw it, that just gave him more time to study bluegrass and old-timey music.

As I sipped some good strong coffee, I tried to hide the need to pick grounds offa my tongue.

"Don't worry about them grounds, son. They'll keep you regular-like," Wallis said.

I didn't like to talk about such things, and Wallis picked up on that. He laughed real big and punched me on the shoulder. He was standing next to me while I was sitting or else he'd never've been able to reach that high.

"Okay, the clock's a-ticking. How can I help you?"

Now that I was there, I felt all nervous. Like I was a kid again, about to give a report on a book I hadn't read.

"WHAT THE FRAK, son? I don't bite. If I did, I'da already taken your head off, right?" He laughed again, and I moved my shoulder some, just in case. I tried to chuckle along with him.

After that I just blurted it out: "I think some murders five year ago were copying murder ballads. And something tells me the two that just happened here are too. But I need proof."

Wallis looked real serious-like. I noticed Keaton poured himself some coffee and headed out the back.

"So what in the H-E-DOUBLE HOCKEY STICKS does that have to do with me?" He held his hands up the way they do in westerns, like I was pointing a gun at him. "I ain't killed nobody, not five years ago or five days ago."

Things weren't going the way I'd hoped. But then he laughed again.

"Oh, well, yeah, you're right. I haven't explained very well," I said. After that, the whole story came tumbling out about Leonard the security guard, "Knoxville Girl," and "Barbara Allen."

I could see his eyes light up at the mention of those two ballads. He went over to a shelf and started pulling out books and papers and setting them on the kitchen table. He poured us both more coffee, and we got to work.

Chapter 19: Abit

Right off the bat Wallis recognized Randleman, the site of our first murder, as the setting for "Omie Wise." "That's one of the oldest American murder ballads," he said. "Never gave that any thought when I heard about the murder, but now, well, you've opened my eyes. We need to take a closer look."

He told me the true story dated back to 1807 when a poor lass named Naomi Wise was drowned in the Deep River by Jonathan Lewis. He was of higher standing than she was, so when he got her in the family way, he couldn't have her running all over town talking about it, the way folks do these days. What really got me going was the fact that the murder we'd had in Randleman was a drowning too.

Wallis looked at the clock over the kitchen sink. "CRAPPITY, CRAPPITY, CRUD. That's all I've got time for today, but you've brought some mighty interesting things to ponder."

"Well, if you have the time, could you check out Kona, North Carolina and anything that might have happened there?"

"Oh, we've got lots more work to do. I've got the tingles. I believe you're right—there's some kind of pattern going on here. Except that 'Barbry Allen' don't fit, at least not with your murder-ballad idea. That may be a real chink in your hypothesis, young Abit," he said just before hitting me in the shoulder again. Not mean-like; more like he was enjoying our hunt for the truth.

I wasn't convinced "Barbara Allen" (some folks like Wallis called her Barbry) was out of step with the rest, but I needed to keep an open mind. I mean, what did I know?

Wallis kept his word to Keaton about mushrooming. As they walked down a trail behind the cabin, he called out, "I need to help Keaton get settled over in Wilkes County, but I do some of my best thinkin' on the road."

I started walking back to my truck, chuckling about how he did that crazy thing people in Mama's church did. They wanted to swear, but they didn't want to break any commandments. Thing was, the words they used instead always made me stop and ask myself which real swear words they were working so hard not to say.

I hurried on home. I didn't want to be late and have Fiona asking what took me so long. I knew she'd say I was playing with fire.

Chapter 20: Della

"Bloody hell, Della! I'm an artist," Nigel ranted as he paced awkwardly in the confines of Coburn's small backroom. "I'm not an effing factory."

"Hmm, would that be called a forge forge?" I asked.

"Oh, you think you're hilarious, don't you? Well, this is no laughing matter."

He was right, but it was one of those laugh-or-cry situations. Nigel had been so cranky all day, even his doting customers were affronted. So when we finally had a lull, I pressed him to tell me exactly what was going on.

"I've never been treated like this in my life. Always with respect—even by that bottle and stopper who arrested me."

"Sounds like you've met your match with this Meeks character."

Nigel sat down heavily and slowly shook his head. "Yeah, all because I got itchy fingers. When I tried to put an end to it, Meeks came out to Abit's and shouted like a mad man. I kept saying I was done, but those blokes know when they've got a good thing. I'm their ticket to untold ill-gotten gains."

I listened as Nigel explained the scheme and where he fit into it. It sounded like a typical small-potatoes scam until he mentioned *real estate*. My ears perked up. I'd seen a story at the *Mountain Weekly* about just such a racket.

Except it was in a reporter's trash can.

I hadn't told anyone I'd gone back to a bit of journalism. The managing editor had stopped by Coburn's a few months ago and asked if I'd do a column for the Wednesday food section. I said yes—with a couple of conditions. One, I'd have a pseudonym, and two, I wouldn't get edited to death. She agreed to both.

I wasn't sure why I didn't want anyone to know about the column. Pride, I suppose, or put another way, journalistic snobbery. I'd worked hard to build my reputation with some of the best papers and magazines, so working for a small-town rag stung a little. I hadn't even told Alex, who would have teased me unmercifully. I could hear the jokes about jello molds and tuna casseroles before he even voiced them.

What I did like was having access to a real, albeit small, newsroom. The energy inside a newsroom is like nowhere else, and I wanted to feel that again. Not all that different from Nigel needing a fix, but at least my situation was legal.

A couple of weeks earlier, while filing one of my columns at the paper, I'd noticed a roughed-out story sticking out of Jessie Walsh's trashcan. While most newspapers had gone digital, many of us still printed out ideas and drafts. The brain sees things differently in hard copy; for me, it was the best way to catch fuzzy thinking and gaping holes in my stories.

Something instinctual made me grab the trashed rough draft and hide it in my bag. I went to the restroom and skimmed it. Then sporting what I hoped was the face of innocence, I asked Jessie how her latest story was coming along.

"I was making great headway with it—then E.J. made me stop," she said with a sad resignation all too familiar to reporters. "He told me it was a dead end. But I know it's not. He got this funny look on his face and told me to cover the festival at The Hicks instead. Nice enough assignment, but nothing I couldn't do with my eyes shut. This other story got the juices flowing. Know what I mean?"

Did I ever. I couldn't believe she'd left it at that, but then E.J. Blakely was a tough editor-in-chief. And some people had more sense than I did.

When I got out to my Jeep, I took a longer look at what I'd found. The names and addresses I could follow up on gave me a jolt. People who sat much higher than Fedora.

I told Nigel all about what Jessie's rough draft had laid out, plus the little bit of research I'd had time for. "There are all kinds of nefarious goings-on in the county's real estate, and this situation isn't going to get any better for you."

Like always, he said he could fix things. "Just leave it be," he added with a big sigh. "I've got a plan."

"Well, don't expect me to sit by and leave this story in some trash heap."

"Oh, Della, don't get tangled up in this mess. Please stay out of it."

"Don't worry, Nigel. I'm coming from a different angle."

On my next day off, I drove over to Cleva's for lunch. I'd been so busy with the store and the newspaper column, I'd been neglecting my old friend. Her granny flat—at least that's what they're called in D.C. Not sure what it's called in an area accustomed to families living together on shared land—was almost as nice as the home she'd lived in for decades. It didn't have the music of the falls in the background, but the mountain vistas were even prettier.

"Honey, so good to see you," Cleva called out from the front door as I got out of the Jeep. When we hugged, I didn't feel that solid, strong woman I'd been hugging for years. Not frail, but not the same. She looked more her age, though still more like 78 than 88. And her mind was as sharp as ever.

I'd brought part of our lunch from the store—all her favorites like Wensleydale cheese, hard salami, fresh baguette, and of all things, cornichons. She'd made a green salad from the small garden she still tended and baked a cake—her famed caramel cake, a rich pound cake with penuche frosting. Almost too sweet for me, but when it came to homemade cakes, *almost* wasn't an obstacle. Since

Lonnie Parker got a promotion and moved to Gastonia with his mother, the county's best baker, we'd all been short on the kind of baked goods Cleva's generation favored. I also brought wine, a lovely dry rosé we both enjoyed.

When we finished, Cleva got up to make coffee. Not the usual hogwash served around here but from freshly ground beans her cousin shipped every two months from Portland, Oregon. Somehow her coffee always tasted better than what I made in the fancy Rancilio Alex gave me for my birthday—more than likely due to the indefinable improvement that came from not having to make it myself. She stirred in plenty of cream and sugar before asking what had been keeping me so busy.

I explained about Nigel, Abit, Alex, and as I was about to add Coburn's, she interrupted. "Enough said. I'd been wondering where you were, and now it's clear. So what's going on with *you*?"

"Well, I found a different baker I'm trying out. Next time I promise to bring a surprise. And I haven't told anyone this, but I have a newspaper gig."

"What's that?"

"Oh, sorry. I'm writing a food column for the newspaper. Maybe you've seen it—Food for Thought? I've got a pseudonym, but please don't tell anyone that's me." She smiled and nodded. "And I also got involved with a story about local money laundering."

"That doesn't sound very culinary."

I laughed. "It's not, but as long as I brought it up, I'd like to get your take on something. It's about …"

"Don't tell me that's why you came over," she interrupted.

My words froze in my throat. Had I? I knew myself well enough to know once I got my teeth into an investigation, everything else went by the wayside, including manners. But this time I didn't think I was guilty. I had honestly wanted to see my old friend; her opinion on this was a bonus. I told her that.

"I believe you, honey. You're a little on edge, you know that? I was just teasing you." She took my hand and squeezed it.

I *was* on edge; the story had gotten its hooks into me. I took a deep breath before pulling papers out of my bag. I laid the most important ones in front of her. Cleva put on her reading glasses; she skimmed most of the content before leaning back in her chair.

"I don't need to tell you we've always had corruption. What place hasn't? But when the price of land started to skyrocket in the '70s, there were lots of shenanigans, or more like machinations, amongst the locals and people from Charlotte and Raleigh. Bankers, loan officers, and higher ups were getting their share of the boom. First from loans they shouldn't have made in the first place—and then off foreclosures. Or worse, money laundering, though I hadn't even heard that term until years later. I lived a sheltered life. I do recall my bank—Westonia—was one of the worst. I learned from reliable sources they were helping make land prices go up to benefit the bank. Lordy, I hate to think how many of us struggled to pay the property taxes once prices kept rising; some even had to sell off parcels from family land just to pay their taxes. Made me so mad, I moved my money elsewhere, though I imagine every bank has its crooks."

Coburn's mortgage was with Westonia. I had four more years to pay off the loan, and I didn't want them coming after me because I was digging around. I'd never let that stop me from getting at the truth, but I knew I needed to work smart.

I really did want to talk about other things, so I asked Cleva about her family. She did the same, asking what Abit was up to. I hedged. I didn't want to get drawn into the murders; the real estate crimes were enough for one day. Besides, Abit's theories were just that: theories.

After a while, I could tell she was getting tired—and a little tipsy. The wine had gone to my head too, but the coffee brought me around for a safe drive home.

Chapter 21: Della

Conor spent the next Saturday with me while the Rollin' Ramblers played at the wedding of one of Fiona's co-workers. The ceremony and reception were set in a popular natural sanctuary just outside the Laurel Falls Wilderness area. Alex and I had attended a party there years ago, and I could still recall how magical it felt within that grove of old trees, a setting that was sure to make their music sound spectacular.

Usually they took Conor everywhere, but Fiona wanted to stay late and have some fun with her colleagues. I was all for that. Those two didn't get enough time alone.

And Nigel had asked for the day off. I'd agreed begrudgingly—only because I knew his request had something to do with Fedora. Then again, I was glad not to have any of that drama going on while Conor was here. Or so I'd thought at the time.

I loved little Conor, but I didn't have a knack with kids. I never had a clue about what they liked. Of course I always indulged him with cookies from the store—he got to pick out the ones he wanted, eat a few, and take the rest home. And I'd picked up a dozen boxes of crayons the last time I shopped in Boone. Earlier he'd told me he didn't like them all rubbed down with the paper torn, and I recalled having a similar distaste. When he asked me why the crayons at my place were always new, I answered with a white lie about a store going out of business. Whatever, by now he just accepted—and expected—that they'd all have fresh points.

Conor kept himself busy in the back with crayoning and eating and later napping on the couch. He didn't seem to mind being on his own. As an only child without ready-made sister or brother playmates, he knew how to entertain himself.

The only thing I dreaded was the inevitable splitting headache. Not because of Conor—you couldn't ask for a sweeter kid—but guilt. Guilt over never sharing with Abit his mother's damn deathbed confession. She'd laid her burden on me, explaining the real reasons Abit was thought to be slow.

To make matters worse, the headaches often conjured that preachy angel-and-devil duo. One telling me I'd promised Mildred I wouldn't say a word, the other arguing my loyalties were to Abit. And it didn't help that I couldn't tell which one was saying what.

I'd never squared this with myself, me playing God and keeping that vital information from Abit and Fiona. But given how well Abit's life had turned out, I worried more about the consequences of their learning of Vester and Mildred's thirty-year coverup. I told myself over and over that the truth would hurt far more than having only one child.

But what did I know? I'd never had the call to motherhood; I couldn't begin to measure their sorrow.

My head pounded while waiting on a slew of Saturday customers. When I hit a lull, I went into the backroom to check on Conor and find some aspirin. He was sitting stiff as a stone statue and almost as pale. I saw the backdoor close.

"Who was that, honey?" I couldn't imagine who'd come in that way. Alex was off on some assignment, and no one else used that door. Conor didn't—or couldn't—speak. After a few beats, he burst into tears. "Conor, who was that?"

"I-I don't kno-o-w." I knelt down next to him and hugged him. I found a tissue and asked him to blow.

"Did he say anything?"

He nodded like only a kid can with big ups and downs. With a little more coaxing, he said, "He told me to tell Uncle Nigel he was in big trouble."

After a while (and more cookies) I asked about the guy's appearance. "Did he look like a gangster?"

"No, a moonshiner."

"And when have you seen a moonshiner?"

"Well, on TV mostly, but Daddy has pointed one or two out, and he looks like them. Kinda weasely." I smiled at his word choice, until he added, "I've seen him before."

Chapter 22: Abit

I heard Coburn's front door bang hard against the wall as I flew into the store. I looked round for a moment, then headed straight for Nigel, who was on his knees stocking some damn thing in the canned goods section. Didn't even speak to Della—who was standing behind the counter with her jaw hanging open.

I grabbed Nigel by his shirt, raising him up to my eye level. He looked so scared that some of the steam went out of my fury; I was an awful lot bigger than him. But I wasn't done with him yet.

"What have you brought on to my family, Nigel? When Fiona and I came to pick up Conor yesterday evening, Della told us about that lowlife coming to the store and scaring the shit outta him. This morning when Conor was sick to his stomach, the little fella burst into tears. He told us about that bastard coming to our farm earlier and threatening you. How could you let that happen?"

By then I'd lowered Nigel so his feet were firmly on the ground; he staggered over to a chair by the wood stove and sat. Even oncet he'd caught his breath he couldn't seem to find his words. I guess I'd scared them right out of him. Della came over and made some soothing sounds, and eventually I felt calm enough to sit in one of the other chairs. I looked round the store and noticed it was empty.

"Well, I'm glad nobody was here to see that," I offered.

"Oh, they were," Della told me. "They left. In a hurry."

I could feel the heat rising up my neck, ashamed of myself. But then I remembered how hard my boy had cried, and I got mad all over again.

Della turned to Nigel. "You never mentioned that Conor had seen Fedora before. Was Conor there when Meeks threatened you?"

Nigel nodded. He looked so woebegone, I almost felt sorry for him. Almost.

Della went in back and came out with tea and teacups. "I'd just made a pot. You Brits always say a nice hot cuppa cures all ills. I doubt this is strong enough for that, but it's a start."

We sat there not saying a word, sipping our tea. I felt like a damned fool—the cup handle so small I had to hold it with my little finger sticking straight up, just to make room for the rest of my hand. I was back to feeling bad I'd been so gruff with my friend. I seemed to always be saying sorry to people who should be apologizing to *me*, but sometimes you had to be the first to make amends.

"I'm sorry, Abit. I never thought it would turn out like this." That was Della. Nigel was still silent as a grave.

"I'm not mad at you, Della—we *wanted* Nigel to stay with us." I looked over at him, but he was studying his shoes. "He's our friend. But this can't go on."

Nigel nodded again. Thing was, we didn't want Nigel to leave; we just wanted Johnny Ray Meeks out of our lives.

After a time, Nigel started talking, though he didn't sound like the Nigel I knew. "It's a right mess, innit? Meeks told me a bunch of porkies, and I dunno how things got so bad. The last time I knew he'd come round was when the boy and I were having a grand ole time making scones. I tried to keep Meeks at bay, but then he started getting rough and, crikey, things went to shite."

As Nigel went on, I could feel the terror Conor must have felt, sure as if I'd been there. I started glaring at Nigel, which made him clam up, and we were at a dead end again. Then Della stepped in and got us back to talking. Della and I kept saying we could help with a plan to get Meeks offa his back, but Nigel shook his head. "I can fix it," was all he'd say.

When the store closed that evening, Della drove Nigel back to our place. She knew I was in no mood to give him a ride.

After breakfast the next day, I walked over to Nigel's room to tell him I was sorry. He wasn't there. I figured he musta stepped out for some fresh air because his flannel shirts and jeans were neatly hanging in the closet, and some books and underwears still lay in the dresser. The only thing missing was the suit he'd been wearing when he arrived months ago. I couldn't imagine him taking a walk dressed like that, but I'd learned the Brits (and the Irish) had their odd ways.

We all expected him to show up any minute, but a coupla days later, still no word. I stopped by Coburn's several times to check with Della.

"Nigel just isn't the type to go off without leaving a note," she said, shredding a tissue. "And to leave his mess for you to clean up. I've been his friend for decades, Abit, and that isn't the Nigel I know."

"Well, you didn't really know him when he was a full-fledged forger, did you? Maybe this is a different side of him."

"But even back in the day, he was known as a gentleman. Always polite to everyone, including the cops. This just isn't like him. And he knows how much I need his help at the store, so I'd expect at least a phone message from the road." She started biting her nails. "Something's terribly wrong. I just know it."

Chapter 23: Abit

I was surprised when I looked out my shop window and saw Wallis' truck pulling up the drive. Shiloh was out there sanding a sideboard, and I heard him greet Wallis like an old friend. I stepped outside.

"OYSTER SHUCKER, young Abit! You're right about one thing—that Kona murder a few weeks ago was the spitting image of one more than a century ago."

Shiloh tsk-tsked us, making some comment about striving for peace before heading back inside the shop.

"That's just SHINOLA, Shiloh," Wallis hollered at him. "We all want peace—not to mention peace of mind by doing something about these GOLLDAD murders!"

I hadn't ever seen Wallis so worked up, but he was speaking my mind for me. This was no time for looking the other way. "Wallis, thanks for coming by," I said. His face was so red, I added, "Could I get you some iced tea?"

"Might be a good idea," he said, unbuttoning the top button on his shirt. He followed me into the kitchen, where Mollie was sleeping. Until she saw Wallis. She greeted him on her back legs with front paws on his chest. I was trying to shoo her away, but Wallis was chuckling. "That's a fine dog you've got there," he said. He gently lowered her and rubbed her behind her ears. She even trilled for him, something not many strangers got to hear.

"Let's go into the living room, and maybe she'll settle down."

"I like her just fine," he said as she trotted next to him, ready for the second act. Which was getting up on the sofa next to him. He stroked her in a way that told me he missed having a dog of his own. Eventually, she curled up with a sigh. He took a sip of his iced tea and gave out a sigh of his own. "I'll have to tell Shiloh I'm sorry."

"Don't bother yourself with that. He's used to me calling him on his high-and-mighty ways. How do you two know each other?"

"His sister used to date Keaton. I bet you didn't know that."

"I didn't even know Shiloh had a sister. She musta been older."

"Yeah, big sister. She'd bring that young'un along on their dates because their family was just a bunch of no counts. He was a shy, sad little fella …." He paused before adding, "and I reckon he still is."

We sat with that a while before I broke the silence. "Speaking of Keaton, where's he been away at?"

Wallis seemed to be off thinking about something from a different time. I cleared my throat the way you do in that kinda situation. "What?" he asked, then my words musta registered. "Oh, just off doing his thing. Which reminds me of your thing—you asked me to check out that Kona murder, and I finally did. Not that I needed much reminding, given how famous it is. I can't believe you didn't recognize the Frankie Silver ballad. That's the one set in Kona."

Of course. Frankie Silver'd killed her husband because of jealousy since he was two-timing her, though others said he'd physically abused her. Either of those things could send someone over the edge, which is where she musta gone when she axed him, the same way that fellow died a few weeks ago. To save face, I said, "It was all the talk about Kona this and Kona that that confused me, and we don't do a lot of murder ballads because our boy Conor plays fiddle with us most times."

Wallis took a long drink and finished his tea. I got up to get him more, but he waved me back down. "I asked round about you. Seems you've done good for yourself. People said your boy plays and sings almost as good as his mama. And I get it that you don't want to sing them lyrics. Some of the more obscure ballads would turn your red hair white. There's a reason why ballads like 'River Bottom' ain't played much. GOB-BLASTED gruesome images and hateful words. And then there's …"

Wallis was heading off track, and I needed to pull him back. "Do you suppose we could be looking for a woman killer, seeing as how the last victim was a man?" I asked.

"Nah, and not because I don't think a woman could do it. I've known some real hellcats who woulda taken an axe to me." A smile creased his stubbly face, and he seemed lost in thought again.

"Wallis?"

"Oh yeah, er, no, if your theory holds up—and I'm not saying it does, yet—them other killings like 'Knoxville Girl' and 'Omie Wise' don't seem like a lady's doing."

I wanted to keep him talking so I brought up "Barbara Allen" again. I was sorry I did.

"Like I told you before, that 'Barbry Allen' don't fit the pattern at all. It was one of them broadside ballads, passed down and preserved through the oral tradition. That makes it hard to find an exact source—more than likely something from the Old Country some four centuries ago and then reworked and set in our land. So the fact that it ain't a murder ballad, and there are so many versions, well, son, I hate to tell you, but that part of your theory is just SAND IN A SANDWICH."

Chapter 24: Abit

"Show me where," Conor shouted as he and Mollie ran round and round the campsite. Fiona had a rare weekend off, and we'd packed up our tent and supplies and headed over to Lake Meacham in Watauga County.

For a couple of weeks, Fiona and I'd been talking about taking Conor somewhere nice after all that mess with Johnny Ray Meeks, not to mention our whispered talk about murders. We both knew he'd found a way to hear, and the lad just hadn't been himself lately. With the murder threat waning, Fiona felt safe enough to spend some time in nature.

We'd chosen to camp in the same place we'd spent our honeymoon. Conor always loved it there and never seemed to tire of the story about our wedding and our long weekend by the lake.

I couldn't imagine asking my parents about their honeymoon. Since they'd both passed, I'd never know if they'd even allowed themselves one. I doubted it. But we'd worked hard to give Conor a different life from how we both were raised. I knew he'd change over time, grow up, and have his own experiences with love and heartache, but at that moment, I just wanted to drink in his precious innocence.

That evening, we played our music round the campfire, and folks nearby came over and asked if it was okay to join in. "That'd be grand," Fiona said. "Music is for everyone."

She got up and gave her chair to an old woman. Conor scooted over on the log he was sitting on and got Mollie to behave herself. She settled next to the old woman, who stroked her while we played and sang.

Around ten o'clock, I watched as everyone headed off to their own camps, happy after an evening of music. I shook my head, thinking how at first I'd thought they were coming over to tell us to pipe down and stop making such a racket.

We woke early, like you do on a camping trip, and I made pancakes over the fire—smaller ones for Conor and even smaller for Mollie. We probably ate too many, but we had such a good time together. We slowly packed up (no one was ready to head home) and talked about what a good idea it was to get away.

The next Saturday evening we had a gig that took us over to Wilkes County—a good ways east of Boone but west of Wilkesboro. Somebody had turned an old barn (were there any other kind round here?) into a music venue, and I was eager to hear how the acoustics sounded with all that weathered wood.

When we pulled up, Marshall was standing next to a little boy who looked scared.

"Got us a new band member?" I asked, as I unloaded our instruments.

"Nah, just my boy, Vernon," Marshall said. "His babysitter had to cancel."

That was the first we'd heard about a boy, but then Marshall kept to himself. Of course, I did too, so I just nodded and said, "Welcome, Vernon. Meet my boy, Conor."

I saw Vernon's little shoulders ease down and the beginnings of a smile when Conor went over and showed him his fiddle. Poor little fella. Musta been hard to be thrust into all the grownups and lights and general carrying on at a concert. "Conor, why don't you show Vernon where the rest of the band is, and we'll meet you over there in a minute." I turned to tell Marshall that Vernon was welcome anytime, but he'd already gone off.

Some other band played first, not so much as our warm-up act, though we liked to think of them thataway. When they broke into "Pretty Polly" (anothern of those murder ballads with a lively tune and awful lyrics), they played so good, I felt envy spike through me. I hoped Conor and Vernon weren't catching the words, but I wasn't too worried. They looked real happy hamboning it. The banjo player strummed a fine break before the whole band joined him for a big finish.

We were all clapping and hollering for more. Except Marshall. "Hey, what's the big deal?" he grumbled when they'd finished. "That wasn't so great."

"Man, were you listening to the same band as me?" Owen asked. "I'd love to add 'Pretty Polly' to our repertoire. I really liked the sound of that one."

"It wasn't only the playing that bothered me," Marshall said. "The guy on vocals was just singing words. You need to sing it like you *mean* it."

I figured, like me, he was having a jealous fit. I'd known my share of envy, not only about music but earlier at school and later over girls. But I'd also come to see that just like there were lots of pretty girls—no one was really the prettiest or needed to be—there were lots of good bands. It didn't feel right to pick on others. I walked away and grabbed my mandolin. "Honestly," I said out loud, "band members are worse than kids on the playground."

"Who're you talking to?" Fiona said, walking up, smiling. When I told her about the band and all, she said, "Oh, Rabbit, be fair. Marshall is the only one who always brings everything he's got to his music."

Man, that pissed me off. Like I just toyed with my music. I hated it when she got like that. I blamed it on those psychology courses, making her all sensible, when sometimes, especially when you were all wound up, you just needed to spit it out to get it out of your system.

I heard the emcee call out "... the Rollin' Ramblers," and tried to shake it off. Didn't work. I hopped up on stage mad at everybody and everything.

Funny thing, though. I played better than I had in weeks, that anger breathing fire into my hands. And when Fiona sang "Too Late to Cry," I had to admit Marshall played the prettiest raindrops behind her.

Chapter 25: Della

I was in the newsroom when the call came in. Two-alarm fire. I said a prayer for the safety of our volunteer fire department. Those well-trained men and women were a lifeline for folks in rural communities like Laurel Falls.

Jessie was throwing her notebook and recorder into her purse when she asked if I could drive her to the fire; she'd left her car for maintenance at Bill Davis' garage. She added an apology for dragging me into this.

You've got to be kidding, I wanted to say. I drove like a demon.

When we got past Hanging Dog, heading toward Beaverdam, I could see the smoke rising in a cove to our right. I parked in a meadow just below the circle of fire trucks and rescue vehicles; we grabbed our notebooks and ran toward them. At the top of the hill, an old shack was mostly burned out, smoke and stink filling the air. The shack was so remote, they hadn't bothered to cordon off the scene, so Jessie and I could walk right up.

Jessie went off to do her reporterly thing, and I nosed around. I could see inside the shack where some charred ropes dangled from what remained of a chair. Not much else inside except three or four pieces of rusted-out—and now burned-out—farm equipment.

After a while, the smell was getting to me, so I motioned to Jessie that I'd be in the Jeep. As I turned away, something apricot-colored caught my eye just outside the smoldering shack. I'm certain my heart stopped for a few beats. I stepped closer and clearly identified two distinct buttons. That and the general tailoring told me it had once been a waistcoat.

Then I heard a loud, mournful sob. It wasn't until Jessie asked if I were okay that I realized it had come from somewhere deep inside *me*. Just a few months ago that waistcoat announced Nigel's arrival; now it might be signaling his death.

Jessie put her arm around me when I asked if the firefighters had found any bodies in the shack. "No, honey, they didn't," she said in a comforting way. "Just a bunch of abandoned junk like they do around here. Can't throw anything away in case it might be needed some day."

But that didn't make me feel any better. Nigel was in trouble—or worse—and I didn't know how to help.

Chapter 26: Della

When Jessie and I left the fire scene and drove back to the newsroom, I didn't want to talk about Nigel, but I did confess about pulling her research from the trashcan and reading it. I waited for her to ream me out, but she said she was glad to have someone believe in her story after E.J. had shut her down. When I filled her in on the machinations of Johnny Ray Meeks and his gang, we bonded. Not quite Woodward and Bernstein, but a good team. No question in our minds that shack was one of the derelict properties involved in laundering lots of money.

The arson inspector found accelerant along the foundation of the now-collapsed building. As part of the investigation, Sheriff Horne made impressions of two sets of footprints at the scene. I called Abit and asked him to bring a pair of shoes from Nigel's abandoned belongings; Jessie and I delivered them to Horne. They matched one of the casts. I filled Horne in about Johnny Ray Meeks hounding Nigel (though I skirted his involvement best I could). Horne nodded with what felt like genuine interest as we explained about the money-laundering scheme Jessie had uncovered. I believed Horne had come to trust my judgment, especially after we'd worked on a case together a few years ago.

I struggled with the reality that Nigel—a dear old man who had always been kind and gentlemanly with me and the oldest friend I had after Alex—was gone, either dead or in hiding. I recalled my talk with Myrtle Ledford about everything going swimmingly and felt even sadder. No wonder people were superstitious!

Abit called every day to see if I'd heard from Nigel, and Alex came down from D.C. He planned to take a longer break than usual after filing several big stories about half of Congress trying to steal the people's Social Security. He needed to get away from all that as much as I needed a break from real estate and fire. And, of course, he was worried about Nigel too.

We took advantage of my day off—sunny for a change—and went for a long walk along the falls trail. As we hiked silently through the forest—even the birds were quiet, except for a pesky brace of crows—the natural calm settled our jangled nerves. Later, over coffee at a small café nearby, Alex tried to cheer me up with pleasant scenarios like Nigel was in the Caymans enjoying himself and his bounty. Or back in D.C. at Churchill Arms, hoisting a few with his mates. But Alex hadn't seen the charred waistcoat.

Late that afternoon, while Alex worked on his famed Tagliatelle Bolognese (though I didn't have much of an appetite, even for something I usually begged him to make), I went downstairs to pick up the day's mail. When I saw the unmistakable British scrawl on an envelope with no return address, my heart hammered while I struggled to open it. I turned the envelope over to make sure the postmark was *after* the fire and sat down on Abit's bench outside the store to read.

Dear Della,

I'm deeply sorry to have worried you so—and spoiled our lovely time together. You and Abit are like family to me. Of course I love those with my bloodline, but the other kind—the family of choice—has an ineffable quality to it.

I'm heading home—my real home in Blighty. Not the clever plan I'd hoped for, but it's a good time to go back and see old friends. My grandson, Jason, who's studying at Georgetown, will be living in my D.C. apartment, so all's well there.

Please extend my deepest apologies to Abit and his family. Jason has agreed to head down soon to clean out the room at Abit's. I left enough of a mess, I don't want to leave one at the guestroom they so generously shared with me.

I'm sure you're wondering what transpired at that dilapidated building and how I got there—and more importantly how I got out. I was kidnapped by that blighter, Johnny Ray Meeks, and oene of his mates. They'd tricked me into thinking we were going out to dinner to celebrate a successful swindle. I thought it was the end of my association with them, which is why I'd dressed up; it felt lovely to wear my suit and waistcoat again! But as the evening played out, it became apparent that in their minds we'd just begun.

When I refused to continue (and I meant it this time!), they dragged me out to that miserable shack and tied me to a chair. As the flames began to lick at the walls, I figured I was a gonner. I started to cry as I thought of the wonderful people I'd never see again. With an instinctual gesture, I reached up to wipe my eyes and realized I wasn't tied tightly. I prefer to think Meeks was just sending a message, trying to scare me. (He did!) I got the ropes off in the nick of time, took off my suit coat and waistcoat and used the latter to bat at the flames and make my escape. Needless to say, I have already called my tailor in London for replacements.

Good news on the RICO front. I heard they caught the thug who'd hired me for that ill-fated forgery. (Aren't they all, I now ask myself.) That means after things cool off a bit, I can make my return to D.C. (He won't reveal my connection because that would just add another charge to what is already a sizable list.) Perhaps you will forgive an old fool and have a cuppa with me (or something stronger) when you come to visit Alex. I should be back in D.C. after Jason's term ends next year. I miss all of you, but I'm sure you've had quite enough of me.

All the best,

Nigel xo

I felt the same way: I missed him *and* I'd had enough of him. For now. I'd heard from more than one therapist that being able to hold two contradictory thoughts at the same time is key to living a serene life. I was working on that. And I was relieved to see Nigel had resurrected his eloquent voice; his last conversation with me and Abit had been a startling regression.

When it finally sank in that Nigel was safe, I couldn't move. I just sat on that bench and cried in front of God and everyone. My customers were well acquainted with life's troubles, so anyone passing by took it in stride. Two women gently laid their hands on my downturned head before walking on. After a while, I went upstairs for a cuppa in Nigel's honor.

No doubt Johnny Ray Meeks had skipped town too. That's what criminals do. Unfortunately Sheriff Horne, like E.J. Blakely, thought the whole affair was just some small-time local caper and, after a few modest inquiries, chose to look no further.

I knew they were wrong.

Chapter 27: Abit

After we met Vernon that first time, I couldn't help but worry about him, probably because he reminded me, well, of me—all shy and withdrawn at that age. We'd learned he was a year younger than Conor, though he was nearly as big. I asked round the other band members, and someone said the boy's mama had run off and left Marshall and Vernon a few month ago. I vowed to help those two however I could.

Before our next gig, Fiona and I talked it over and decided to ask Marshall if Vernon would like to spend some time with us, especially on the weekends. I put Fiona up to asking because I seemed to piss off Marshall, more often than not over music decisions and such. I was having to learn to give in more to others' ideas, and I wasn't doing such a good job of it.

The next evening when she asked, Marshall looked funny at first, then his expression turned to what could only be described as relief. "That would be great for me," he said and actually smiled. Then he added real quick-like, "Oh, and for Vernon too."

Conor loved having an extra kid round, and Mollie was over the moon. Two more hands to pet her and throw her rope toy. And I could tell Fiona was happier too. Just having one child—and that was only because of an accident—had hovered over our lives. I'd been afraid our children would turn out like me—and afraid I'd carry on the Bradshaw tradition of treating them like shit. We'd dodged heartache when Conor turned out so fine, but I just couldn't risk it again.

Fiona sacrificed the most. She'd always said she wanted a big family, and she'd gone along with having just one because she loved me. But I wasn't blind to the shadow that sorrow cast over her life. Especially when Conor took such an interest in children he met when we were on the road. He wasn't just a pint-sized showman on the stage; he seemed to know what to do with other kids, like he'd done with Vernon—talk nice to them and show them round wherever we were, even when he didn't know much about the lay of the land himself.

We'd tried to make sure Conor got to be with other kids, like those things they call playdates. He enjoyed a little girl named Henny at his school, so we called her mama to set one up for them. But we had a devil of a time ever finding a date that suited everyone. (It made me laugh to imagine, back when I was a kid, Mama on the phone, calling round to set up play times for me.) Anyway, having Vernon come over regular-like worked a whole lot better.

We'd arranged to pick him up the following Friday evening at the cabin they'd rented near Newland. Marshall had made a nice home for the two of them, and Vernon seemed more relaxed on his own ground. He showed us a birdhouse he was building with Marshall's help, and though it was a little outta square, I knew a pair of bluebirds would like to settle there and raise a family.

One thing did irk me: I had a hard time with them naming him Vernon. It was almost as bad as Vester, but I got that noose round my neck more than thirty year ago, back when people did things like that. Fortunately, for now, Vernon seemed too young to mind. When he was with us, we called him Vern. That still sounded like an old man—but at least it was better.

I wondered what his middle name was. It would be funny if it were James or John because he could go by the same initials I did, V.J. (for Vester Junior), back before I gave up trying to fight the name Abit.

Chapter 28: Abit

We had anothern.

It'd been a couple of month since the last murder, though it'd felt longer. As word spread like wildfire, it burned up any calm we'd begun to feel.

At supper that evening, Fiona passed me some cutlery and a paper napkin. In an instant that concert came back to me, the one when someone wrote "Tom Dula" on a napkin with red lipstick. I recalled the Dula murder had taken place somewhere out near Wilkesboro. The newspaper said the one we just had was in Ferguson, but I had no idea where that was.

I ran from the kitchen to a bookshelf where we kept an atlas of North Carolina. I riffled through the pages, my fingers feeling thick and useless when the pages wouldn't turn fast enough. I finally found Ferguson—it was in Wilkes County, due west of Wilkesboro. Then I grabbed my notes on the Tom Dula story and found that murder was in Ferguson too. I picked up the phone to call Wallis, but of course I couldn't.

"What's going on, Rabbit?" Fiona called out.

I returned the atlas to the shelf and slid my notes back into the box where I kept them. And tried to act normal-like. I didn't want to upset her before I knew what I was talking about. "I just need to go see Sheriff Horne about something."

"Oh, Abit, *please* don't go to the coppers." When I grabbed my truck keys, she kept at it. "I've seen how peelers on both sides of the Troubles did terrible things with the truth, depending on who they were loyal to. You just never know."

"Shug, we're not in Ireland."

"Well, I don't want you getting that involved. You have a *family* to think of." She crossed her arms like she did, and I knew she wasn't budging.

"Then why'd you help me with the computer, finding out more about the Tennessee killings?"

She didn't say anything, long seconds turning into minutes. Finally, she sighed. "I know I'm all confused about what's the right thing to do. But everything's getting too big for the likes of us. I'm scared, and I don't want any of this to rain down on our family. Please don't go to the coppers."

"Okay, for now, but if what I think is going on, Wallis and I can help with where the killer might strike next."

I was too antsy to just sit around and worry; I had to get out and talk with someone. No way could I make it out to Wallis' in the dark, but maybe Della had time for me that evening. I gave her a call.

When I pulled up, she came out on the landing at the top of the stairs to her apartment. She had on her bathrobe, so I knew I'd disturbed her. She gave me a hug and showed me inside.

"I'm sorry I got you outta bed, Della."

She laughed. "I wasn't in bed. I'll be up for hours— Alex is coming in late tonight. I just got comfortable. You're like family, so I didn't bother to change and make a fuss."

But she had. There was fresh coffee and slices of apple cake on a plate. Turned out we needed those refreshments because we spent the next two hours on her computer, looking things up. Not having a computer and not feeling particularly comfortable round them, I was amazed at what it could cough up.

At some point she stopped and looked over at me. "Abit, sit here and type in that ballad you were telling me about."

"I can't type."

"Everyone can hunt and peck. Take your time. Just type in T-O-M space D-U-L-A."

I had to admit it felt like magic to hit Enter and see all kinds of things come up for that. Some were for Tom Dula the state senator in Oregon or Tom Dula the gardening expert, but eventually we found what we were looking for.

"Abit, you need to get with it. You should get a computer at home and an email account."

"What for?"

"Well, for one, you wouldn't have to drive down here at night to look things up." She was standing behind me and patted my back. "I love seeing you, but you and Fiona could email while she's away at work."

"Why would I need to do that? She'd be home soon, or I could call on the phone if there were an emergency."

She bumped my shoulder. "You're hopeless! Okay, what did you find?"

We went back to work, and a little later I left with what I'd needed before talking with Wallis again.

I didn't get home 'til midnight. Fiona was fast asleep, so I tiptoed through the house. I peeked into Conor's room, where he was all curled up in bed, the bedcovers twisted round him. I straightened them and watched him sleep for a while. He woke oncet and mumbled, "Hi, Daddy," and I forgot all about murders.

Too bad that didn't stop me from having wild dreams. Nothing I could remember, but they made my sleep uneasy. Around dawn, I had to untangle myself from my own bedcovers before I could get outta bed. Fiona was still sleeping, so I tiptoed downstairs to start breakfast. I was drinking my third cup of coffee when she came down. I thought she'd give me hell, but instead she hugged me.

"I know you're doing this because you can't help yourself, but also for me and Conor—and all the others who could get hurt."

While she sipped her coffee, I brought her up to date with what Della and I talked about. When little Conor came downstairs, I started cooking French toast. He didn't know anything bad was going on, at least not all the details, so we had a nice breakfast together.

When I started on the dishes, Fiona came up behind me and whispered, "Go on, honey. I'll do the washing up. I know you're busting to get over to Mr. Harding's."

I kissed them goodbye, and as I was going out the door, I heard Conor ask, "Where's Daddy going?"

"Oh, just to see an old man about some music."

Chapter 29: Della

Not long after Abit had pulled away, Alex drove in from D.C. It was late in the day when he'd gotten out of town, and by then weekend traffic had ground to a virtual halt; the rest of the drive down had been slowed by a stalled truck and an accident. We stayed up past two o'clock, catching each other up on our news.

When we went to bed, Abit's tales and all the other upside-down news of the world kept going through my mind. I just lay there, worrying about not sleeping, which only made matters worse. I finally did fall asleep, because next thing I knew I smelled coffee. I opened my eyes and saw Alex holding a cup under my nose, trying to help me wake up so I could open the store before customers started honking their horns.

By the time I came out of the shower, he had an omelet and toast waiting for me. We both ate quickly. I had to get down to the store, but I wondered what his hurry was. He said something vague about an appointment and that he'd be away until late. I didn't have a clue what that was all about, but I was too busy to worry. I kissed him and trudged down the steps.

As I made my way through Friday—stocking shelves, skipping lunch, solving tiny problems that only seemed big to customers—a soothing resolve came over me. No way was I going to pursue that real estate story. In my twenties,

I would have jumped at the chance, but by this time in life, after witnessing so much crime, it felt hopelessly repetitive: a vicious cycle of greed and corruption in which the bad guys came out on top, more often than not. Oh sure, maybe some new law would be enacted to stop them, but somehow they'd find a way around it. *Why bother?* I asked myself. *There would just be another and another after that.*

I'd hoped Jessie would get involved, like she'd said earlier, but when I'd asked her recently, she'd mumbled something about being too busy and not wanting to go against E.J. She seemed content to settle for local council meetings and the occasional fire.

After I closed the store, I looked forward to a quiet evening by myself. Two things put that on hold.

As I headed up the stairs to my apartment, I spotted a little dog shivering under the steps. He couldn't have been more than eight or nine pounds, and his fur was so matted, it was hard to make out his coloring—maybe beige and white, once upon a time. One ear looked chewed to bits, the other frayed on the tip. His little chest was going up and down like bellows.

I went back into the store and found the few emergency cans of pet food I stocked—just enough if someone ran out and didn't want to drive into Newland for their regular supply. I opened a can and put a couple of spoonsful in a bowl for the little fellow. It was gone before I'd pulled my hand away. I put a couple more spoonsful down—I didn't want to make him sick—and got another bowl for water. I pulled an old blanket out of the Jeep, put it down in a sheltered corner, and patted it. He slowly moved into the middle of it, and I covered him just enough to help stop the shivering.

"Well, little one, I hope you have a good evening. I've got a bottle of Malbec waiting for me."

Upstairs, I opened the wine and plunked down on the couch. After a couple of glasses, I was ready to face dinner. Just a salad and some leftover Tagliatelle Bolognese Alex had made on his last visit. (I'd frozen the leftovers for an evening just like this.)

I was carrying my plate to the dining table when I heard something that sounded like a rat scrabbling through the walls. As it grew louder, I began imagining a rodent the size of a cat. Then I realized the sound wasn't coming from the walls but the front door. Great! They're asking to come in now.

I opened the door and the little rascal from downstairs trotted in like he owned the place. A woosh of chilly night air followed him and softened my hardline stance. "Okay, you can stay tonight, but tomorrow we'll see if someone's missing you." He didn't look well cared for, so I doubted I'd have an easy time finding his owner.

I couldn't let him up on the couch, even though he was eyeing it like a pro. He was dirtier than I'd realized in the fading light downstairs, and once inside, a strange smell emanated from him.

I hadn't bathed a dog since my buddy, Jake, now more than seven years ago, but for some strange reason I still had an old bottle of dog shampoo under my bathroom sink. I opened it to make sure it wasn't moldy; all I smelled was oatmeal and aloe. I drew a warm bath and went to get him.

"Okay, you, follow me."

He jumped off the couch and came to me.

"Now hop into the tub."

He looked at me for a second or two. I nodded my head toward the tub and after a pat on his behind, he jumped in. It didn't take long to clean the little guy, though tomorrow I'd need to cut out those mats. I went downstairs to get his blanket and bowls. While down there, I remembered I hadn't checked my mailbox.

As these things have a way of happening, just when I'd given up on that real estate wild goose chase, I got a message in the U.S. mail.

Chapter 30: Abit

Wallis' drive was empty as I approached his cabin. I hung round on his porch for a while, but after a time, I gave up and walked back to my truck. I was easing on to the road when I saw his pickup heading my way.

He pulled up next to me, and we rolled down our windows. "I just heard, young Abit. I was over helping Keaton settle in when a neighbor brought the news. Come on back to the house. We need to talk.

"GOB-BLISTERED WORMFOOD!" he shouted when we got inside. He pointed to a chair for me and plunked down on the couch, a saggy old thing that almost swallowed him. "It's a terrible injustice to our beloved music. I just know these murder ballads and murders are all tangled up together, but who could be this mean? Or should I say crazy?"

I didn't quite follow his way of thinking. I hated the way the murder ballads were being acted out, too, but Wallis had skipped over the fact that these ballads were about awful murders in the first place. I waited a beat before saying, "I've been studying the 'Tom Dooley' story. It fits with the recent murder, doesn't it?"

"Does it fit? Like a halter top in a whorehouse. This whole Ferguson thing is right outta the Dula story. You *do* know that the real name is Dula, right? The way local people pronounced Dula made outsiders misspell it. Anyway, he was a randy SO-AND-SO, and the murder of Laura Foster was brutal. With a mattock, if you can imagine, which is a lot like a pickax—just like the poor woman two days ago." He folded his hands over his lap and added, "Oh, this makes me sick to my stomach."

I felt relieved Wallis and I were of the same mind, but I worried we still didn't have what we needed. "Do we have enough information to go to the sheriff and not be laughed outta his office?"

"In a word, no. It still doesn't pass the WHAT THE FUDGE test."

"I'm not following."

"We can't answer how linking our murders to murder ballads helps *catch* the SON OF A MONKEY. That's what we've got to figure out before you set yourself up for public ridicule. Those lawmen types don't take to us civilians telling them their business."

Back home, I made myself go out to the woodshop. I was all keyed up and thought working on a dining table I'd promised for next week would help. It didn't. I'd mentioned early on how I tended to put off working on the dining table orders "for some reason," but that wasn't exactly true. I *did* know why.

It was the same kinda table I'd made for Fiona, back when we broke up, before we married. She'd left me for one of the doctors at her hospital. To add to my misery, Dr. Gerald Navarro pulled up in his Porsche one day, swept into my workshop, and in a voice that wouldn't melt butter ordered a dining table for her. "Fiona speaks so highly of your woodworking skills," he'd offered like a preacher's blessing, as if I'd been just her handyman. All those troubles came up because of my fear of having young'uns of our own.

Everything worked out in the end, but to be honest, that doctor never really left me. Deep sorrow does that. A stubborn ache in the heart that hangs round like a living thing, ghostlike 'til something wakes it up. I reckon some things you never get over; you just learn to live with them. Not that his memory took anything away from the love I felt for Fiona and Conor. Not a bit. But some days that old pain sure cast a fine dusting of hurt.

I'd thought about not making that design any more, but I just couldn't let Dr. Navarro rule my life thataway. Not to mention it was my best seller. I just wished I didn't think of him every damn time I worked on one.

I gave up on the table and moved on to a corner cabinet. After a while, my mind drifted back to Dula and that lipsticked cocktail napkin. Not a good idea while running the table saw; I almost cut myself. I stopped and took a walk down by the creek to try and clear my head. I needed to be more careful if I wanted to keep all ten fingers. (There was a reason a furniture plant over near Franklin got the nickname "Finger Factory.")

When I came back, I switched jobs to something safer—wet-sanding a small table—and I let my mind drift back to Dula. Just as I was finishing up, a thought slipped past like a wraith. Hadn't I heard someone recently mention Wilkes County? Not the Ferguson murder, but in a different way? I stopped to think, but nothing came to mind. It wouldn't come 'til suppertime.

Conor was taking a bath and getting ready for an evening of supper and a little TV. I was alone in the kitchen and got busy chopping vegetables from the garden. I kinda jumped when Fiona came in from work and dropped her purse on the kitchen table.

"Sorry to scare you, Rabbit," she said as she hugged me from behind. We smooched a little while our boy was busy upstairs, but then she wanted to talk about the latest murder before he joined us. As I started to fill her in on what little I knew, a terrible weight came down on me. "Why are there so many awful people in the world?" I asked.

"It's just one in a million, darlin'." She was trying to soothe me, but I knew she was upset too.

"Still, how could you live with yourself?"

"Well, some folks are mentally ill, and others, depending on how they were reared, grew up with some pretty crazy people—like you did." She kissed me again. "But not everyone takes the fork in the road you chose. Some just want to hurt others back the way they were hurt."

That stirred something in me, a mix of shame and regret. I knew I wasn't as good as Fiona made out. I had plenty of dark thoughts lurking under the surface. I always tried to stuff them down deep, but what she'd just said put me on edge.

Fiona musta picked up on my mood, because she was awful quiet when we sat down to supper—one of Fiona's fine cottage pies and the salad I'd pulled together. But pretty soon we were laughing about Conor getting some mashed tater on the end of his nose. He was getting to be such a little imp, I wouldn't've put it past him to have put it there on purpose. I loved how his sense of humor was coming along. (I don't believe I said anything funny—on purpose, anyways—till I was 17 or 18 year old.)

As Fiona leaned over and playfully wiped his nose, she said, "No telling what you might get up to next! You are one crazy son."

And that's when it hit me. Wallis' *son*, Keaton, had moved to *Wilkes County*. And he'd been back for several months after being away for *five year*. And he knew a lot about our music. I didn't want to think he could be the murderer—Wallis had become my friend—but the facts stared me in the face. Not to mention he was creepy.

But for the second time that evening, I pushed unpleasant thoughts away. Surely that was all just coincidence.

By the next day, though, the notion wouldn't leave me alone. I was in my shop fretting over it when Shiloh asked me why I was frowning so.

"Just something on my mind. Nothing worth sharing." He looked offended, like I didn't trust him, but this wasn't the kind of thing you told someone without thinking it through. "Sorry, Shiloh. Nothing personal, but it's bigger than I can handle."

"Then share it—you won't be carrying the burden alone." That sounded like one of his Zen sayings, which often made sense to me, or at least made me want to think more about them. But I needed to honor Wallis more than Shiloh. I shook my head.

"The noble-minded are calm and steady. Little people are forever fussing and fretting," he said before going into the other room I'd built to help keep dust offa everything out front.

I tried not to bite, but after a few minutes I called out: "Okay, who said that?"

He turned off the sander and shouted, "You don't think I could have come up with something that insightful?"

"I'm sure you could with time, Shiloh, but not on the spot like that."

He laughed and said it was Confucius. I mumbled something like I knew who that was. (I *had* heard of him, just didn't know the particulars.) We went back to our respective chores and worked together contentedly for the rest of the afternoon.

That evening, Fiona had the second shift, so oncet I put Conor to bed, I was alone with my thoughts. Instead of fussing and fretting, I just sat quiet with them, the way Shiloh would've. And sure enough, with time I knew what I needed to do.

Chapter 31: Della

Saturday morning, I closed the bedroom door quietly so Alex could sleep longer and turned to find the little rascal curled up on the couch. Last night he'd crept up there as soon as my back was turned, so why would I think he'd sleep all night on his makeshift bed on the floor? Besides, now that he'd had a bath, what difference did it make? I'd long given up trying to keep dogs off furniture.

After breakfast I cut out a bagful of mats from his coat, but my unprofessional trim made him look awfully raggedy. On his morning walk, passersby glanced oddly at him or offered something noncommittal like, "Oh, I see you have a new dog." I found myself rooting for the little guy. Maybe his coat would grow out soon, and he'd look good enough for someone to adopt him.

Alex was still asleep when we returned. I was dying to show him the note I'd gotten in the mail—I was asleep when he got home—but that would have to wait. I let the dog off his leash, put down some extra food, and hurried to open the store. Another busy Saturday when my mind was elsewhere. Not just the money laundering and the recent murders, but more personally, I wondered why Alex was away until after midnight. Of course, I told myself, he'd always kept late hours, and his body clock traveled with him.

Around eleven o'clock, he joined me downstairs, looking beat. He remained mysterious about his day away, but we'd agreed years ago to give each other plenty of space. I wasn't really worried about his philandering again, and his health had been fine since his treatment for prostate cancer several years ago. I knew he wouldn't come down here to secretly go to the doctor; our medical care was far inferior to what he could find in D.C.

"Whose overgrown rat is that running around your apartment?

"Oh, that's Rascal."

"You've named it?"

"Well, he *is* a rascal. And having a proper name makes an ad more effective, easier to find him a good home."

He mumbled something I didn't quite catch, though I definitely heard *already has*. But he was wrong; I was in no position to take on the care and welfare of a dog. I'd always felt as though I'd neglected Jake once I bought the store. I'd given him a good life in D.C., but down here, I spent too many hours inside the store, afraid to let him hang out in back because of random visits by the health inspector.

I brought Alex a cup of perked coffee and showed him the mysterious note from my mailbox. The evening before, after retrieving it from my mailbox, I'd cleared off the kitchen table so I could study it with a large magnifying glass.

Whoever sent it had gone to a lot of trouble to tear words from a newspaper in different sized fonts. Seemed like a lot of drama and toil, but I guess a whistleblower couldn't be careful enough. And I had to admit the note had style; it piqued my interest.

When I showed it to Alex, the look on his face cried *Really?* "Go on, take a closer look," I said.

The note was oversized with a large photo of the burning building we'd feared had taken Nigel's life. Just six words below that: SO MUCH BIGGER THAN YOU THINK!

"So what?" Alex asked. "You already knew that. What are you supposed to do now?"

Alex was right. I didn't have a clue about what to do with this strange proclamation from some mysterious—and perhaps disgruntled—whistleblower. But I also sensed something off with Alex, his usual reporterly demeanor missing in action. I took back the note, folded it, and returned it to the envelope. I asked him what he was up to today.

"Just got to run out again."

"When will you be back?" My patience was stretching thin.

"When I come back to take you to the best dinner you've ever eaten at the Inn at Jonas Mountain." Normally, I'd be delighted, but this sounded more like asking forgiveness than generosity. But then I thought, *Oh, to hell with all the suspicion.* I loved eating out, especially on Saturday night after a long work week.

Even on a busy day at the store, there were always lulls, and around three o'clock it was so quiet, I struggled to stay awake. I went in the back, put the kettle on, and picked up the magnifying glass. As a last-ditch effort to glean something from the mysterious note, I closely studied each word. I didn't find anything special in the first five words, but on the sixth, I caught a break. Just a small one: THINK (the exclamation point had been cut out separately) seemed to be from a headline, and in a small font at the very top I could just make out the letters "BSERVER." Had to be from the *Charlotte Observer*, which told me something. The person was from around here, generally speaking. Perhaps fairly literate, someone who actually read a newspaper from a town known for its banking and finance.

After the initial rush, though, I heard a voice in my head repeat Alex's question: *SO WHAT? What can I do with this?* Thanks a lot, whistleblower, for just stirring up trouble. No way could I start an investigation as the *Mountain Weekly* food columnist. Gone were my credentials and my bravado for such undertakings, even if my curiosity was as strong as ever.

All that was forgotten on the trip up the Blue Ridge Parkway, decked out in its lush wardrobe of summertime green embroidered with sprays of wildflowers.

Even after so many years living in the mountains, I still felt conspicuous in Alex's Mercedes as it puttered up the parkway. But the smooth ride soothed my jangled nerves, as did the bottle of Champagne we ordered at the inn. No special celebration other than it was Saturday night and neither one of us had to work the next day. I ordered the mountain trout dinner, and Alex tried the chicken scallopini.

We talked some about the message I'd received, but neither of us had any fresh ideas about what to do next. I decided to let it go, the proverbial brick wall. After dinner and a couple of cups of coffee, I was good to drive. We got home safely and, as they say around here, hit the hay.

I awoke Sunday morning with an idea floating through my head: *place a classified ad in the Observer online.* So much for giving up on my hard-to-figure whistleblower. But then again, why not give it a try? Roll the dice and see what happened. And while I was at it, I could place an ad about Rascal.

I got up, turned on the Rancilio, and headed over to my computer. The *Observer* offered several choices of where to place my ad—legal, real estate, or just wanted. I hedged my bets and chose both "legal" and "real estate wanted." Editing my words a time or two delivered a cheaper yet more effective ad: NOT FAIR, MR. BIGGER THAN YOU THINK! TELL ME MORE. Rascal's ad included a photo and some details along with my phone number.

It was a long shot the whistleblower would ever see the ad, let alone reply, but I felt better for trying. I paid for an entire week to boost my chances on both ads. I told myself that if I hadn't heard from the whistleblower after seven days, the hunt was over.

I wasn't clear on which way I hoped it would go.

Chapter 32: Abit

"Wallis is in the hospital."

I nearly fell off the stoop when Keaton opened the cabin door and delivered the bad news.

Earlier, I'd decided to put my suspicions about him on hold and head over to the cabin to talk with Wallis. I wanted to go deeper into how the old ballads matched up with the current murders.

Keaton just stood in the doorway, not asking me in. He looked all uppity in his big-city clothes—suit pants, white shirt, tie—an odd sight in a rundown cabin. Then again, what else could he wear but what was in his closet?

When I heard Wallis was sick, though, I put all that behind me. "What happened? Did he fall? Where is he?" I rattled on, torn up about my friend.

"His heart. He's had heart trouble for years. I took him to the hospital in the middle of the night on Thursday. Over in Spruce Pine, where his doctor practices."

Keaton seemed genuine in his concern. We chatted a while, though he never did invite me in. I just stood there while he told me about the tests Wallis was having and that he'd be in the hospital at least a week. I asked Keaton if he planned to visit Wallis that evening.

"No, I'm going to Boone to do some research at the university; then I'm attending a music recital. But I'm sure he'd be glad to have your company." Like he was relieved

I'd be doing what he shoulda been doing. I could tell he wanted me to leave.

"Whatcha researching?" I asked just to piss him off.

He looked down his nose at me. "Oh, something for my latest project."

That could mean anything. My mind started racing again.

Wallis' cabin was dark when I came back. I'd worked my way through the woods, sticking close to the stand of laurel that surrounded his cabin. I'd parked a ways away so nobody would see my Chevy truck. It stood out with those beautiful wraparound curved windows in the back, the way they made them in 1950.

I'd gotten Maizie, a neighbor girl, to babysit Conor while Fiona was at work. We'd had her stay with Conor a time or two, and they seemed to get along fine. After she said her howdy-dos with Conor and got settled in, I told her I'd be back as soon as possible. "Oh, and don't say anything to Fiona, okay?"

She looked at me funny and I blurted out, "Oh, I'm not stepping out on her or anything."

We both blushed like teenagers caught in the backseat. I felt bad drawing Maizie into my lie, but if Fiona knew what I was up to, she would've had my guts for garters (one of her favorite sayings).

I wasn't worried about Conor mentioning anything. He was still young enough to think mostly about what lay right in front of him. If he did, I could just say I had to make a delivery. Kinda lame. Who needs a sideboard delivered at eight o'clock at night? Then again, I wouldn't put it past some of those second-homers.

I'd feared Keaton, with his city ways, might've deadbolted the door. I tried the knob and let out a big breath when it opened. Oncet inside, I headed straight for Wallis' work corner. I had this nagging feeling Keaton was hiding something, and I needed to see if Wallis had letters, clippings, anything that would tell me more about where Keaton had been for five year and why in the hell he chose to settle in Wilkes County. The same county as our latest killing—and not that far from the othern.

I couldn't believe the mess. Papers everywhere. I put my flashlight in my mouth and dug round with both hands in different piles. Toward the back of the table I came across a few yellowed clippings, and one of them told about Keaton winning some kind of award for a book he'd written on Appalachian culture. I looked on Wallis' bookshelf to see if the spines had the Harding name, but I couldn't find one. To be honest, I was so nervous, the flashlight was bobbing up and down and making me feel queasy.

I took it out and held it in one hand while I rummaged round best I could with the other. I felt something thicker and heavier below the stacks of papers: *English Roots of Appalachian Music*. Sure enough, it was Keaton's new book, which I figured he could have written while in prison for five year. There was Keaton's name in big bold letters on the cover. I leafed through real quick-like and saw a whole chapter on murder ballads.

As I put the book down, lights fanned across the front window. I peeked out and saw two headlights accompanied by the grind of a four-wheel vehicle coming up the drive. It had to be Keaton; Wallis wasn't in any shape to be driving himself home, not to mention his pickup was sitting out front. Maybe the hospital called and Keaton had gone to bring him home. Or worse.

I fussed with the papers a little, trying to put them back the way they were. I wasn't too worried; I figured no one but Wallis would ever notice anything out of place. I'd met people who had desks that messy and yet knew where everything was. But they were always the person who'd made the mess in the first place. I didn't think Keaton could make any more sense of it than me. I crawled on all fours over to the bedroom closer to the work area.

"Damn hicks. I'd like to kill those halfwits," Keaton growled as he slammed the front door. He kicked a stool, which made me flinch. Luckily not enough to knock anything over.

Keaton went into the other room, what I figured was his bedroom 'til he moved to Wilkes County. I thanked the heavens I hadn't chosen that room to hide in. Then he flipped on a light, and I could hear his footfall getting closer. When it stopped, he musta been standing right at the tables.

Oh, no. He did *notice the mess was different.* I heard what sounded like a book or two coming offa the shelves. Then footsteps away, the front door slammed again, an engine roared before the SUV ground its way back down the road.

To be safe, I stayed in my cramped position for ten more minutes before straightening myself out and running for the front door. But then my curiosity got the better of me. I went back to the bookshelf, curious about what he'd taken. I could see Keaton's book peeking out under the papers where I'd replaced it. As for the bookshelves, I hadn't had a good enough look at them to notice anything missing. The books round the blank space Keaton left were John Parris' *These Storied Mountains* and "Movers & Makers: Doris Ullmann's portrait of the craft revival in Appalachia," some kinda exhibit catalog. I sure would've liked to look through both those books. Especially Doris Ullmann's. Her photographs lined the hallways at The Hicks, and my heart always stirred at the way she captured the dignity of work and creativity of mountain folks. But there was no time for leafing through picture books. I needed to get out of there and go home, where I belonged.

Chapter 33: Della

Since I didn't subscribe to the *Observer,* I'd picked up an extra roll of quarters at the bank so I could buy copies at the newspaper box in front of Blanche's laundromat. I suppose I could have studied the classifieds online, but I needed to pore over every square inch of them. I didn't expect the whistleblower to make it easy on me.

I hitched up Rascal, and we walked down to buy a paper. (No calls yet about *his* ad.) Blanche stared at me out the big plate-glass window, more than likely wondering why I was suddenly patronizing her newspaper box. I was surprised she hadn't tacked one of her infamous signs on it, like those inside warning us about misusing her washers or misbehaving in general. I'd expected to see signs like WASH YOUR FILTHY HANDS BEFORE USING THIS BOX or THIS NEWS ISN'T FIT TO READ. Then again, maybe she had and the delivery guy kept tearing them off.

To be fair, she might have been looking out to admire Rascal. Nah, she didn't like dogs, which, as far as I was concerned, closed the book on her. Or maybe she was looking for Nigel. She may not have heard he'd left the country and hoped he'd come back to see her. I was with her there. After a few weeks without him, I was back to missing him.

I had some time before I had to open the store, so I spread out the newspaper on the counter. I'd planned to study the classifieds while Rascal checked for invisible crumbs in both rooms, but I ended up watching him. After he'd eaten all he could find, he wandered over to where I'd piled up a blanket, turned a time or two, and sank down. He was going to make someone very happy.

I finally got down to business with the classifieds, but I couldn't find anything from the whistleblower. We carried on this routine for the next three days. After perusing the classifieds on the fourth day, I still couldn't find any response to either ad. I figured I'd wasted my money, but so what? I hadn't spent more than the equivalent of a few movie tickets, and this was a lot more fun than the films that came to the Hen Theater.

I folded up the newspaper just as some customers filed in. Through the open door, I could see the postman putting a sizeable envelope into my box, considerably larger than the usual circulars and bills.

Autumn 2005

Chapter 34: Abit

After that crazy night at Wallis' cabin, I'd decided to wash my hands of all that murder business. I didn't have the stomach for it. Fiona knew something was up when I was off my food for a coupla days. I told her I just had a bug, but it was more than that; I was sick at heart from all the hate and violence and fear.

Instead I finished orders I'd put on the back burner. It felt good to make pretty dovetail joints, thanks to what Shiloh had taught me and a new jig I'd bought. I got lost in the beauty and smell of wood and felt happier than I had in ages.

Later that week I got a call from a second-homer I'd promised an oak bed to. The husband told some long story about relatives coming over from Germany and wondered if there was any chance the bed would be ready in time for their visit. I told him that wouldn't be a problem as I was almost finished. But then he explained the bed was needed in their home in Greensboro—not the one in Beaverdam. Could I deliver it by the following Friday? When I paused (I was trying to stifle a big sigh, but I'm sure he musta heard it), he offered to pay me $200 to deliver, plus mileage. Hard to pass up, so I said yes.

That oak bed gleamed after Shiloh finished sanding it and rubbing it with a special oil concoction he'd made. By Thursday, I took some photos, wrapped it with padding, and loaded it onto the truck. The next morning, I headed out before dawn. My family was still sleeping; even Mollie only lifted her head to say goodbye.

I caught an awesome sunrise on my trip east and stopped for coffee round Yadkinville, where I reread the directions and discovered the customer lived south of Greensboro, which made the trip even longer.

I found their home (more like a mansion) with no trouble, and the husband helped me unload and install the bed. They asked me to wait while they made it up pretty as you please with a comforter and throw pillows. His wife was so happy she clapped her hands. I had to agree. I took a few more pictures for my book.

He handed me a wad of cash, which he said included the balance due, estimated mileage, and the $200 delivery fee. Out at the truck, I realized he'd tipped me an extra $50, so I felt pretty rich with all that money in my pocket. Time to celebrate with a big dinner; I was starving.

I decided to backtrack and get on U.S. 64, where I'd have better luck finding home cooking instead of the fast food along the interstate. Not long after, damned if I didn't see a signpost for Randleman, the site of our first murder. I got a funny feeling, like it was an omen, and drove in that direction.

I stopped at a barbeque place outside of town and asked my waiter about the murder. He shook his head, claiming to know nothing about it. A man at the next table leaned over and kinda whispered, "It's just past town a bit, going south. Turn left at a house for sale and go a short ways down. You'll see the crime tape."

I plowed into my pulled pork dinner like a workhorse with a whip to its flank. It included turnip greens, pinto beans, cornbread, and I finished things off with homemade blueberry pie and coffee.

I didn't feel too confident about the directions and worried about Fiona needing me home before she left for work. But I'd gotten such an early start, it was only a little after noon; I had time to spare. I found the turnoff just fine and pulled up to where the crime tape hung in tatters. It was a sorry sight, abandoned and forgotten. I figured five month ago the river bank was run over with cops and lookers, but now, everyone had moved on with their lives, except those still grieving.

There was nothing much to see, but I sat a while on a rocky bluff overlooking the river and listened, paying my respects and hoping to get some kinda nudge about what to do next. I imagined the poor women—both Omie Wise and the one this spring—taking their last breaths here among the fragrant cedars and pines where birds chattered about how good life was. I sat a while longer before hitting the road.

I figured as long as I was in the truck, I might as well swing by Ferguson, not quite a hundred mile due west and on my way home. I didn't have any trouble spotting that crime scene. The cops were still there, their black SUVs and vans and tents scattered across the site. I couldn't get close, so I went up the road and parked. I sat there a while, but again, nothing special came to me.

Since I'd made good time to Ferguson, I decided to swing by Kona, just to complete the tour of these godforsaken places. I'd begun to feel like the trip was a bust, but at least I'd gotten it outta my system while getting paid for the drive. (And I knew Shiloh would appreciate his share of the tip.) I came up on Kona, just a slip of a place on the North Toe River, and drove through town. As I was looking round, wondering where in the world the crime took place, I had to slam on my brakes. Up ahead, Keaton was getting outta his SUV. What in the world was *he* doing here?

I stayed back and found a shady place to park. I watched him go into a café and waited. After thirty minutes, my truck was getting hot, and I worried about Fiona. She'd be wondering where I was, but I didn't see a pay phone anywhere. I started to pull outta my parking place just as Keaton left the café with a Styrofoam cup of coffee; I could almost taste how bad it was, old and stewed on a burner since breakfast.

I followed him to a pretty little holler with a white church surrounded by Mountain Ash and bull thistle and the odd mullein popping up here and there. No one else was anywhere round, so I had to be careful he didn't see me. Luckily there was a sheltered place I could park and watch where he was walking. He marched off in one direction, like he knew just where to go. That was when I spotted the crime tape, flapping in the breeze.

I felt so sad for Wallis I couldn't watch any longer. I cranked the truck and hurried home.

Chapter 35: Abit

I couldn't remember when I'd had a good night's sleep. That night I kept going over the world of hurt Wallis was likely facing, that on top of his bad heart. I got up early and put on coffee. Fiona was sleeping in after a late night at the hospital, so when Conor got up, I made us breakfast, wrote Fiona a note, and loaded him and Mollie into my truck. I felt unsettled and needed to get out and do something.

Coburn's wasn't open yet so I kept driving. I never liked knocking on Della's apartment door unannounced when Alex was there. They didn't have much time together as it was. I pulled up in front of Blanche's laundromat to use the payphone.

"I don't want to go in there," Conor said.

I started laughing. I'd made my peace with that woman, but I knew she musta looked like the wicked witch from one of his storybooks. I'd taken him in there oncet when we had a bunch of blankets to wash, and she scolded him a coupla times before I had to have a talk with her. After that, she just watched him like a hawk.

I ruffled his hair, which needed a trim, though I'd never make the little fella do that now. I had no idea why he hated having his hair cut, but he made a fuss every time. "Don't worry, I'm just going to call our friend, Alex, from that payphone."

Alex answered on the first ring, like he was expecting a call from someone else. He said he was sorry, but he couldn't meet me 'til Monday. That messed up another work day, but hey, I'd take any time I could get. I needed someone to talk over my ideas with, and Alex got me better than even Della.

Not to waste a trip into town, I drove over to Tate's Dry Goods. I'd noticed this morning when Conor came downstairs how high-water his pants had gotten. We'd bought him new clothes before school started again, but he was growing that fast.

"You know, Conor, you're getting too big for your britches. Let's go to Tate's and get you some new ones." He didn't know that was where Johnny Ray Meeks used to work, so that wasn't a problem. And it was fixing to rain, which made it cool enough for Mollie to sleep in the truck for a short while.

Most kids don't like shopping, at least that's what Fiona told me, but Conor didn't get to do it often enough to mind. Not that he was crazy about picking out new clothes, but I bribed him with a visit to the toy department afterwards.

As we came out of Tate's, damned if I didn't see Keaton walking toward his SUV with a big coil of rope. That guy was everywhere! A shiver came over me, something Fiona would've said was a sign. But this time, it felt more like a natural reaction to all the worrisome things going on.

Conor and I got in the truck and gave Mollie a treat for waiting on us. I tossed two new pairs of jeans behind my seat and cranked the engine. Conor studied his new Matchbox truck all the way home.

Monday morning, after Conor was off to school, I told Fiona I needed to visit Wallis in the Spruce Pine hospital. It was her day off, and I could tell she was grateful for the luxury of time to herself.

I'd been putting off going to see Wallis because of Keaton, not to mention how much I hated visiting people in hospitals. But I also hated *not* visiting them. When does someone need a friend more than when they're inside such a cold, weird-smelling place?

I opened the door to Wallis' room and stuck my head in. He was dozing, looking all shriveled in his bed. And rough. His hair was a tangle of white fluff, though they had given him a clean shave. I stepped in quiet-like, but he musta heard the door close behind me.

"Huh? Who's there?" he said, fumbling for his glasses. I handed them to him, and he settled them on his face. He looked up at me and smiled. "Young Abit."

"I hear you're getting out soon," I said, even though I didn't know that to be true. I figured that was always a good thing to say in this situation.

"SON OF A GOAT, you'd better believe it." He pulled the covers off as though he were about to get up and leave right then. His spindly legs looked pitiful sticking outta that hospital gown. "The food here tastes like a CRUD MUFFIN. You don't have any snacks on you, do you?"

I'd picked up some grapes, something Fiona told me she always took when visiting folks in the hospital. I held out the brown paper bag, and his face lit up. When he opened it, he looked awfully disappointed. But he thanked me and began munching on some, offering me the open bag. I took a few to be polite.

Wallis settled back down, pulled the covers up, and surprised the hell outta me when he asked, "You know, I've been wondering why you asked me what Keaton had been up to the past five years. What are *you* up to?"

Oh, man, I didn't see that coming. I'm a terrible liar, but I put on my best straight face. "Just curious. He looks like someone who's seen more of the world than me, and I wondered where he'd been to. Why?" Della'd taught me it's always good to answer a tough question with one of your own.

Wallis studied me a while, and I tried not to swallow too hard. I ate another grape.

"Okay, just wondering, what with all this talk about 'Knoxville Girl' *five years* ago and now Tom Dula over in *Wilkes County*." He left it hanging there like a bad note at a concert.

"Have you had time to ponder the killer's choice of ballads?" I asked. Keaton wasn't off the hook with me, but I had to shift things away from him.

"I've had nothing but time to think on it—when they're not sticking me with needles or wheeling me somewhere scary for a test. I was able to determine that the 'Omie Wise,' 'Frankie Silver,' and 'Tom Dooley' killings were exactly seventy-three days apart. That's bound to be important, but I can't tell you why." He started staring at me again. I wasn't sure I'd dodged his bullet, but I was breathing a little easier.

"Well, I sure don't know about such things. What I *do* know is the Tom Dooley murder took place twenty-five day ago. If you're right ..." Wallis gave me a sharp look. "I mean thanks to you, we now know we've got forty-eight day to stop the next murder."

And just like that, Wallis went from suspicious to all worked up, in a good way. "Yeah, but how? We don't know SQUAT about how to stop this MOTHER TRUCKER, and that's the only reason all this research matters."

He was nearabout shouting now, and that musta sent a message down to the nurses' desk because all of a sudden, a big guy came in and told *me* not to excite Mr. Harding or I'd have to leave. Wallis started nodding his head up and down like a teacher's pet. When the door closed behind the nurse, his face went back to normal, and he started in again.

"This is what them fiction writers call the ticking clock. We've only got so much time, so we've got to get busy."

He pointed to a stack of three books on a little table. "Keaton brought these the other night. He was fixing to go to some recital up in Boone, but they had a typo in the newspaper notice—the wrong DADBURN date, if you can imagine." So that's what Keaton was so mad about. I just shook my head like I couldn't imagine. "Gimme that other one, the one on the bottom, the one by Alan Lomax. No one knows more than him."

I handed him *Folk Songs of North America*; I remembered studying it some at The Hicks. While Wallis looked through that one, I opened one of the other books. It covered most of the important murder ballads and told a lot of sad stories. What with that and the fact that I hated hospitals, my skin began to feel like bugs were crawling over it. I got up to leave.

"Don't go, young Abit. Not yet. I'm just getting to the good stuff. He set aside the Alan Lomax book and asked for the one called *Traditional Tales of True Crime Ballads in the Southern Appalachians*. I'd sworn to myself I wouldn't bring up Keaton, but a question was burning a hole in my gut. "Didn't Keaton write a book about mountain music and murder ballads? Why don't you use that one?"

Wallis looked funny at me again. I stared right back at him, holding my breath. Finally, he nodded, like I'd passed his test. "I helped him write that book. HORSE HOCKEY, I wrote it! He did some of the research and editing, and I figured he needed the book credit more than me. So I need information I *don't* know. Now hand me that other book."

He read to himself for a while, nodding and mumbling things I couldn't make out. "Here now, I want you to listen to this," he said, his finger running along each line in the book as he read aloud. "It says here that in the 19th century, there were all kinds of songs about violent death. They used old tales from ancient ballads back when there were knights with swords and ladies who dropped their underwears in front of the wrong guy."

"It doesn't say that!" I said, laughing.

He laughed too but then got real serious. "Well, nearabout. Instead of all that lady and lord HOGWASH, they started writing these ballads right where they were living. These ballads became like newspapers, telling what had happened but making it even juicier and gorier, sometimes adding a moral lesson."

He quit talking and read to himself a while. Then he started lecturing like a teacher. "This is about us—in the Southern mountains. I'm sure it will come as no surprise to you that a lot of our music came from Scotland and Ireland, and because our kinfolk settled in the hollers, it says here 'we kept to ourselves and stayed *pure*.'" He looked up from the book. "Ha! I'd never use that word for round here, but I know what it's saying. We didn't marry a bunch of Norwegians or Swedes or Italians. But we did hold on to all that personal honor BULLPOCKY left over from the knights, along with the idea that it was okay to resolve our problems with violence. Brother, does that ever ring true. Even a dispute over where someone dug his fence posts can result in a shooting. Oh, looky here. He calls our ancestors moonshiners and feudists. The only thing I'd disagree with there is that he said 'ancestors.' We're still a-doing it!"

Wallis was on a tear, and he began waving his arms round, which pulled out something stuck in one of them. Just then a different nurse slammed into the room.

"What do you think you're doing, young man?" she barked at me.

"We're talking about saving lives," I answered, my voice not as strong as I'd've liked.

"Well, leave that to us. You can save Mr. Harding's life by going home. Now get out!"

I gave Wallis an apologetic look, but he just chuckled and waved goodbye.

As I rushed outta his room, I couldn't believe who I almost ran into: Dr. Gerald Navarro. The very one. His name hadn't been mentioned in our home for a good eight or nine year.

That was about to change.

Chapter 36: Abit

"Keaton's been missing for five year," I told Alex, as though that made my case against him. Alex wasn't having it.

As promised, we met Monday afternoon at Adam's Rib. While we waited for our order, I filled him in on the rest of my evidence: Keaton had been back long enough to have killed our three victims, and he wrote a book about mountain music and murder ballads. (I left Wallis outta the book business to bolster my case.) "And I need your help because I can't go to the law about this—or to Wallis. He'd never speak to me again, either way the truth plays out."

"Okay, Abit, we'll go back to Della's and look into this. I'm sure we can find out something on LexisNexis or some of my other resources."

When the waiter arrived with our dinners—barbecue chicken plate for both of us—we ate in silence for a good while. Oncet Alex was halfway through his meal, he started asking me more about Keaton. After I told him all I knew, I felt a little better. Especially when the waiter arrived with our pecan pie and coffee.

I'd known Alex since I was a kid, and he hadn't changed much, except for a few wrinkles each year and more streaks of gray in his hair. (The same went for Della. She stood tall and still had that pretty reddish gold hair, though by now I reckon she was helping the color along.)

Alex loved what he did, and more than likely that kept him younger. He talked about working out in a gym, which sounded awful to me. Between chopping and sawing wood, lifting heavy furniture, tilling and tending a garden, and lugging music instruments and equipment, I couldn't imagine adding workouts in some gym. But then I didn't sit at a computer all day.

I tried to hurry him up, but he ordered more coffee. Finally, he slipped a twenty on the table and left before I could argue about who paid the bill.

I waved to Della on my way past the store and took the steps two at a time. Alex already had two computers fired up. "Abit, I'm happy to help, but you know, you could learn how to do this and do it whenever you needed. You can use the extra computer I leave here anytime you want." I shrugged my shoulders, and he laughed. "Don't pull that aw-shucks stuff with me, Abit. You can learn how to do this."

Now it was my turn to laugh. He had me there. "I'm sure I'll learn when the time's right. But just this oncet more, please?" He was still looking at me when I told him I'd think about it, which was what I always said just to get him offa my back. I think he knew it too.

We started with the "Omie Wise" murder over in Randleman in Randolph County. Alex worked a while and cursed colorfully a time or two. I knew the woman killed in April had drowned, just like Omie, but Alex said first she'd been struck with a tire iron. And she wasn't pregnant like Omie. Those new facts bothered me, but I needed to know them; Airhorn (that's what we called the sheriff behind his back on account of his loud voice) would bring them up—and more.

Alex kept digging. After a while he said, "The first victim did work as a housekeeper for a family in Randolph County, which does jibe with the ballad's backstory."

My heart started banging when we moved on to checking out Keaton. I gave him Keaton's full name and the title of the music book he wrote. Alex put his head down and typed and clicked and cursed some more. Then he looked up. "Abit, I'm glad you didn't tell anyone else those ideas you're harboring about Keaton."

"Why? Is the FBI already looking into him?"

Alex smiled, the kind you do when you're tolerating an idiot you happen to like. "Looks as though he's been serving his country for the past five years, some of that time in Afghanistan. He was in special ops, so no wonder there was a bunch of secrecy surrounding his whereabouts. Besides, I don't have to tell you that mountain folks keep to themselves."

He worked a while longer. He didn't seem to mind me looking over his shoulder as he brought up all kinds of new leads. "Here's something about his book. Hey, you didn't tell me his father co-authored it. Anyway, it was well reviewed in *Now & Then* magazine out of East Tennessee State University."

I was sorry for Keaton, having lived through a war and all, but I still wasn't convinced he was innocent. I kept seeing the way he crept outta the room at the first mention of the murder. "Okay, but what about five year ago? Was he stationed in Tennessee, maybe?" I was thinking about "Knoxville Girl" and "Barbara Allen" over in Chattanooga.

"Nope. When he was stateside, he was based in Fayetteville, on the other side of North Carolina."

"He coulda driven …"

"Come on, Abit. What have you got against this guy? That's way out in left field."

"But he was carrying a coil of rope and, well … he's creepy." The words were barely outta my mouth before I shuddered. I thought about how I'd feel if I'd spent time fighting strangers in Afghanistan. To be honest, I couldn't even imagine it. His shying away from murder talk now seemed only natural.

Alex and I talked some, and he eased me back on track. "Look, just because it isn't Keaton doesn't make the mystery go away. Somebody's killing people, and your theory about the murder ballads seems sound to me. Look for other people who are familiar with bluegrass."

"Well, technically, it's folk music, and in these parts that doesn't narrow it down much," I said. "Guys you'd figure couldn't recall their own names know the exact year Bill Monroe formed the Monroe Brothers and the year Earl Scruggs and Lester Flatt left the Blue Grass Boys to form Foggy Mountain Boys."

All this made me wonder if maybe I did need to learn about computers. Sure was easier than sneaking round somebody's cabin to find info—and coming up with wild and hurtful ideas. You could probably still find crazy notions on a computer, but it wouldn't take the toll of time and trouble.

Alex sat quiet-like as I worked out my feelings. He was good like that. After a while, I thanked him for his time and our dinner. Then I slipped out, chased by feelings of shame.

I noticed the store wasn't too busy, so I stopped by to say hey to Della. She was looking over some papers at the counter, but when she saw me, she put them down where she stored paper bags. I wanted to ask about them, but I had more important things on my mind. I told her what had just happened with Alex.

"I can't believe I almost accused an innocent man who'd been fighting in a godawful war of committing five murders." But then something hit me. "Hey, but what was he doing in Kona? And why did he have a big coil of rope?" Della looked baffled, so I brought her up to date on my Keaton sightings.

"Sounds to me as though he's a researcher," she said. "Probably writing an article. And didn't you say he was moving? More than likely he needed rope for that."

I started fiddling with the coffee cup she'd given me. "Man, I've gotten everything wrong. I wished I'd never started looking into all this."

"Oh, come on, Abit. Only Alex and I know what you were thinking, and we don't count. Don't let this misstep stop you. Like you keep saying, your ideas, in the right hands, could save lives. Share them with Sheriff Horne. He's a fair man. He'll listen to you."

"I'm not so sure."

"You're headed in the right direction. Keep at it. I was reading in the paper just this morning about how clueless, in the literal sense, law enforcement is about these murders. Go talk to the sheriff. Get it off your chest and then get back to your real work, the work you love."

"I can't seem to get up the nerve," I said. "It always feels like someone is looking over my shoulder, ready to cut me down or find fault. You ever have that happen, Della?"

"Not really, honey. I'm afraid that's your cross to bear."

"Okay, but will you go with me to see Sheriff Horne?"

"Make that *two* crosses to bear."

Chapter 37: Della

When Abit left, I pulled out the envelope the postman had delivered and carried it to the backroom. I sorted through pages and pages of names and deposits from Westonia Bank printed on an old dot-matrix printer. I didn't know those were still around, but I imagined my guy—I'd given him the moniker DEEP POCKET—had chosen it and his cut-out words to make everything harder to trace. And he'd likely worn latex gloves while handling it all. I thought about taking these documents and those I'd found in Jessie's trashcan directly to the authorities, but before I did, I needed a better understanding of what I had.

The bell over the door had been jingling, and from the rising level of chatter I could tell the store was filling up. I spent the rest of the day out front. The store didn't clear out again until right before closing time. Once I locked the front door, I grabbed a cup of lukewarm coffee before settling down again with the packet.

Three pages contained long lists of small deposits into dozens of accounts—what I'd learned was a scammer's way of avoiding regulatory thresholds. That must have been where Johnny Ray Meeks and his crew of small-time crooks came in. Another page contained a list of names, some of which I recognized: people of influence and money in the area. My heart did a tap dance as I pored over the remaining pages that included photographs of property for sale and other real estate transactions.

But in the end, what did I have? Just a lot of suspicions, nothing I could take to local authorities, who I reminded myself had already signed off on the burned shack that nearly took Nigel's life. I couldn't help but worry that county officials, maybe even Sheriff Horne, were somehow in on this, or at least looking the other way for kickbacks.

Other transactions I recognized as properties Nigel had forged documents for. No way could I mention those to Horne; Nigel was lucky to have gotten out of the country without that tagging along after him. Or keeping him from ever returning.

Dammit. This all felt like crazy tail-chasing. I stuffed the papers back in the envelope until I could talk with Alex. He was upstairs packing to go back to D.C., but I'd see what we could figure out tonight after dinner.

I used to feel sad when Alex left, but not so much lately. I worried there was something cold about that, but I figured we'd been together long enough for a lazy comfort with one another to infiltrate our lives. Maybe that was *why* we were still together.

I *would* miss his cooking. For our farewell dinner, he was making shrimp scampi with linguine and a late-season tomato salad on lettuces from my back garden. I'd hired Louis, Elbert Totherow's grandson, to plow a good-sized section of the meadow behind the store after I'd found an old copy of Ruth Stout's *How to Have a Green Thumb*

Without an Aching Back on Elbert's front porch; he let me take it for the barter of a dozen tomatoes. I covered the soil with a good foot of *rotted* hay (Louis taught me that—so I wouldn't grow a lush garden of fescue grass) and planted a salad garden—five kinds of lettuce, tomatoes, cucumbers, and herbs. Our summer had been a wet one, so I hadn't needed to water the garden. The results were more than satisfying.

After dinner, Alex brought out port and a small chunk of Stilton he'd brought down from D.C. (I used to stock it, but it never sold well.) I didn't know if feeling tipsy would hurt or help our musings about DEEP POCKET, but I was about to find out.

Not surprisingly, Alex had written a series on money laundering several years ago. That was the reporter's mantra: "I wrote a story on that …," which usually cued friends to roll their eyes or leave the room. The situation he wrote about was different—more money, bigger crooks—but the M.O. was the same.

"I lucked out," Alex said. "Like Nigel was for you, my source was one of those culprits-turned-expert. He'd been convicted of money laundering, and once he'd served some time, he switched sides. That began an impressive career in the identification and detection of financial crime with a focus on money laundering. I was grateful for his inside knowledge, though I've got to tell you, that guy rankled me. He oozed decorum and charm but I knew he'd graduated from White-collar Crime University. With dishonors."

When Alex stopped to sip his port, I broke in. "Johnny Ray Meeks forced Nigel to be a part of something similar. Best I could tell from what Nigel said, they also involved shell companies in other states."

"Yeah, and your lazy sheriff refused to look deeper." I hated to lay that on Sheriff Horne, but I couldn't disagree. "Now let's see what your whistleblower sent you."

The document that proved especially helpful was a four-page primer DEEP POCKET created for me about what made real estate deals easy and profitable for money launderers. Compared to other methods, real estate was less complicated and required little planning or expertise.

I felt myself getting steamed by the ease with which these crimes could be pulled off. "Why don't the banks and government agencies do something about this?"

"Lobbyists outnumber representatives, and banking has one of the biggest cadres of lobbyists. They *know* this is going on; they just choose to look the other way."

The primer included other ways money launderers did their dirty work, such as overpriced renovations on high-end properties that can be resold for way more than their worth. Or taking advantage of mortgages, something DEEP POCKET called the money launderers' favorite "safe" method. Once approved for the loan, the mortgagor settled the debt after a short period, thereby getting rid of tons of cash "legitimately." Other crooks chose successive selling, which meant exactly what it sounded like: selling the property many times to confuse the audit trail.

"Time to stop, for now," I said, leaning over and kissing Alex. I was thinking about his leaving early the next morning and how riled we were getting over the boldness—and abundance—of these scams. "I really appreciate your helping me with all this. It's hard to get my relatively honest head around these machinations."

"You're welcome, babe. But I want to know why this whistleblower chose you. Why not go to the authorities?"

"Maybe he did. We both know whistleblowers who were blown off by authorities, sometimes for good reasons, sometimes not. As for why he chose me, I have no idea. I've never covered financial stories in D.C., though it was well known I had excellent sources in various government agencies. But that was ages ago. No one would remember me now."

"It's got to be someone from Charlotte, though maybe with ties to D.C." He looked lost in thought before adding, "But you don't really need to know, do you? It's not about the whistleblower—assuming you trust him—but what he's delivered. That's the story."

And there it was again. That frisson of excitement that fueled the almighty story. I guess I wasn't ready to give up, after all.

While I was still on a roll, I wrote out a new ad for the *Observer*: I GET IT. NOW WHAT, DEEP POCKET?

I looked over at Rascal curled up on the couch. His little head popped up, curious about what was next. A walk? A treat? His coat was growing out in the cutest way, which boded well for his adoption. I placed an ad about him too.

Like clockwork, the postman brought an envelope the fourth day after my ad ran. When I opened it in the backroom, I saw a simple dot-matrix note attached to more printouts.

DEEP POCKET? Ha! I remember your sense of humor, but don't think this is a game. You're playing with fire.

I felt a chill work its way down my spine—and back up again. He remembered me? Just who was I entangled with?

At six o'clock, I locked the front door, poured a glass of pinot, and read his latest report: more pages of names, but these included phone numbers and account numbers. I'd start calling tomorrow, my day off. For what, I didn't know. Yet. But if it meant enough for DEEP POCKET to send it, it must be important.

Chapter 38: Abit

The next evening, Fiona finally got a night off from the hospital. I usually looked forward to our evenings together, but not that night. I couldn't put off Dr. Navarro any longer; I'd been stewing long enough.

Vern was staying over, and we'd had a nice supper I'd made of fresh squash and tomatoes from the garden alongside macaroni and cheese—a recipe I'd gotten from Eva and Lurline, the cooks at The Hicks. They were two of the finest cooks I'd ever met—even if they were a coupla wildcats. I still had the scar where they accidentally cut me when I broke up their fight with kitchen knives.

We were clearing the table and doing the dishes; the boys were upstairs, doing more horseplay than homework. I screwed up my courage and said, "I see the doctor's back." Fiona flinched. She didn't need me to explain *which* doctor. "I wished you'd told me so I wasn't surprised when I saw him. And it would help me think it didn't matter to you. But you hiding it, well …" I turned my drying towel inside a glass so hard I was surprised it didn't bust.

When I thought she wasn't gonna answer, just leave this big black cloud hovering over us, she spoke. "He's only working part-time in Newland, the rest of the time in Spruce Pine." As if that made any difference. "And I *was* thinking of you. I didn't want you to get upset."

"I'm not the one you should be thinking about. Think about little Conor whenever you see that doctor, and think about who his daddy is."

"I know who Conor's daddy is. He's the man who didn't want to have him." She left me standing there, not moving, just holding on to that towel for the longest time. It was all twisted up when I used it to wipe my eyes.

I was surprised how fast that old pain seared my heart again. I felt sick to my stomach. But as I went over and over what Fiona had said, I could see how her big sadness just had to come out. Fiona wasn't talking about only Conor but also the children she'd never have, thanks to me.

I went out to my shop to work on something, anything. I picked up some wood for the spindles of a rocking chair I'd started. I turned a couple, and then as I turned anothern, I noticed how a weevil of some kind had burrowed into the wood. I was afraid I wouldn't be able to use that piece, but when I looked closer, I saw it hadn't gone deep enough to ruin the wood. In fact, it'd made it more interesting, adding texture and a hint of color before it stopped chewing.

That seemed like such a small thing at the time. But gradually, as I shaped and sanded that wood into something good, it came to me that my problem with the doctor wasn't all that different. I needed to stop the hurt from burrowing any deeper and let that seven-year-old heartache color my life in a good way, with gratitude for how things turned out.

I liked how that sounded. The hard part would be living into it.

Chapter 39: Abit

Fiona and I made up late that evening, though a stillness hung heavy throughout the house. It felt cold lying in bed next to her, like being underwater too long.

First sign of dawn, I got up, made coffee, grabbed a biscuit, and drove over to Spruce Pine to see Wallis. We needed to make some decisions. When I got to the hospital, he was sitting on his bed, dressed in a faded flannel shirt and overalls.

"I'm going home," he said, his words filled with relief. "Finally."

"Can I drive you?"

"And make me hike all the way to the FRIGGIN' cabin?" Then he chuckled a little. "Just kiddin' with you, young Abit. Keaton's coming. We both have four-wheel drive so we can actually navigate my road. Maybe I'll get it graded and graveled, though don't count on it, boy. I've been saying that for a long time." I asked when Keaton was coming. "Not 'til later this afternoon, after work."

I was about to ask what Keaton did, but I decided to let that lay. Besides, I wanted to spend our time together talking about the murders. "Can I buy you a cup of coffee— and get you the H-E-DOUBLE HOCKEY STICKS outta this room?"

"Now, don't you go stealing my swear words. Think up your own! And yes, hand me my boots over there. Let's get the FRANK outta here."

I bought us each a coffee and a decent-looking blueberry muffin. I noticed Wallis sipped his weak coffee as if it were fine wine. "Ah, real coffee," he said, "even if it is weak as cat piss." He looked over at me and winked. "No pretend word for that one—and no, I don't know what cat piss tastes like."

He had me laughing with crazy things like that. He musta felt like a guy just let outta prison, and I was glad to see that side of him. When I turned the conversation round to the murders, I asked if he'd had any more inspiration while he was on all those drugs.

"Not that much more than the last time you were here, but I know we're close. And so is our deadline. The fact that he strikes every seventy-three days means we've got only twenty days before …"

"So we've got to get moving," I interrupted. "Are we ready to go to the sheriff?"

"Right on *one* count. As I was saying, we've got only twenty days before tragedy could strike again."

"What's the other count?"

"I don't know who this *we* is you're talking about. You're on your own with the sheriff, young Abit."

That evening we had an early gig in Spruce Pine. (Seemed to be the only place I went these days.) We were playing first, which meant the crowd was cold, and we warmed them up for the next act. But on weeknights, early was just fine. Those of us working or going to school the next day could get a decent night's sleep.

The band arrived in dribs and drabs, and we'd just gotten tuned up when Owen asked if we could play "Arch and Gordon." None of us had even heard it before. "It's from Kentucky," he added with a pride that made me think that must be his homeland. But then I remembered he grew up down near Murphy. Didn't matter. Thanks to Bill Monroe, Kentucky held a special place in the hearts of all bluegrass players.

He showed the band the music and lyrics, and I wasn't surprised we'd never heard it. As Fiona read over the music, her eyebrows shot up a time or two where the lyrics went on about dying sons and such. "The music looks too slow and dreary," I said. "It'll put the audience to sleep."

"We can fix that," Owen shot back, "with a little practice."

They were going back and forth when I interrupted. "We've got to go on in a minute. Let's talk after the show." I wanted to let the others decide, especially since I'd already made up my mind. I hated those lyrics; I was sick and tired of murder and death.

Chapter 40: Della

I had the day off, and I wanted—no, make that *needed*—to do something fun. Get out into the woods or maybe drive up to that new café in Banner Elk. Rascal picked up on my energy and started following me everywhere.

First, though, there was something I wanted to check in DEEP POCKET's latest report. I'd looked it over last night, but it wasn't until this morning that it struck me something was off about the names. Sure enough, William James on one list became James Williams and Liam James on others. Allen David became David Allen and Nella Davis. They couldn't even come up with fresh names? Then again, why bother? Regulatory oversight appeared to be a joke.

That led me to take another look at some strange-sounding companies—likely the LLC shell companies money launderers favored. I found a few of them on the Internet, but most either had no presence on the Web or the barest of home pages. And no answer when I called the phone numbers listed.

Same with the lists of individuals. Mostly no one answered, but when someone did, they told me they were just visiting—renting a mountain home for a few months. One even asked if I could come over and unblock the toilet. I hung up.

When I checked the clock, what had started as a quick look turned into another shot morning. This whole mess was crazy; I had to get out. I called Cleva. She was up for lunch but insisted on making it. I just had to bring wine and something from the new baker I'd told her about.

I packed the Jeep with a couple of bottles of her favorite white wine—Gruner Veltliner—and a coconut cream pie. And Rascal. She hadn't met him yet, and I planned to ask her to spread the word among her sizeable cadre of friends and family that he needed a new home.

She'd made some of her favorite vegetable dishes—yellow squash casserole, corn pudding, ratatouille. I worried the pie might be too heavy after all that, but neither one of us complained. Afterwards we were sipping a silky brew of Arabian Mocha-Java when Cleva asked to see the documents I'd brought.

"How did you know?" I asked.

She just smiled. I *had* brought the lists from DEEP POCKET just in case I got the opportunity to run it by her. She scanned one, then another. I didn't expect much since she seemed rather blasé, turning the pages quickly. Maybe that's what happened when you turned 88.

Wrong again.

"Some of these addresses caught my eye," she said. "I'm certain they're all out Beaverdam way. Really nice second homes overlooking the Black Mountains. May I mark on these pages?" I gave her a pen, and she circled some addresses while she talked. "I used to wonder about whether these homes were rented out too. Does that thing say anything about that?"

She was referring to the primer I was leafing through. "Yeah, it says they can't lose money on real estate deals and probably make a bunch more through rent and appreciation—all while laundering sizable fortunes."

"And I'd always thought those rich folks were just treating themselves to a mountain getaway." She handed back the papers. "I think we need a road trip."

We drove to Beaverdam, looking for addresses on our list. Not as easy as it sounded. Out in the country, people knew where each other lived by ancestral names or landmarks like "the old school yard" or "J. B. McCutchen's daddy's place." Once 911 was introduced, the county assigned everyone an address to help EMTs and firefighters find them. But that was rarely painted on a mailbox, if you could even read the name and address through all the bullet holes. (Apparently new mailboxes made for irresistible target practice.)

These days GPS helped, though too often, way out there, it sent you to the edge of a cliff or you couldn't even get a signal. Thanks to Cleva's keen eyes, we managed to locate the cluster of second homes on our list and several shacks. The records showed that two of the shacks with surrounding land sold last year for more than $700,000.

This chicanery seemed so obvious to me I couldn't believe they could get away with it. But as I kept reading, I learned there were virtually no reporting requirements for suspicious deals. Add in busy loan officers, shady lawyers, and no telling how much palm greasing, and I could almost smell the steaming pile of illegal transactions in and around our county.

"This is giving me a bad case of the jitters," Cleva said. She reached over and patted my hand. "But I sure am enjoying the countryside—and your company. And Rascal's."

At the sound of his name, Rascal stretched from the backseat all the way to the console, positioning himself for some petting that Cleva generously supplied.

We weren't ready to head home, so I drove down curvy mountain roads 'til we came to a stunning overlook. I stopped and turned off the engine. Rascal jumped in the front seat and sat on my lap. Now we could both pet him. We sat there for the longest time, not saying much. Not needing to.

After I dropped off Cleva, I drove home under a cloud of gloom. I was long over the notion that I'd escaped D.C. for an idyllic mountain community, but this blatant fraud was a new low. Not only did it line the pockets of greedy crooks, but they forced poor and hard-working families to fork over money to pay jacked-up property taxes.

I got madder and madder on the drive back to Coburn's. By the time I arrived, I couldn't wait to place another ad for DEEP POCKET.

Chapter 41: Abit

I sat outside the sheriff's office in Newland, unable to make myself get out and go talk with Airhorn. I mean Sheriff Horne. Man, that was the last thing I needed to do—slip up and call him Airhorn to his face.

That morning, I'd asked Fiona if we could meet up for our midday dinner together since the sheriff worked in the same town as her hospital. Things had been tense round the house, and I wanted to do something different to help break the spell.

My heart sank when she said she never knew when she'd get a break. "Never mind, then," I said, sounding like someone closer to Conor's age. But I'd been counting on having something to look forward to after talking with Airhorn.

"Well, if you don't mind waiting for my call, Rabbit." Then she acted like she'd just thought of something. "Oh, wait. You don't have a cell phone." She looked so smug, I turned to walk away. She grabbed my arm. "I'll do my best to make it by one o'clock," she said, smiling. "But bring something to read in case you have to wait."

Our former Deputy Sheriff Lonnie Parker had gotten a promotion, though I had no idea why. He'd never showed a bit of gumption except a time or two when he got Della some information the previous sheriff didn't want her to have. After Parker moved to Gaston County, two women took his place, one a deputy and the other some kind of office manager. I walked toward the one with the kinder face, which happened to be the deputy.

"I'm Abit Bradshaw, and I've got some important information to share with Sheriff Horne."

"He's with someone."

These people never gave out more information than they had to. "Can I wait?"

"Of course you *can*, but you *may* not want to. I don't know how long he'll be."

I didn't know what she was on about with that *can* and *may* business; I'd have to ask Della. But I figured since I'd screwed up my courage, I'd better wait. I sat down and pulled out a notebook, where I made some notes about what I wanted to tell him.

Airhorn wasn't a bad guy. I'd gotten to know him when Della and I worked together to try to find that missing mother a few year ago. He'd worked hard on that case, and he was nice enough to me, mostly because Della wouldn't have it any other way. But on this day, he made me wait over an hour. I tried being reasonable—maybe he really was busy, and after all, I didn't have an appointment. But when he came out, no one else was in his office, and he had crumbs on his chin. Okay, we've all got to eat, but it was just after eleven o'clock.

"Hello, Bradshaw. What can I do for you?"

"I've got information about the murders."

The office woman stopped typing. The deputy's head shot up from whatever she'd been reading.

"Did you do them?" he asked. That shook me; I felt myself jump back a little. Then he started chortling. Like that was hilarious. And of course the women tittered right along with their boss. The only consolation was they didn't really think I'd killed anyone.

He showed me into his office and motioned toward a couple of chairs. I sat in the one opposite his desk. "So Sherlock, tell me what you've discovered." He did that bunny-ear thing with his fingers round that last word, like he was just pacifying a fool. I couldn't figure out why he was in such a foul mood. I knew if I'd been Alex Covington, he would've been nicer, which irritated the tar outta me. But by now I was an old hand at dealing with this shit.

"Listen, Sheriff Horne. I know you think this is funny, a man like me telling you your business. But I'm trying to save lives. Wallis Harding and I have been working hard on this, and we know when the killer will strike again, though I wished like anything we knew where." His sneer got bigger and he actually sighed. "But me and Mr. Harding are still studying on that. Whatever you've been doing hasn't worked. Just ask the families of that poor man in Kona or that woman in Ferguson."

He nodded, letting me know he wanted me to go on, I reckoned to finish hanging myself. So I told him everything Wallis and I had come up with. I explained how we were trying to take the pattern further, to find the where and how of the next one. When I finished, I felt spent. But I looked Airhorn right in the face and waited. And waited.

After what seems like forever, he smiled a scary smile and tented his fingers under his chin. I knew I was in for it. "First, I'm sheriff of *Avery* County. I have no jurisdiction in Mitchell or Randolph counties. Second, you don't know what I *have* been doing. And third, I don't think much of your Nancy Drew detective work. Any questions?"

Man, that guy had a burr up his butt; I barely recognized the man I oncet knew. But I also knew I'd let Airhorn get my ire up, especially when he called me Sherlock, though I believe even Shiloh would've taken offense. Any way you looked at it, I'd blown my chance.

As I drove over to the hospital for dinner with Fiona, I was dreading telling her how much I'd screwed up. When I got there, the only parking place was a ways from the front doors, but I was early, so I took my time.

I was already feeling bad enough, but when the sliding front doors opened and that awful hospital smell came wafting out, my stomach did a flipflop. I didn't know how Fiona stood it, but I guess she got used to it, like I was used to Shiloh's finishing oil. I gave the woman at the information desk my name and told her Fiona O'Donnell was expecting me.

"Oh, Mr. Bradshaw. She left a note for you."

I opened an envelope and took out a quickly scrawled note saying there'd been an emergency she had to help with. All kinds of things ran through my mind, wide open to hurt after the beating I'd taken from Airhorn. Then I read "And get a cell phone so I can let you know proper-like." She drew a smiley face and signed it.

To be honest, I was relieved I didn't have to tell her right then about me and Airhorn. As I walked back to my truck, I saw Dr. Gerald Navarro drive off in his Porsche—alone. At least one of my fears was gone: she wasn't having lunch with *him*.

Chapter 42: Della

FOUND LOTS, CALLED #s, NOTHING ADDS UP. WHAT NEXT?

It'd been three days since I'd placed that ad in the *Observer*. No answer yet.

I was in the back wrapping four-year aged gouda wedges when two men in white shirts and narrow black ties walked into the store. I knew immediately who they were. Especially since the younger one was a Black man, and we didn't see many of them in Laurel Falls.

They picked up bottled water, dried fruit, and mixed nuts. Healthy types, and their waistlines backed that up. When they came to the counter, I felt like a 25-year-old reporter again. I wasn't about to let this opportunity go to waste.

"Just passing through?" I asked. The older one nodded. The young man smiled and said yes. "Headed for Ferguson?" That got their attention. I figured I needed to dive in before they turned to leave. I purposely hadn't taken their money yet.

They just looked at me, thinking their steady gaze would put me off. Not a chance. I'd dealt with the FBI more times than I cared to remember. It was part intuition and part know-how that told me who they were.

"How do you know that?" the older agent asked. He was a good-looking guy, in spite of his military-style haircut and stance. His partner had the fresh face of a relatively new agent, around Abit's age or a little younger. I felt for him; I'd written several stories about Quantico and the training they put new recruits through.

"Well, I don't believe you're Mormons, and I know you're not Jehovah's Witnesses," I said. "And we've had three murders in this neck of the woods. Seems like a reasonable guess. What I can't figure out is why you're on our windy road, since I assume you're up from Charlotte."

"Well," the older one said, "you know that assume makes an ass of 'u' and me."

I burst out laughing and stuck out my hand. "Della Kincaid. Sorry to be such a smartass, but I have a friend with a strong theory about these murders, and I'd love for you to meet him." I figured I owed it to Abit—and any potential victims—to strike while I could.

"Thanks, but we're on this," he said. He did shake my hand but didn't give me his name. I couldn't let that go, either.

"Okay, got it. But I gave you my name. How about yours?" They mumbled Ezra Stoltz (older) and Curtis Maynard (younger), more out of innate politeness than any professional obligation. I made their change and thanked them. "Oh, and I may have something else to run by you."

"Trouble in paradise?" Stoltz said, with a rather adorable smirk that brought out his dimples.

"Oh, yeah. Looks are deceiving. And good luck with the case. People around here are scared."

They did what those guys do best—nodded—and left. As I saw their black SUV turn into the road, I wondered why the FBI was getting involved in what appeared to be a state investigation.

Chapter 43: Abit

"My da is sick. I need to go see him."

Fiona had just come out to my workshop. Shiloh was there too, and he looked genuinely sad for her. Truth be known, I reckon he liked Fiona a lot more than me.

"What's wrong with him?"

"What do you think? His liver."

I flashed on our wedding party, where he drank a bottle of Jameson and sang the IRA fight song. I figured he hadn't stopped doing either one. But when he was sober, he was a jolly sort, and I was sorry he was doing poorly.

"And you know, not a day before the call I got a shiver, like a goose just walked over my grave." She shivered again.

"Shug, don't go thinking the worst, goose or no goose. Your dad will be fine, especially oncet he sees you."

"You mean us."

"I wish I could take off but …" I looked over to Shiloh for support, but he had a funny look on his face. I realized he'd gotten her meaning before me. "Us?"

"Well, yeah. Conor's going with me. The school has an autumn break in a week, and he can catch up when we get home. I want him to see where I grew up and meet his other family."

"What about Vern?"

"He has his own da and a babysitter. They can manage for a couple of weeks—just like they did before we started having him over." She stamped her foot. "My da needs me."

"But they have good insurance over there."

"That they do. A lot better than here, but still, I'm family, and I'm trained to help."

"That you are—but I still wish you wouldn't go."

"Why are you acting thisaway?" We just looked at each other for what felt like forever, then her face softened. "Aw, Rabbit, sure, I know you're gonna miss us."

I couldn't say a word. It felt like if I spoke, a dam would break and I'd make a fool of myself. Instead, I managed a weak smile. I always gave in to that lass. Besides, who was I to keep her from helping her daddy? I had trouble understanding feelings like that toward a father, but I knew people had them.

Fiona came over, nudged me toward a chair, and sat on my lap, putting her arms round me. Shiloh had the good sense to go back to work in the other room. We sat like that for some time. Then she got up to pack.

I drove them to Asheville a couple of days later. That dam feeling came back when I hugged Conor goodbye, like my words were caught in my throat. "Don't worry, Daddy, we'll come home soon," he whispered before letting go.

I didn't want to ruin his fun, so I pulled myself together and smiled. As they made their way through the security line, he waved at me as long as he could see me. Then Fiona held him up one last time before they disappeared through a coupla doors that went only one way.

When I'd finished my work for the day, I didn't want to spend the evening in an empty house. I called Mollie, and we hopped into the truck and headed to Coburn's. Della had a half hour before she could close up, but she welcomed us with a beer and a biscuit. She brought down that little fiest, Rascal, to play with Mollie. Everything had been so crazy, the two dogs hadn't met yet.

While they got acquainted, Della told me about her white-shirt-and-tie visitors. And what she'd said to them.

"You want *me* to talk to the FBI?" I asked, my voice cracking like a teenage boy.

"Abit, this isn't about you. It's about your having a terrific—in all senses of that word—theory. You'll know that you did all you could."

"You wouldn't be encouraging me if you knew what a bad job I did with Airhorn." Her eyebrow went up. I sipped my beer and went on. "Okay, he made me mad. Calling me Sherlock and making bunny ears. And smirking."

She kinda chuckled. "So what did you say?"

"I told him Wallis and I were trying to save lives, which was more than he'd done when it came to Kona and Ferguson."

"So?"

"What do you mean, so?"

"So what? Okay, it would have been helpful to have Horne on your side, but he's small potatoes. He's only the sheriff in Avery County, and there hasn't been a murder in our county."

"Oh, believe me, he made that perfectly clear." I looked away and took another swig.

"And now you're giving up? What happened to your high-and-mighty proclamation of saving lives? If I'd given up every time I made an ass of myself, you and I would never have met. I'd still be living in D.C., only I'd be writing for the free shopper news. You've got to keep at this, Abit."

We went on like that for a time, but she finally wore me down. Besides, with Fiona and Conor away, I didn't have any excuses. "Will you come with me? To talk with the FBI? I mean they'd recognize you and all."

Della thought about that. I was sure she was fixing to say no, but then she took mercy on me. "We'll see."

Chapter 44: Abit

A coupla days later, Della invited me to midday dinner on her day off. Mollie raced up the apartment steps ahead of me to see Rascal; they'd really taken to one anothern.

After a while, we sat down to some homemade vegetable soup, fresh bread, and a coupla cheeses. I'd learned that I liked some of the stinkier ones she carried and noticed she'd remembered which ones.

When I'd finished my soup, I kept whittling on a cheese called raclette. It spread on the French bread as good as soft butter. After a couple more of those, I mentioned something I'd been stewing on. "I don't know how you do it—saying goodbye to Alex all the time. Fiona and Conor being gone made a big hole in my life. Is that what you feel when Alex goes away?"

She gave me the saddest look. "No, honey, it's not."

"But you love him."

"I do. And I miss him when he leaves, but we've spent too much time apart to feel the rift you're feeling now. And the damage that was done when we divorced took something out of me. I don't know if this makes sense to you, but some sorrows just don't go away. Not fully. We learn to live with them, we even have days we forget all about them, but they're still there, like someone living in the basement who keeps to himself, though you always know he's there."

I assured Della I knew exactly what she was talking about. In fact, I had enough men in my basement for a bluegrass jam session. But I went on to explain I was also missing the smaller things. Like when I'd catch a glimpse of Fiona rustling through her special Irish box and sneaking a wheatmeal biscuit when she thought no one was round, enjoying it and a good memory from back home. Or seeing her leaf through a catalog, looking for something pretty to wear. "Those times are so tender, Della, they're hard to describe."

"No need to, honey. I get it. Like when you see someone hungry eating a meal or smiling when offered a kindness they're not accustomed to. Times like that remind us we're all one, not separate."

After that we didn't say much as we worked together on the dishes. When she put her towel down, she asked, "Have you ever noticed the way a lot of old people seem so world-weary, dragged down by life?" I nodded; my parents sure did, though they didn't wait 'til they were old to get thataway. "Now that I'm catching up with their age, I've been asking myself what causes that. All I can figure is each of life's heartaches takes a piece out of us, and something hard and dark can slip in to fill that hole. After five or six decades, the dark places begin to outweigh the good."

She paused. I was about to say some stupid thing to cheer her up, but she beat me to it. "One way I've found to overcome the darkness, to not let it slip in and petrify my heart, is to make new experiences. Like you just said, they don't have to be big—just small things. Being kind to a stranger, trying a new café, driving somewhere you've never been before. They often lead to something fresh, filling those holes with light."

"Not much new round here."

"You haven't been looking hard enough. Let's take Mollie and Rascal for a walk somewhere new—like Stone Mountain State Park. A couple of tourists stopped by the store for drinks on their way home and said it was amazing. Afterwards, we can get supper at a place we've never been before. My treat."

I liked her plan, but I should have known she was cooking up more than a walk in the park.

Chapter 45: Abit

For some reason, Della took small, windy roads to get to the park. "They're prettier," was all she said when I asked why. Okay, I gave her that. Goldenrod and purple asters hugged the roadside while red-leafed dogwoods and witch hazels, blooming yellow now, hovered over them like protective parents.

The trip gave us time to talk, and we managed to get in a few laughs. I started to feel so good I sang "On and On," a lively tune I loved, even if the lyrics were kinda sad about his darling leaving him. But that was okay; I knew my family would be coming back to me.

With a sudden jerk of the steering wheel, Della turned off the main highway on to a gravel road, like she knew just where she was going. She pulled into a field where black SUVs, cars, and a van were parked willy-nilly.

That's when it hit me. Della'd driven us to Ferguson. Where Tom Dooley murdered Laura Foster in 1866 and some monster axed a woman two month ago. The same place I'd swung by on my trip home from Greensboro.

She found a shady place to park for the dogs, lowered the windows, and put a bowl of water in the back. Then she smiled at me. "Come on, Abit, let's go meet these bottles and stoppers."

By the time I'd straightened myself out after slouching in the Jeep for over an hour, Della was already chatting with some guy who looked official. Her reporter skills hadn't left her.

"Listen, you can't just walk up here like that. Who let you in?"

"More like who was there to stop us? Security is pretty lax around here." Man, she had some nerve.

"Ms. Kincaid, please step away from the scene."

In spite of my nerves—or maybe because of them—I had to work hard at not laughing. That guy sounded right out of a TV show. He stood a little taller than Della, about her age and looked good for his age. His short hair had turned salt and pepper, and his eyes were so dark brown they looked almost black. The only color was his face—an angry red.

"Okay, okay, Agent Stoltz. But I want you to meet my friend, Abit Bradshaw." She did her arm like a game show host in my direction. Stoltz's eyes followed, and his frown deepened.

"What is going on here? What are you playing at?"

"Playing at? Really, Agent Stoltz? Like I mentioned at the store, we're here about finding this damn serial killer before he kills again. We're here about *saving* lives."

I guess what I'd told Airhorn might've done some good, after all, since Della nearabout quoted me. What I'd told her the other day had made an impression.

Another agent walked up while she was talking; I assumed he was the younger one Della'd met at the store. That made two FBI agents too many, and I turned to leave.

Not Della.

She started in on how she knew from her crime-writing days in D.C. that the FBI didn't just show up on cases like this. Local lawmen had to have asked for help from the FBI. "So here's some help for *you*," she said, again pointing my way.

Stoltz looked at me like I was dog dirt on his shoe. "Oh, please. Enlighten us. Then maybe this crazy woman will drive off and leave us to do our work."

I had trouble finding my words, but after a time, they tumbled out. I managed to make my case and give credit to Wallis Harding, who I explained was an *expert*. I gave them all the details we'd come up with, including seventy-three days—now with only twelve to go. I was extra polite and *yes sirred; no sirred; you're right, sirred* whenever Stoltz asked me something. I told them everything—except the one thing they were looking for.

"So how will all this help us *stop* the next killing, God help us if there is one?"

I felt the color rise up my neck. I couldn't answer.

When we got back into the Jeep, we rode along forever without saying a word. Della was lost in thought, and I felt like a fool. Stoltz had practically patted me on the head and sent me home. And the other guy, Agent Maynard, just stood there, studying the ground.

But after a while, I let all that go. I reminded myself that I was on a road trip with Della, like the ones we'd taken so many year ago. The weather was still sunny and warm, and we were headed to a park I'd never been to before. We rode along quiet-like until I asked, "You know how Fiona and I decided to have only one child?"

Della clenched the steering wheel so tight the Jeep swerved a little. She righted it and nodded. I'd noticed she tensed up whenever I brought up the subject of kids. I reckon that was somehow a heartache in her life too.

"Well, it wasn't just because of my genes." I waited a beat, but she kept staring straight ahead. "When I was little, I used to say to myself that I couldn't wait to have my own kids so I could push them around, you know, like I was."

Della looked over and let out a big sigh. "Oh, honey, everyone's had thoughts like that. That doesn't mean anything in the long run. How old were you?"

"About 8 year old or so."

"I rest my case. I'd hate to think of what all went through my mind when I was that age. Don't beat yourself up. When we're young, we think all kinds of crazy things. That's why they call it growing up."

"So why didn't you ever have kids?"

She took her time answering. "Oh, lots of reasons. I couldn't see bringing a child into this crazy world, but you've changed my thinking on that." She looked over my way. "When I see children like Conor, I know the world will go on in spite of mean-spirited politicians and crazy serial killers." She gave me the saddest smile and turned back to watch the road. After a mile or so she added, "And besides, I didn't trust Alex to stick around."

"But he's great."

"Yeah, in lots of ways. And to be fair, it wasn't just that. I loved my job. It was dangerous and time-consuming. I couldn't see chasing a story about a mob gangster and going home to make pablum."

"You'd've been a great mother."

"That's easy to say now, Abit. Maybe I would *now*. But not back then." She looked at me again. "You'll just have to be my kid, okay?"

"Fine by me."

Stone Mountain turned out to be a giant rock sticking outta the earth, big and smooth and hard to fathom. A sign explained that over time, all the softer layers of rock washed away, leaving it to stand proud, six-hundred feet in the air.

The dogs were excited, and I was glad to get outta of the Jeep. I'd started having a delayed reaction to that damn FBI agent. "You oversold me, Della."

That came outta nowhere, but she knew exactly what I was talking about. "Hold your horses, buster. I got you an audience with the chief honcho, and he's not likely to forget you or what you're trying to do. You know how men like that are—ego all caught up with being first, being the best.

He knows you now, and I believe I saw some respect for your ideas."

"You were seeing things."

"No, honey, I wasn't. He nodded a time or two. Coming from an FBI agent, that's tantamount to a papal blessing."

We took care of Mollie's and Rascal's needs before we settled into a quiet walk, only saying stuff about the wildflowers or birdsong. A hawk shrieked off in the distance. I never liked that sound, a cry of loneliness.

Walking in the woods made me think of church, in a good way. The trees rose up toward the heavens while protecting us here on Earth. We walked on a path made soft with pine needles and leaves, hugging a stream where frogs carried on in harmony with a chorus of chittering birds. Everything felt right.

Until a big tattooed guy came up behind us with a blaring radio. Some kind of mishmash country music—nothing like the good stuff the Rollin' Ramblers played. I made a face at Della, but she just shrugged her shoulders. Rascal took my side and gave a low growl, though that guy never heard him over his noisy radio. We slowed down and mercifully the brute moved on. The music drifted behind him for a while, but soon joined him round the bend.

The trail led us to the middle falls and later the lower falls along Big Sandy Creek. It was pretty, but I liked Laurel

Falls better. I thought to myself, *that sounds just like Mama*, but it was the truth. Whatever, the walk did all four of us good.

We found a nice little café for supper. After we gave the dogs some fried chicken scraps, they slept most of the way home, and I almost did. I made myself stay awake to keep Della company, but she was lost in thought again. After a while, she broke the silence.

"When do you think you and Wallis will figure out the killer's pattern? You've come so far, surely you two can take it the next step."

"If I knew that, I'd be at Wallis' right now."

She chuckled. "I guess you would. It was just that you did such a good job of explaining the chronology of everything to Stoltz. It's like 'shave and a haircut, two bits.' You've got the shave and a haircut part, now what is the two bits?"

Something she said gave me a start. I tried to follow that feeling, but it had already drifted away, like that awful country music.

Chapter 46: Abit

A gunshot made me bolt straight up in bed. Mollie lifted her head and looked over at me like *what in the world is going on?* (With Fiona gone, there was plenty of room on the bed for Mollie, and to tell you the truth, it felt pretty good to sleep with her back against mine.)

I lay back down, listening to see if I heard it again. The clock said five o'clock; too damn early to get up. Mollie didn't have a bit of trouble getting back to sleep, making little snoring noises I envied. I lay there quiet-like, and eventually I came to understand that gun's report was making sure I paid attention to something I'd dreamed about.

I lay there a while longer before I got up and made Mollie's breakfast and cooked myself some scrambled eggs. I did a real good job of them; Alex had taught me how. The trick is to cook them pretty quick. Just as they start to thicken, move the curds off to the side and keep doing that 'til they're almost done. They'll finish cooking on the plate, which I'd warmed on the woodstove. The mornings were already cool enough that a little fire felt good.

I sat down with my toast and eggs, eating some and sharing some with Mollie. Mostly I drank coffee, thinking about what I was going to do next.

"Didn't expect to see you, young Abit."

I guess not, given that Wallis was in his bathrobe—in the middle of the afternoon. I'd worked in my shop on some pressing orders, so it wasn't 'til after my midday meal that I drove out to his cabin. I was worried he was sick again and asked if he was doing all right.

"I'm fine. Just the most comfortable thing I own. And with Keaton off on his own again, I didn't see any good reason to get dressed."

"Makes sense to me," I said, even though I couldn't imagine not getting dressed by that late in the day. I almost snorted as I pictured myself out in the woodshop, sawing a big board down to size wearing one of Nigel's silky dressing gowns.

Wallis invited me in and went to put on regular clothes. He came out wearing his usual flannel shirt with ironed overalls and headed straight to the kitchen to put on some coffee. I needed anothern after my early start. As he put a mug down in front of me, he asked, "So what's so ALL-FIRED important that you came all the way out here?"

"I need your opinion."

"Fire away," he said, frowning. He definitely had a case of the grumps today, but I reminded myself he wasn't long outta the hospital after heart troubles.

"A gunshot woke me early this morning, but I believe it was from a dream, trying to grab my attention so I wouldn't let something important slip by." He seemed to understand what I was saying. "Later, while I was carving some oak leaves into a sideboard, I realized it had something to do with what my friend Della said to me yesterday." I told him about the FBI, and he looked wide awake for the first time since I'd arrived. "She was telling this stuck-up agent about the *chronology* of everything. At the time I got one of those funny feelings, but I didn't know what to make of it. Now I think the murderer is choosing ballads based on when *they* happened."

Wallis jumped up and grabbed *Traditional Tales of True Crime Ballads in the Southern Appalachians*. He started leafing through the book real fast. He read for a while and then hit himself in the head. "STORM AND THUNDER, young Abit, you've done it!" He plunked it down on the table between us and took a big swig of coffee. "If I weren't such a MUTTONHEAD I'd've seen it too. Looky here."

He turned a few pages and pointed to a timeline of the murders near the front of the book: Omie Wise, 1807; Frankie Silver, 1833; Tom Dooley 1866. "It appears the author has chosen to cover the biggies—there's only so much room in a book, you know—and now, thanks to you, what I'm thinking is this maniac plans his heinous crimes following the best-known ballads in the order they happened."

"If we're right about 'Knoxville Girl' and 'Barbara Allen,' what years were they?"

He scratched his stubbly beard, which was growing back in after his stay at the hospital. "Oh, those are too

BLASTED old," Wallis said. "Long ago—from the Old Country. Fifteenth, seventeenth century. Let's not bring them into this; besides, I'm still not sure how 'Barbry Allen' fits in."

I was irked he'd brought that up again. "You SON OF A BISCUIT, quit dismissing 'Barbara Allen.' She's in there somehow, I just know it."

I expected him to get mad, given the mood he was in, but his mouth twitched at the corners and he nodded at me, acknowledging his approval of my made-up swearword. That made me laugh.

He waved me off and jabbed his finger again on to the page. "So if we stick to these all-American ballads, look at the chart. At least this author—and we have no reason to argue—has listed the next in line as 'Poor Ellen Smith' and 'The Peddler and His Wife,' 1892 and 1895, respectively."

"I've never heard of 'The Peddler and His Wife.'"

"Oh, I have, but that's not the point. The point is this author lists it, and if the killer has this book too, which is likely since there's not all that many books out there about murder ballads, the odds are good the next victim—or victims—relate to one of these ballads."

"Yeah, but which one?"

"That, young Abit, is the $64,000 question."

Wallis said he could give me one more hour, and by the end, we knew we were on to something. The next murder would be over in Winston-Salem if it were fashioned after "Poor Ellen Smith" or up in Harlan County, Kentucky if he chose "The Peddler and His Wife." I didn't say this out loud, but I hoped it was the first one, because the story in Kentucky was a *double* murder.

"The Peddler and His Wife" told the story of a Jewish couple—what would be a traveling salesman and shopkeeper today. In 1895 the man and his wife were both shot while riding in a wagon, robbed for their gold.

In 1892 Ellen Smith was shot in the heart by her former boyfriend, Peter DeGraff, while in the garden of the swankiest hotel in Winston-Salem.

"Which one would you choose, if you were trying to catch this guy?" I asked. "My bet would be on the next one year-wise—'Poor Ellen Smith.'"

"I don't know," he said in that mountain way that reeked of contrariness.

I bit. "Okay, what would you do?"

"I'd tell those G-men to stake out both sites. Sure, 'Poor Ellen Smith' is next chronologically, but it's in a big city, right downtown. This killer don't seem like the type to go traipsing round a metropolitan area."

"What about Chattanooga?"

"Well, those murders weren't in town but out in the nearby countryside. Still, to be on the safe side, I'd tell the G-men to cover both. I bet you could help them find some

Jewish merchants in Harlan County. Remind me where in the SAM HILL that is." He was so hepped up he didn't bother to wait for me to tell him. "I plan to go to the library and find out what hotel in Winston-Salem is the finest today. Then you take that information over to them, and tell them BLASTED BANDITS they need to pay attention to you. Us. We are right about this."

For maybe only the second time in my life, I'd wished I'd had a computer and could get on the internet. I coulda helped Wallis find that hotel in no time. But he was stuck in his ways and probably wouldn't've listened anyway. He could read ads in the Yellow Pages at the library or one of those fancy travel brochures they keep on hand. Too bad that wouldn't work on finding Jewish peddlers.

When Wallis and I finished up, I hurried home to get Mollie. She was good about staying round the farm, so it wasn't like she needed to be let out, but I missed her. And she was such a people dog, I knew she was feeling as lonesome as me.

When I drove up, she bounded over. We wrestled a while and then I fed her. Being back at home made me long to write Fiona on the email. So much had happened since she'd been gone. She'd called oncet, but I knew that musta cost a fortune; I think her daddy paid for that call. I wanted to talk to her *now*—even if just in writing.

Chapter 47: Della

I finally heard from DEEP POCKET. The last message I would receive from him arrived in a small envelope—just two letters cut out of a newspaper and glued to an index card: DC. Short, but I knew exactly what he meant.

He *did* know me, and somehow he knew I used to have contacts in D.C., or maybe that Alex still did. What he didn't know was I had a direct connection to a couple of FBI agents, who I planned to ask for help when the time was right. Until then, I needed to get the story straight in my own head. And I didn't want to get in Abit's way. He needed their full attention—or whatever he could garner—for the serial murders.

I was in the back of the store, closing up when I heard the bell over the door ring. Dammit. I hated latecomers. I stuck my head out front and laughed. "Well, speaking of the devil."

"Why am I the devil? And what's so funny?" Abit asked. Mollie trailed in after him just before he closed the door, which brought Rascal running in from the backroom.

"Oh, just that one minute I was dreading another late customer—or the health inspector—and the next I was happy to see *you*."

"What's going on that's so unhealthy?"

"I'm not supposed to have Rascal down here."

"Well, as Wallis would say, FUDGE the health inspector. That dog belongs here."

"That's what I've been thinking."

"What does that mean?" Abit asked, that crooked smile of his creasing his face.

I looked down at the little guy playing with Mollie. "Oh, just that I don't think I'll place any more ads about him."

I wanted to get out of the store before someone else showed up late. I ushered Abit and the dogs outside, locked the front door, and headed up the stairs. "What brings you to town?"

"I want to learn the email."

"Okay, first thing you need to learn: there's no 'the' in front of the word. It's just email."

Abit chuckled. So different from the lanky kid I'd first met who would have given up right there and then. I'd loved that vulnerable man-child, so full of wonder and hurt. But even more, I loved how he'd forged a life remarkably different from what everyone expected.

Mollie and Rascal settled on the couch in the living room while we worked in my office/guestroom. I pulled up my email and asked for Fiona's address. I was worried Abit hadn't understood that you didn't just send a message out into cyberspace, but he reached into his back pocket and pulled out a folded, well-worn piece of paper.

"I got this from her about three month ago, and I've been carrying it round with me."

"What were you waiting for?"

"3,600 miles."

Abit gave the keyboard a serious frown. I reminded him that hunt and peck worked just fine. "Alex still does a variation of that and look how much he types. I'll leave you to it and go rustle up some supper. And dinner for the dogs."

"Mollie's had hers," he mumbled.

"Won't hurt her to have a small encore." I started to leave him alone—then turned back. "See that line called subject line? You'd better type something like 'Hi from Abit' or Fiona will think something awful has happened to you if she sees my email address. I know how she worries about her family."

I made a quick pasta with fresh tomatoes and basil and a salad. We could rummage in the store for dessert. (I enjoyed that as much as my guests.) I called Abit to dinner.

"Could you come look at this thing?" he shouted back.

"You don't want me reading your little love note."

"Nah, just make sure I did this right."

He had. He hit send and stared at the screen as the message disappeared across the ocean.

"What time is it in Ireland?" I asked.

"Half past eleven o'clock. She should still be up, given how late she works some nights here. She has trouble going to bed early."

We were about halfway through dinner when I heard a chime announce a new email. When I was a reporter and sat at my computer all day, I turned that annoyance off. But now I rarely used that computer, and I liked knowing whether Alex or some other friend had written me. We raced to the computer. His face lit up when he saw Fiona's name.

I left him to read in private. As I closed the office door, I heard a knock on my front door, and the dogs did too.

Chapter 48: Abit

I nearly dropped my teeth. Curtis Maynard was sitting in Della's living room, drinking a cup of coffee outta one of her fine china cups. The FBI had come a-calling.

"Abit, you'll catch flies with your mouth hanging open." That Della; she always had some wisecrack. Curtis laughed, put down the cup, and walked over to shake my hand.

I still hadn't found any words when he said, "I wanted to talk further with you, but I didn't know how to reach you. I remembered the way to Ms. Kincaid's store and drove over. Lucky for me you're here too."

I couldn't for the life of me imagine what he needed to talk to me about. I settled into one of Della's chairs and waited. And waited. We were all looking at each other kinda strange, but I didn't begin to know how to start this conversation.

Finally, Curtis said, "I got to thinking about what you told us the other day, and I believe you might be on to something interesting. At least worth hearing more about."

"That wasn't the impression I got earlier," I said. Della frowned at me, her sign language saying *lighten up*. "Not that that was your fault," I added real quick-like. "Agent Stoltz was the one."

"Well, you sure yessired him enough, maybe too much. You suck up to Agent Stoltz like that and it tends to backfire." I cringed at Curtis' description of how I'd acted, reminding me of Fiona's damned complex father stuff. "I mean, he's *not* always right—he just acts like he is. In a word, he's a bully." He stopped. "Oh, never mind all that. I shouldn't be talking out of school. I just wanted you to know I thought your ideas had potential and ..."

He kept talking but I was off thinking about that word. Bully. It hit a nerve, opening a flood of memories I'd tried to keep buried. I musta been lost in thought because I heard Della say something kinda loud.

"Abit, I asked you a question."

"Sorry, what was that? I didn't hear you."

"I asked if I could get you something. Water? Coffee?"

They were both drinking coffee, so I figured I'd better catch up.

Oncet we got back to talking about the murders, Curtis said he couldn't share much (on account of some FBI oath), but he did agree the cases appeared to be the work of a serial killer. Well, that was so obvious it hardly seemed worth the drive over. But he went on to explain how our murder-ballad idea had piqued his curiosity. I filled him in on some details I'd left out while Stoltz was giving me the evil eye. When I mentioned the chronology of the ballads, Curtis' eyebrows dove together.

"What?" I asked.

"Why didn't you mention this the other day?"

"Wallis and I just discovered it." I went into how I'd gotten the notion from Della and then confirmed it with Wallis. "The next likely ballad choices are 'Poor Ellen Smith' and 'The Peddler and His Wife.' And as I told you and Stoltz, they happen every seventy-three days."

"Yeah, we noted that too. Strange number. It must mean something to the killer."

"Wallis said the same thing, though neither him nor me have a clue what to make of that."

I looked over at Della, feeling bad Curtis and I were firing questions back and forth, leaving her out. She could always read my mind and waved me off in a way that said she was fine just sitting this one out. Like the dogs—who were sound asleep at her feet.

"I think it's some kind of numerology," Curtis said. "A lot of people just play at it, but the real deal is fascinating—and complicated. Basically, the letters in names are assigned a number, and those letters are like a puzzle that can be put together in different ways. It takes a computer program to do it from this angle—start with a number and discern names or other clues from it—but I'm going to look into that." Then he stopped talking and looked troubled. "Abit, you know the people around here and their mindset a lot better than me. What do you suppose the payoff is for this serial killer?"

I just shrugged. I couldn't get my mind round a guy wanting to kill people. I was about to say he was crazy when Curtis asked, "Does he love or hate country music?"

"It's bluegrass, or in the case of the murder ballads, more like folk music."

"What's the difference?"

"Never mind that, for now. It's clear this killer knows a lot about murder ballads, though I'm not sure what his choice of music says about him."

"We don't even know for sure it's a man, though I'm with you—it likely is. I hope we can get some clues from this numerology report. *If* we get the report." Della did her eyebrow thing and he went on. "My request needs to pass through Agent Stoltz, and I'm pretty sure he won't go for it."

"Why's that, Curtis?" Della asked.

"You know about chain of command, ma'am. Everyone's life is ruled by it, but in the FBI, if you're young and black, well, you don't get listened to very much."

I knew how folks round here talked about Black people. When I first learned to drive, Mama and her church folks told me to be careful, and to never, ever drive through Lantana, the part of town where Black folks made their homes. It was a good shortcut on the way to Crossnore and Newland, so I never paid them any mind. One wintry February day, I cut through Lantana, and sure enough, the Merc conked out. The cold slapped me in the face when I opened my door and whipped round as I looked under the hood. I couldn't figure out what was wrong and had no choice but to knock on a door.

An old Black man answered and urged me to come in and thaw my hands by the fire; he pointed to the phone and said I was welcome to use it to call for help. He musta been pushing 70 himself, and there he sat in the living room, next to a hospital bed where his mama lay dying. After I called Bill Davis, we sat together, in silence, warm and safe. I've never forgotten that man's kindness—both to me and his mama.

Curtis and I talked a while longer. Then Della started yawning real big (I could tell she was hamming it up to make sure we got the message). Curtis started yawning too. I asked, "Where are you staying?"

"Over in Wilkes County, near the site. We're still working the area."

"That's a long, windy drive. There's room in our barn, if you'd like to hit the hay sooner, rather than later."

Curtis just stared at me for the longest time. Then he jumped up, almost dropping his china cup and saucer on the floor. "What the hell are you talking about?"

I didn't know what to say. Or more to the point, what I'd said. Thank heavens Della stepped in. "What Abit means, Curtis, is they have a lovely guestroom on one end of their barn, overlooking a beautiful mountain vista."

When I realized what he was thinking, I started laughing. Curtis was still glaring at me, but pretty soon he managed a small smile. "Okay, Abit, I'll take you up on that barn. I've only been drinking coffee, but like you said, it's a long drive in the dark."

We thanked Della, who seemed happy we'd both come over—and happy we were leaving.

Curtis followed me home in his car. I pulled the truck in next to the barn so Curtis would know where to park. As soon as I opened the truck door, Mollie jumped out and raced to the door, beating us there. Oncet I unlocked the room, she jumped on the bed and wouldn't get off. She was trying to get Curtis' attention, and I believe she did; he looked awful worried he might have to sleep with her. That made me nervous he'd still think I was putting him out with the livestock, even if that was only Mollie.

"Mollie, come on, girl. Let's go to the house." I clapped my hands a coupla times, and she trotted to the door. "Oh, and the sheets are clean, though they've been on there a while. I hope they're not damp from all this rain."

"Goodnight, Abit and Mollie," Curtis said through a big yawn. "Thanks for putting me up." He looked round the room and added, "Did you do this yourself?"

At first I thought he was saying it looked homemade. But then I saw a tenderness in his face, and I realized we were brothers, of a sort. He hadn't always known a lot of kindness, either.

Chapter 49: Abit

That night a woman's scream woke me round three o'clock. While my heart was trying to scrabble outta my chest, I reached for Fiona, thinking she was hurting. All I felt was dog fur. Then I thought about Curtis out in the barn, worried he might've been in trouble, or at the very least freaked out hearing screams in the middle of nowhere.

When I heard it again, I jumped outta bed. By then, Mollie had a worried look too. The third time, though, I knew: mountain lion. They sounded just like a woman crying out. I grew up hearing them all the time, but I hadn't heard one in ages. All the building and bulldozing in the county had driven them deeper into the woods.

We still saw deer, turkeys, raccoons, and all kinds of birds. I wanted to add more animals to our farm, like banty hens and a rooster. Maybe someday we could stop leasing the hayfields to other farmers and have livestock of our own.

I got back to sleep round five o'clock. By eight I was frying eggs and bacon and baking biscuits for breakfast. Curtis came wandering in and told me not to make a fuss, but I couldn't let him leave hungry. I asked if he'd heard the mountain lion, but he shook his head. I don't think he believed me. He went about cleaning his plate. (I didn't know he was vegetarian 'til later, when Mollie was happily panting in my face while I laced up my boots, and I realized Curtis had given his bacon to her when I wasn't looking.)

When we finished breakfast, I got up to clear the dishes. Curtis stood to help. "I can't thank you enough, Abit. It gets lonesome on these cases."

"Why's that Stoltz guy so hard on you?"

"Oh, just a few things like rank, personality, race. And did I mention race?" He chuckled without humor. "But also because I'm not like most recruits. I don't swagger, at least I hope you haven't seen any of that." I shook my head. "I got into the FBI to help people, not to prove how tough I was."

I hadn't ever had a friend my own age, except for Fiona. Everyone was fifteen, twenty, even thirty year older than me. Maybe you needed to have some wisdom about life to see my worth. Whatever, Curtis seemed different. "You know, my wife and boy are away for a while yet, and I could use some company too. Would you like to come to dinner, say, next weekend? Will you still be up here then? You could stay in the barn."

We both laughed at that, then Curtis said, "We're back and forth from Charlotte, depending on where we're needed. There's a good chance I'll be around. But I insist on meeting for dinner at a restaurant. My treat. My mama would skin me alive if I didn't honor your hospitality."

Later that evening, Mollie joined me on the bed, me under the covers, her on top of them. I petted her for the longest time, hoping her sweetness would come through and fill me. But all I could think about was that damned word—bully. I started recalling all the ones from my life, Agent Stoltz on back to people at Mama's church and Mr. Donnelly, principal at the elementary school. Every time I closed my eyes, hoping to drift off to sleep, I'd see one of them looming over me, meaning me harm.

I'd believed they knew what they were talking about, and that'd caused me to tiptoe through life. But none of them were round to make me do that now, and yet I carried on, picking my way. That was no way to live.

While I lay there, listening to Mollie's deep breaths in sleep, I remembered what a counselor at The Hicks had taught me: Don't run from bad memories—stay with them; let them play out in your mind.

It wasn't easy, but I hung out with those assholes for some time, like we were in a staring contest. Eventually, as I held their eyes, it was like a sword started cutting away the layers of hurt from the schoolyard, my classrooms, Coburn's, carving right on down to the source of it all: Vester Bradshaw. Daddy.

With each cut, I felt tears slipping down my face on to the pillow. By the time I finally felt sleepy, I had to turn the pillow over.

Chapter 50: Abit

Even with all the crazy stuff taking up my time, I still felt at loose ends with my family so far away. I turned to my woodwork and spent long hours in my shop with Mollie close by.

Shiloh seemed to sense my restlessness and tried to cheer me up with his jokes. They were all pretty bad, but I appreciated the thought and laughed for real a time or two. Like "So what if I don't know what Armageddon means? It's not the end of the world." I wished I'd heard that one while I was going to Mama's church. His other jokes reminded me of the corny sayings in the Christmas crackers Fiona's father shipped over every December.

It wasn't 'til late in the day that I started wondering what Shiloh meant by a couple of the jokes: "Tell your boss what you think of him, and the truth shall set you free" and "When a man tells you he got rich through hard work, ask him whose." I never really thought of myself as his boss—we just worked together, even if I did pay him every Friday—but it sounded like he was trying to tell me something.

When I shut down everything in the woodshop and turned out the lights, instead of going straight to the house, I headed over to the guestroom. As I opened the door, the smell of long ago wafted out. Even after all the changes, all the paint and new flooring, something from its past lingered, in a good way.

Before I closed the door, I called for Mollie. She stuck her head round the corner of the house and gamboled over, always happy to get inside somewhere different. We both got up on the bed and wrestled for a while. When she curled up with her head on one of the pillows, I laid back crossways on the bed and started recalling how nice it had been to have Nigel visit (except when that weasel-faced gangster came round, scaring our boy). Over the years, Nigel and I'd grown close during my visits to D.C. and even closer while he lived in our barn. I felt more of a loss than I'd expected when he left for England.

Nigel's grandson, Jason, had come down as promised to tidy up. He was a nice kid and spent the night in the room before heading back to D.C. Even though he'd cleaned it real good, the room still carried traces of my old friend. I got up and started poking round for no good reason. I found a tie clip with a sixpence coin that I'd need to mail him when we got an address plus a coupla bottles of British beer in the back of the closet. I opened one and drank it while rocking in the chair. The beer was on the warm side, but Nigel said that's how he drank it back home.

I reckoned Nigel would return to D.C. in a year or so, when the heat was off. Or who knew? If he couldn't come back, maybe he'd invite us over to England for a visit. We could go on to Ireland too.

That set me to thinking about Fiona and Conor again. They should be asleep now, what with the five-hour difference. I pictured them in their beds, Conor all snuggled up like he does, clutching the blanket tight, a worn-out stuffed puppy under his arm. I saw Fiona in her bed, maybe the one she'd had as a child. Like my family, hers had never moved from the old homeplace.

I spent the rest of the evening playing music in the guestroom. Those notes, especially the sweet, mournful ones, lifted me outta my life. I got swept away by a coupla songs that got their start right where Fiona was.

With her away, the band hadn't gotten together to jam but a time or two. We were lucky we only had to reschedule one gig. We'd all agreed the audience would've felt ripped off with substitutes for Fiona and Conor, our stars. I missed our tearing round the countryside playing at different shows, so it felt good to get the notes under my fingers again and make that pick earn its keep. I cradled my mando and played songs like "Liberty," "Soldier's Joy," and "Red-haired Boy." They were merry tunes, but damned if that last one didn't get to me anyway, thinking about my own red-haired boy.

Chapter 51: Della

After DEEP POCKET's two-letter advice—DC—I knew I'd need Agent Stoltz's help. A living, breathing FBI agent could cut through red tape a lot faster than me poking around next time I visited Alex.

There was no way I could write that story. I wanted to check out a few more leads, but I was sure even after that I wouldn't have sufficient facts for a story worthy of publication. And in its current state of anecdotes, lists, and hypotheses, it was over the heads of anyone at the *Mountain Weakly*. (Yes, I'd thrown off my journalistic solidarity, resorting to the paper's snarky moniker. I was disappointed in Blakely, who'd refused to run what we could use as a follow-up to the fire. And in Jessie. Even though I'd piqued her interest with the latest developments, once again she'd said no thanks.)

As for Sheriff Horne, he'd made it clear he couldn't (in my book, *wouldn't*) do anything with the information. Not only did he agree with Blakely that the story ended when Nigel and Fedora left the county, he was in such a foul mood lately, he'd become unapproachable. I asked around and found out his marriage to Mary Lou was on the rocks. I'd wondered why *she*'d been in such a good mood lately. Turned out she and her ex, Abit's and my friend Duane Dockery, were getting back together. Duane had stopped drinking, gone back to school to learn masonry, and pretty much had his act together. Their kids were grown, and they were ready to try again.

But I felt obligated to do *something* with the information DEEP POCKET had risked his career over. Seemed I had no options other than to drive over to Ferguson, where I could talk face-to-face with Agent Stoltz.

When I arrived, no one was in the outer office. I knocked on Stoltz's door, and I heard his voice call out, "Come in."

I opened the door and saw him talking on the phone. I stepped back and started to close the door, but he motioned me in, pointing toward a chair opposite his desk. After he said his goodbyes and hung up, he smiled. "You and I got off on the wrong foot."

That surprised me. He didn't strike me as the type to apologize, if that's what he was doing. But I was grateful for any break in the ice. "Well, I can't even imagine the pressure you're under, and I appreciate your seeing me now, especially since I didn't make an appointment."

"We're busy, but not that formal out here."

"It's about something completely different. I know you're already swamped, but I just want ten minutes of advice."

"Fire away. Maybe you can help wake up my brain. I'm determined to find this SOB and break him like a wedding vow in Vegas."

I laughed. "That's a tough line to follow." Thanks to my reporter days, I was able to encapsulate the story into five key points, starting with Nigel's debacle and ending with DEEP POCKET's envelopes and final instruction.

"Man, this *is* a real Peyton Place," Stoltz said.

"Tell me about it. I thought I was escaping all the crime in D.C. only to land somewhere with a higher crime rate per capita."

"I doubt that, but there *are* more crooked and craven dealings that I'd anticipated."

From there, we traded career stories. He started out in D.C., and thanks to a broken marriage—she also worked in the Bureau and had seniority—he was sent to Charlotte. After that we quizzed each other about D.C., asking all the typical questions like *Where did you live? Did you ever go to La Fourchette on 18th NW? What about La Taberna on I NW?*

We were laughing and enjoying our memories. I was about to launch into one of my favorite D.C. stories when I saw Abit standing at the door. Stoltz had left it open for some air.

"Hey, honey, what brings you up here?"

"I need to see Curtis, um, Agent Maynard about something."

Abit gave me the most curious look. I wondered what that was all about. I planned to ask him later. Right now I had other things on my mind.

"Hey, you two. I made a picnic and thought if you had time, we could head up to Stone Mountain," I said to Stoltz before glancing at Abit to include him. I'd brought the food in case I needed to sweeten the deal with Stoltz for getting help in D.C., and I was glad I'd made extra so Abit and Curtis could join us. "It's only an hour or so away—but it's a world away from crime and overwork. I've always found a break in nature to be good for jump-starting my thinking."

"Maynard's over at the crime scene, but he's due back soon."

"What do you say? It's almost quitting time for us civilians. How 'bout it?"

"I could use a break. Thank you, Ms. Kincaid."

"Della."

"Okay, Della." He smiled at me and then nodded at Abit, who looked like he'd just spent the entire day with Blanche Scoggins. Honestly, I didn't know what had gotten into him.

"Abit, I hope you can join us," I said. "Do you have plans?" He just shook his head and kept glaring at me.

"Is that no you don't have plans or no you can't join us?" He turned around and walked off, presumably to find Curtis.

Stoltz grabbed his cell phone and called someone. When he closed the phone, he said, "Let's go get Agent Maynard. Looks like we could all use a break—somewhere, I hope, cooler than this damn office."

Chapter 52: Abit

Earlier, I'd told Curtis he should be the one to tell Stoltz what Wallis and I'd discovered about where the next killings might be. I was hoping he'd get some extra credit. Besides, the idea sounded more believable coming from an agent, junior or not.

I saw Curtis coming my way as I walked across the parking lot. He looked as pissed off as I felt and made a thumbs-down motion.

When we shook hands, he didn't smile. "Stoltz shot down the chronology idea," was all he said. I shrugged, likely more used to put-downs than Curtis. "What brings you over here, Abit?"

"I'd hoped to get these to you before you talked with Stoltz." I handed him a packet of notes Wallis and I had made earlier that day, fine-tuning the timeline and what might happen next. "Now the trip seems like a waste of time." We didn't say much as we headed toward Della, who was waving us over.

We all piled in her Jeep, Curtis and me in the back like a coupla kids. Up front, Della and Stoltz were carrying on like old friends. After we'd been riding for a while, along windy roads that made me kinda car sick, Curtis asked in a pouty voice, "When are we gonna get there?" I wanted to laugh—he sounded just like Conor—but I couldn't muster even a smile. I tried rolling down the window, but the air blew gritty against my face.

Oncet Della laid out the picnic, my appetite came back. Man, she knew how to do it. The food was up to her usual standards—fried chicken, Waldorf salad, and homemade chocolate chip cookies. She'd brought beer too.

Della and Stoltz got all caught up in their D.C. talk, so I figured it was a good time to ask Curtis more about what Stoltz had said. We turned so they couldn't hear us.

"It backfired," he said softly. He nodded his head toward Stoltz. "He thought it was a faulty idea, too farfetched for us to pursue. When I wouldn't let it drop, he started saying we didn't have enough manpower to have teams in both Harlan County and Winston-Salem." He stopped and looked even sadder.

"What else?"

"Oh, it's just that if I bring something up, he's sure to cut it down. I don't know why I let you talk me into telling him about this. It would have gone over better coming from you."

"Don't kid yourself. He's not crazy about me, either. Wonder why he's so ornery?"

Curtis looked over at Stoltz and shook his head. "Let's talk about this later."

I did what I did best and went back to the food and beer.

After dinner, Curtis and I found the Cedar Rock Trail that led to the top of Stone Mountain. The views were amazing, and we could talk more freely. When I asked how he became an FBI agent, his lip curled a little. "Well, it sure wasn't because my daddy paved the way like Agent Stoltz's did. Someone told me his father was a real J. Edgar Hoover Junior. Strict, weird, and mean. Stoltz was probably treated that way when he was growing up—like drill sergeants who think they have to humiliate in order to make someone stronger."

The evening had turned cooler, the air soft against our skin. I didn't want to dwell on our troubles anymore. For almost an hour, we walked without talking. I'd found that either soothed the soul or brought up things you needed to recall. That evening it did both.

When we walked back, I could see Stoltz and Della at the picnic table, their faces up close to one anothern, like teenagers telling secrets. I didn't know what had gotten ahold of her. As we approached, they started chortling. That stuck-up FBI guy could actually laugh.

Della drove us back to the FBI office, and Curtis and I suffered again in the backseat, not saying a word. When she pulled up to where our vehicles were parked, I got out, pissed off that no one, namely Stoltz, had even mentioned the chronology. Like we all just knew each other from Kiwanis or church, getting together for a little outing.

I felt disgusted and wanted to get away from them all. Even Della. I was about to slink off to my truck when I stopped, my heart hammering. I surprised myself when I spoke, my voice beginning high and breaking like a boy's.

"Before you all run off, I wanted to talk about the chronology of the murder ballads."

Stoltz stared at me. "Yeah, Agent Maynard spoke to me about that." He paused, and I knew what was coming. "I think it's a classic case of deductive reasoning."

When Della started in with, "What he means is …" I interrupted. "Thanks, Della, but this is my concern, and I'll ask Agent Stoltz myself what he means."

It was like someone farted in church. Everyone looked round, not saying a word. Finally, Stoltz began to explain.

"Deductive reasoning is like tunnel vision—everything stems from one premise or hypothesis. In this case that the murders are related to murder-ballad stories. Given the M.O. of the homicides, not a bad start. But you go too far with your conclusion that the killer mimics those ballads in a definite order. What about 'Knoxville Girl'? How does that fit into your chronology? And what makes you certain that the next one is a specific choice you can pinpoint? It could be twenty different ballads."

"Because I just know—and because it's in *Traditional Tales of True Crime Ballads in the Southern Appalachians.*"

"So?" he asked, all smug.

"With so few books on this subject, Wallis Harding and I reckon the killer is using the same list we're looking at." When he didn't acknowledge that, just kinda shook his head, I added, "Look, I get it that you can't go to your boss with something that Abit Bradshaw said, but this is worth *you* thinking about."

"I appreciate your concern about these crimes," he said, his tone a little nicer. "These are your people, and I can tell you have a big heart when it comes to their—or likely anyone's—welfare. But I can't see the merits in going with a list of songs, for Chris …" He stopped himself.

I jumped in. "Okay, what have you come up with better?"

"We're still working on that."

"Oh, great. And we've got ten days 'til he'll strike again."

"You don't know that."

"You don't know that's *not* true. Just tell me a better plan, and I'll go back to my holler and never bother you again."

"Well, that's something to work toward. You act like we're not doing anything. I won't stand here and justify our work. We have profilers studying these crimes both here and Quantico. We've explored every angle—from how the victims might be related to how the killer knew them. We're talking to everyone within a reasonable radius in these remote areas, and ..." He stopped himself. "Like I said, I don't owe you any explanations."

He got this smirk on his face that was like a match to kerosene. "I'll grant you that you don't owe me an explanation for what you *are* doing. I'm talking about what you *aren't* doing. I've mentioned this before, but you're not listening. You've closed your mind. What are you waiting for? Anothern? More dead bodies? You need to take a good look at our idea so you can catch someone *before* he kills again. The folks round here are dealing with a world of heartache. This is your chance to catch this monster *now.*"

Stoltz's face turned a shade of red I don't believe I'd ever seen before. I reckoned he was fixing to arrest me. We stood like that for the longest time. Just him and me. Everyone and everything else seemed to have slipped away.

Finally, he let out a big sigh. Next things I knew, Curtis was scooting off, waving and offering a weak thanks as he almost ran to his SUV. I waited for what came next. I knew I'd ruined the picnic, but that wasn't high on my list.

Stoltz mumbled his thanks to Della, turned, and headed for his office. Della and I were left alone in a dark parking lot.

"Well, I knew you were working on speaking your truth, and I believe you did," she said, smiling. "And I'm *glad* you did. Your ideas are better than anything Stoltz has come up with. I hope he'll come to see that. Soon."

"I'm sorry I ruined your picnic."

"You didn't ruin it, honey. I had a great time. And I loved seeing you stand strong."

"Well, you out did yourself."

"Oh, it wasn't any trouble. I'm glad you could join us."

"Would you have rather been alone with him? Is that why you made such a nice picnic?"

"Hey, you might be taking this truth business a little too far." But she chuckled and squeezed my shoulder. "I was just being friendly to someone who can help me out with a big story."

"You were flirting, Della."

"I was not." She looked dead serious now.

"I may have been a shy boy when I was growing up, but I know flirting when I see it."

"Oh, go on. I was just paving the way for the help I need. And you too."

"Maybe."

"Not maybe. Definitely." She looked so hurt, I agreed with her just to make that awful evening end.

As I drove off, I could see her in my rearview mirror, staring after my truck.

Chapter 53: Abit

The next day, I went into town and stopped by Coburn's. Oh, who was I kidding? Coburn's was the only reason I went to town. I'd decided, just like every time I ever disagreed with someone I liked, I'd been out of line. I wanted to see if Della was still my friend.

When I pulled up at the store, Agent Stoltz's SUV was sitting out front.

I could see Della through the front window laughing, her head thrown back in a full chortle while her hand rested on his arm. I snuck back to my truck and waited for almost half an hour before Stoltz pulled on to the highway. I walked to the store, opened the front door, and for the first time ever, felt I might not be welcome.

"Okay if I come in?"

"Of course it is, Abit. And why are you asking permission? Don't tell me you're sorry about speaking up. That negates what you accomplished."

"When is Alex coming back?

"Why are you asking *that*?" I could sense her good cheer fading.

"Because he needs to get back here to save you from yourself."

"Oh, stop that. And since when are you my keeper? Seriously, who are you to stand over me and criticize? I know I've gotten in your business a time or two, maybe more, but I was always looking out for your wellbeing."

"That's what I'm doing."

"How?"

"Well, I love you. And I love Alex. And I don't know what's going on."

"Nothing is going on. Even if it were, that would never affect our love for you—or, I hope, the other way around."

"Yeah, but I love you *together*."

I turned and slipped outta the store, back to the quiet of my truck and home.

Chapter 54: Della

That night I replayed my squabble with Abit over and over. First while staring at the ceiling, later in my dreams. By morning, I felt sad and embarrassed. To be honest, I wasn't sure what had come over me. Of course, loneliness was never far off; I think I was born lonely. But my current state had a sharper edge. Alex was gone again. The summer had been wet and gloomy. I felt old and forgotten in my apartment above a store in the middle of nowhere.

My dark mood hovered close the rest of the day. I wanted to lock the doors and stay away from everyone until it passed, but I had a store to run and a story to run down.

I tried. But after struggling through work that day, I wanted a break from *everything*. I got Mary Lou to handle the store for the next few days.

On the first one, I pulled the blinds, turned off my phones, drank hot tea, ate scones, and loved on Rascal. I only took him out early and late, when I knew no one would be around. The second day, I spent more time on the real estate scheme. I was counting on Agent Stoltz to come through with a contact so I could unload this pile of research into the right hands.

By the third day, I woke in a lighter mood. The sun streamed in my window at six o'clock and woke me too early; after so many dark, rainy days, I'd forgotten to pull the blinds. But I welcomed its bright rays. The birds seemed to feel the same way.

I fired up my Rancilio and enjoyed a dark, rich latte with chocolatey overtones. A day-old brioche loaf made perfect toast. And fresh applesauce on yogurt tasted as good as an ice-cream sundae.

As I got ready to go out in the world again, I looked in the mirror and said out loud, "You're not dead, you know. Not even close."

I knew a lot of people who as soon as they approached their sixties started saying things like, "I'm giving all my books away and don't plan on getting more." Or, "I don't need anything for my birthday; I need to get rid of stuff, not acquire it." That used to depress me; now it just made me mad. I'm no spendthrift, but the idea of never buying anything new—something meaningful or pretty or creative—felt like packing your bags for the funeral home.

The same for love and sex. My father's mother had proudly proclaimed that the Kincaid women didn't remarry. No, according to her our lot was to lead abstemious, prudish lives. Well, count me out of that family tradition. I wasn't dead and so what if I'd had fleeting feelings for someone besides Alex? Big deal. We didn't run away together; our feelings didn't even run away. But I'd enjoyed feeling alive, noticed, appreciated.

I made myself another coffee. As I sipped it on the couch, Rascal curled up next to me. I started to feel better—until my old friends the angel and devil began making noises again. I'd always liked the devil better; he seemed more fun. But this time the angel caught my attention when she asked: *Does your behavior over the past week remind you of anything?*

No, I said, again out loud.

How about the way Alex acted so many years before?

I nearly spilled my coffee. My first reaction was *Not in the least.* Really? That was absurd. But as I sat there, stroking my little dog's rather glorious new coat, I drifted back to those troubled times. I thought about how I'd always assumed Alex had gotten too full of himself when he'd won the Pulitzer. Was it possible he'd felt lonely and lost the same way I was feeling now? Back then I was often out of town on investigative stories, just as he is now. He always contended he'd made a terrible mistake, but I'd dismissed that as simply the confession of a scoundrel. Maybe he was, but maybe things weren't the way I'd imagined. He'd been a fine companion for years.

Then I felt silly. All this fuss over a little banter and coy behavior. Nothing had happened to be ashamed of.

Rascal let me know he needed to go out. As we walked down the stairs from my apartment, I heard the devil ask: *Then why won't you let the past go?* Now they were both ganging up on me.

That night, alone in my bed, I went over all that again. And again. Those two had opened the door to an awful period in my life, unleashing long-buried rancor I didn't know I harbored. But when I asked them for help, they went utterly silent.

Chapter 55: Abit

We didn't have many good restaurants close by that stayed open past three o'clock, so even though Curtis was a vegetarian, we ended up at Adam's Rib. He was a good sport and found macaroni cheese on the menu along with a big salad. I got the roast chicken special. We both drank the beer on tap—Coors. Nothing like the British brews Nigel had spoiled me with, but it went down good enough.

By the third one, we were swapping stories so sad they'd've made a murder-ballad songwriter weep. Curtis' father had been a mean SOB and his mother just prayed all the time that things would get better but never stepped in to help Curtis. *Whatever happened to "pray to God and row to shore"?* I wondered to myself before asking, "Are you sure you haven't read *my* file?"

"Do you have a file?"

I laughed. "Well, not yet, but if I keep up all this snooping round, it can't be far off. If that happens, can I call on you to help?"

"Grease my palm, brother. Grease my palm," he said, chuckling. Then he got a serious look on his face. "So I take it your parents were a lot like mine."

"From what you just said, I'd say we could be cousins." He put his arm against my arm. "Well, you never know what's going on in families."

Curtis' eyes turned sorrowful. "That's for sure. Sad growing-up stories like ours are a dime a dozen. Have you ever thought about how strange it is that so many men delight in beating the crap out of their children? What's with that? I guess it's some kind of passed-down rage, generation after generation, that works its way into fists and on to little bodies."

"I can't figure it, either. I *can* tell you that kinda rage has stopped with me. Little Conor has never seen my fist, not that he's done anything to bring it on. Do you have any children?" Curtis shook his head. "Well, you've broken free of your daddy's unholy hold in your own way and made it to the FBI."

"We'll see. It's not easy being there—even though it's an organization that stands for the law."

I held up my beer glass. "Let's toast to the big surprise the FBI has in store when you rein in the murder-ballad killer."

"I'll drink to that," he said. Just as we clinked bottles, his cell phone rang. He answered and started nodding and saying *yessir, okay, yessir.* When he hung up, he said, "Stoltz wants to see me … and you."

Chapter 56: Abit

"We need to get over to Harlan County and Winston-Salem, Agent Maynard." That was Stoltz telling us what we already knew. "And Bradshaw, I brought you over to make sure we're all clear on your hypothesis."

Stoltz's change in attitude threw me. All I could figure was he'd either finally seen the light or had failed to come up with anything better. I did know he believed in the seventy-three days between killings, which meant only a matter of days till the murderer would strike again.

I managed to stand up in front of all those agents and explain what Wallis and I were thinking. I started to relax some when folks at the meeting nodded and asked questions I could answer. I added that I didn't know a fraction of what they did when it came to catching criminals, but I believed Wallis and I were on to something important.

When I finished, Stoltz took over again. "Maynard, I need you to work on the details. Get more from Bradshaw— any logistics he may know." (I hadn't let on I didn't know much about eastern Kentucky, though I was pretty sure I knew more than anyone else in the room.) "I'm sending personnel to each location to scout it out. I'll let you know what they report." Then he looked at me. "If you're right, we have only a few days."

At last something was happening, though I felt a little sick knowing my ideas had better work out or more people would die. Soon.

On my way home, I swung by Della's. It was late, but I knew Alex was still away, so I wouldn't be bothering them. I knocked, and when Della opened the door, her face looked a little scared. I felt sick all over again.

"I want to send Fiona an email," I said, still standing on the stoop. "I want her to know I'm helping Stoltz, and we're making progress. And I'm not afraid of him like he's my daddy."

She stood there so long with her arms folded, I was afraid she was gonna say no. Then she moved her hand, as if to say come on in.

"Della, I'm sorry …"

"Well, I'm *not* sorry," she interrupted.

"Okay, I'm glad you're not 'cause you didn't do anything to be sorry about." That seemed to take the fire outta her. She nodded, so I went on. "But *I* am sorry I butted into your business. I think I got scared."

"Well, nothing to be afraid of, Abit." She let out a big sigh as she walked toward her office. "I think we've worn out this topic. Let's go send that email."

It took me forever to write, but I wanted Fiona to know that I got what she'd been talking about, what with Daddy hounding me from the grave. I waited a while for her answer, but I knew it was awfully late in Ireland. I talked with Della a while longer before heading for the front door.

"Don't you want to check one more time before you leave?" I turned to go back to her office and saw on the table near the front door that Della'd wrapped up some cake slices for me to take home.

Just as I sat down at the computer, I heard it ping. Fiona. We talked like that, back and forth, for some time. When I asked her why she was up so late, she said she was still on home time. Home. Not Ireland but here. That felt almost as good as a kiss. And she didn't say I told you so or anything like that about Daddy.

But she did have more to say: *When I was in nursing school, I read a book about the benefits of a lousy childhood. It made a difference for me. That speaks to both of us. Without all that happened, you wouldn't be Rabbit— or Abit or even Vester Junior. You wouldn't be the person who Della and Alex love, who Shiloh appreciates, who I love and Conor adores. And Mollie too. You might still have become a musician and a woodworker, but you wouldn't have the depth of feelings that the harsh ways of your parents and teachers and preachers carved into you.*

She knew me better than I knew myself. I wrote back: *I miss your music.*

Oh, darlin' we'll be home soon—and you've got the band. Are you jamming?

Not that *music.* Yours. *The sounds you make as you fix supper. The sweet words you whisper to Conor while you bathe him or help with his schoolwork. All those lovely things you murmur to Mollie. And me.*

Not long after that we said good night. I felt full again.

Chapter 57: Della

"I've got something for you," Stoltz said when I answered the store phone.

"Hmm … sounds interesting. Can you come to the store?"

"I'm needed here. I'll be here 'til late. Maybe you could come after you close?"

On the way over to Ferguson, I felt as though Abit were in the car with me. Yeah, we'd buried that hatchet, but something felt off about driving up to see Stoltz. I kept telling myself I needed his FBI contact person—and that I hadn't done anything wrong. I hadn't.

When I arrived, I played it cool, though friendly.

Stoltz looked tired, the skin under his eyes bruised from overwork. He'd met me on the porch of the makeshift office and offered no smiles or niceties, what I took to be his official FBI persona. We just stood there making small talk.

Until he kissed me. The big kind, with pounding hearts and arms encircled.

"There. We got that out of the way," he said when we broke apart. We both nodded, tensions eased. We knew this, whatever *this* was, couldn't go anywhere. After a moment, he said, "Okay, I've got that name you asked for. Our last meeting was rather rudely interrupted by your amateur sleuth."

I hated that term, but I wasn't about to nitpick now. He walked inside toward his desk, pulled out a notepad, and while he was writing said, "I don't mean to sound like a chicken shit, but don't tell her who gave you this."

"History?"

"Wife."

I could feel my eyebrows go up. "So what happened to *fidelity* in the FBI motto 'Fidelity, Bravery, and Integrity'"?

"EX-wife. I still forget to say that sometimes. It's only been six months. But she's nice and smart and she'll listen to you. Do you go to D.C. often?"

"Yeah, my ex-husband lives up there." I didn't bother to tell him he was my current boyfriend, or whatever you call it. That kiss didn't mean a thing.

He tore off the piece of paper and walked back to where I was standing. He pushed it into my hand, and folded my fingers around it. "You know, I shouldn't do this. I don't really know anything about your research, but I trust you, and I've come to see that there *is* trouble in Peyton Place." I smiled. We stood there not knowing what to say next. Stoltz broke the ice. "So you go up and visit him in D.C.?"

I didn't want to get into all that. Instead, I stepped closer and kissed him. Like the last one. It *was* the last one. "There. We're even. And done with all that."

I drove home thinking more about the phone number than the man who gave it to me.

Chapter 58: Abit

"That's what everyone makes me."

Seemed mac cheese was all anyone who wasn't a vegetarian could think to serve Curtis for dinner. When he said that, I recalled it was the only main dish he could order at Adam's Rib. I felt bad, but I'd made it because it was Conor's favorite and one of my better recipes.

Curtis noticed. "That was rude of me, Abit. I didn't mean it the way it came out—just an amusing observation. I'm not one of those card-carrying vegetarians, all up in your face. And I happen to love mac cheese."

We were having our Sunday midday dinner together. That was a special time for Fiona and Conor and me when we sat round the table and shared stories and music. I was awfully glad to have some good company.

Curtis had come over early to help me pull together the meal. Not much to do besides the spinach salad; I'd made the mac cheese already, and the day before I'd run into town to get a pumpkin pie at Coburn's.

It wasn't even noon when we finished our prep, so we drank some coffee and talked for a while before dinner. Curtis was easy to be round. We'd moved on from the bad stuff in our pasts and talked about what we liked. We both loved music, even if his favorites were rock and hip hop and mine bluegrass and old-timey.

"Music lifts me outta my world," I told him. "That used to be especially important when I was younger. But now, even with the comfort of a family, who doesn't need to rise above everyday life?"

I grabbed my mandolin and played "Foggy Mountain Special" for him. I could tell he liked its lively rhythm, and I was pleased with how good I'd gotten my tremolo (or as Bill Monroe called it, tremble). I told Curtis about each of our band members and what instruments they played. I added Vern, who joined us sometimes on stage, keeping time on his hambone.

And I told him about that harmonica the drifter had left for our boy. Conor always had it in his back pocket, ready to practice any chance he got. I had to put my foot down about him playing it with the band, though; harmonica does *not* go with bluegrass. But when we played "Wabash Cannonball," he got to let that old harp rip.

Curtis was into collecting something called pullback motor cars. I'd never heard of them, but he showed me some pictures on his cell phone. Some kind of wind up car he'd gotten first when he was a kid. Then I mentioned my hub cap collection, which was different but kinda the same.

We were going back and forth like that when his phone rang. I could tell it was Stoltz from the look on his face and all the *yessirs*. When he hung up, he said, "The agent checking out Harlan County got a tip from the sheriff about a strange man poking around Harlan County, asking if any Jews lived there."

"Oh, man! That is exactly what Wallis and I were saying." I was both excited and scared.

"Stoltz told me to invite you to our meeting up at the office." He grabbed his jacket. "That's a big deal, you know, Stoltz inviting you again." He took one look at my face and added, "But don't get any ideas about being part of the team. He'd never go that far. And this could just be local folks taking it out on a Jewish stranger making his way through town. You'd be surprised—then again, maybe you wouldn't—at how often sheriffs get called about things like that."

We threw the mac cheese and salad into the fridge and grabbed our coats. I quickly made Mollie a treat ball to keep her busy while I was gone. I felt bad how much I'd left her alone lately. As I was stuffing a big biscuit into it, I changed my mind. I'd take her with me; I could do with the company on another long drive. I started to put the treat ball on the counter, but Mollie gave out a little yap. I dropped it into my pocket for the ride. Then I went back to get the pie; I figured those FBI guys needed it more than me.

"I forgot to mention," Curtis said as we walked toward our vehicles. "We name our operations, and Stoltz got Operation Murder Ballad approved by headquarters. You and Wallis can both take some comfort in that."

"I won't be taking any comfort 'til we get this guy. But thanks for sharing that."

Curtis sped on ahead of me in his SUV. My old truck wasn't up to that, so I took it easier. By the time I got over to the Ferguson office, they were already meeting. I stood in the back, just listening. The latest was some stranger had asked a Jewish woman if there was anywhere he could bed down. Turned out she ran a small store while her husband did some traveling sales for a hardware company. I didn't like how closely they matched the story behind "The Peddler and His Wife," and I reckoned Stoltz didn't either.

The wife was known to be kindly, offering her barn to passersby, the way Fiona and I shared ours. Apparently after she did that outta her good nature, she thought more about how he looked—a dark hat covering much of his face, his head down, just mumbling his words. She got worried and called her husband, who called the sheriff.

Stoltz explained how one team was heading to Harlan County while anothern went to Winston-Salem, where they planned to stake out some expensive hotel. Again, just like "Poor Ellen Smith," who died in a garden behind whatever hotel was the fanciest in 1892.

I wasn't sure why Stoltz had invited me, especially after the meeting broke up and I was left standing in the back while everyone else headed out. I could tell he wasn't about to let me ride along, like Curtis had warned, but that didn't mean I liked it.

"Glad you could make it, Bradshaw," Stoltz said as he patted me on the back. He was smiling. I guess he was used to this kinda thing, but to me it was serious business. "I wanted you to see for yourself that your theory has been a big help."

You'd've thought that would be enough for me, but I needed more. "And that's it? I'm supposed to go back home now? Why did you have me drop everything to come all the way over here? A coupla hour drive or more, round trip."

"That's just how it is in the real world, Bradshaw. What did you want me to do?"

"You could've written a thank-you note," I said, sarcasm dripping offa every word. "Would've saved me a lot of time and trouble."

Stoltz laughed, but then he saw the look in my eyes. "Well, son, there's nothing more you can do for us. I just thought you'd like to know the latest—thanks to you and Mr. Harding."

"You *need* me there. I know these people. You're from Charlotte, for God's sake." I said the name of that town like it was a curse word. Nothing wrong with it, as cities go, but it didn't prepare him or his agents for dealing with folks in Harlan County.

"Listen, Abit, we have procedures. Some civilian can't just step into the investigation."

"I'm not just some civilian—I figured it out."

"You *think* you figured it out." He turned to join the other men. I gave up and started to leave when Curtis came running in, holding a bunch of paper. "Jonathan just faxed me the numerology report."

"Dammit! Am I in charge here or are you two Keystone Cops running this operation? Maynard, I told you I wouldn't authorize that report. Is it coming out of your budget, which, oh by the way, you don't have?" Stoltz's face turned that deep red again.

"Okay, you can yell at me later, sir," Curtis said. "For now, look who's on the list."

"Well, who?"

"Right there, sir. It jumped off the page at me."

Chapter 59: Abit

Marshall White.

I nearly choked when I saw that named circled in red.

Just like Wallis, Curtis had gotten a funny feeling about exactly seventy-three days between killings, and he'd worked out its numerology. Or make that a computer had. Curtis explained that according to this guy Jonathan, real numerology involved a lot of calculations, and they figured Marshall, like a lot of folks, was just playing round with it. Luckily, Jonathan had the experience to know how an amateur would grab on to something like that and then work from there.

Even after Curtis explained everything to Stoltz, my head was spinning. Marshall White. A serial killer. I hadn't had a clue. "How'd you even know that name, Curtis?" I asked. "You haven't heard our band."

Stoltz answered for him. "Agent Maynard has one of those legendary memories that will serve him well in his career."

"Not exactly legendary, at least in this case. The other day you were telling me about your band members. I was just lucky his name showed up on page two of all these." He held up a messy stack of pages and went on. "Another question, Abit. I checked out the two murder ballads you and Mr. Harding came up with as the next possibilities, and

I did a little research. Both strongly feature the banjo, White's instrument."

"That they do. But Marshall doesn't like to play murder ballads any more than me and my wife do. He always voted against playing the ballads. I just can't figure it." But as I said that, something came to me. I thought about it for a moment and added, "I'm not sure about this, but now, looking back on things, I can see how Marshall acted kinda protective of the music. Like he thought nobody could play them as good as him. Or that nobody else *should* play them."

"Hold on, now," Stoltz said, trying to get the conversation back under his control. "There's always the chance White's name showing up is just a coincidence."

Curtis and I shook our heads. No way. Curtis looked down at his notes. "Do either of these ballads, 'Poor Ellen Smith' or 'The Peddler and His Wife,' feature the banjo more than the other? I'm hoping one does so we can focus on that locale."

I shook my head again. "They're both strong on banjo."

"We're planning to cover both locations," Stoltz said. "Though that's not easy; lots of other crimes going on with more definite needs."

"All the more reason I need to go to Harlan County," I said. "I *know* the lay of the land better'n any of you."

"No way in hell. If you know Marshall White, that's all the more reason you need to stay away," Stoltz shouted.

"Sir, I agree with you on that count, but I'd like to have him close by to advise," Curtis said. "He could stay safely with the husband and wife. If this Marshall guy goes off the deep end for some reason, Abit may prove invaluable with our negotiator."

Curtis told me to follow him. Stoltz shouted at both of us, "Hold on, hold on. I need to think about this."

We stopped and waited. I was about to pipe up with another plea when Stoltz caved. "Okay, you can join them in Harlan County, but stay out of their way."

"*Their* way? They'd still be scratching their heads if it weren't for me and Wallis."

Curtis grabbed my arm and tugged me away. I saw Stoltz point a finger at me and shout, "Don't get a big head, Bradshaw. And I mean it. Stay out of everyone's way— unless they ask for your help. Maynard? Get with Agent Fitzgerald and make sure Bradshaw has what he needs."

Curtis and Agent Fitzgerald ushered me into an office. They gave me a map with directions and made me take a cell phone, and this time I *wanted* one. From stuff Della and I'd gotten ourselves into, I knew these things never went the way you hoped.

When I got to my truck, Mollie's big ole face was staring out the driver's window. I wished I hadn't brought her along; she'd already been cooped up way too long. I told Curtis I needed to swing by home (it was on the way) and drop her off; I'd meet them there. Curtis and his buddy hopped into an unmarked SUV and sped off.

As I drove home, I was in that kind of shock that lets you do things you'd never think possible. I'd had it come over me before, like when I was carrying Conor to the emergency room when he broke his leg and that time I took Millie, our dog before Mollie, to the vet for the last time. You just go into motion, somehow knowing what to do, not thinking about anything but what lay before you. I didn't notice the beautiful countryside. I didn't hear a bird whistle. I just drove.

Oncet I got Mollie settled in at home, I took backroads up and over toward Harlan County. We were having strange weather—the sun winking in and out of angry clouds in a way that felt eerie. Then again, everything felt thataway.

Curtis had given me good directions to the homestead where the "peddlers" lived. When I got to the end of them, I could see the house and barn up ahead. But I couldn't see Curtis' SUV. What with my detour to drop off Mollie, I was surprised I'd beaten them. I pulled into a wide spot where a stand of pines formed a sheltered circle. I planned to stay well out of the way, and I didn't want to scare the couple. I just needed to be nearby where I could be on the lookout for any trouble. I cut the engine and waited. And waited.

Where in the hell is Curtis?

Then I heard a woman scream, and it wasn't no mountain lion.

Chapter 60: Abit

I used the cell phone to call Curtis, but a no-service message flashed. I tried again. Same thing. I couldn't just sit there, not with someone screaming for help.

I snuck out of the truck, leaving the door open in case it creaked, and inched toward the barn, where the scream came from. As I got closer, I could hear a woman's voice begging for mercy. My heart cramped when I pictured what she was up against. A crazy man that no pleading, no treasure could sway. He just wanted to kill.

A man came running from the house, likely the husband. I motioned him back with everything I had. I knew I looked like a wild man myself; I could've just as easily been the killer. But he did what I asked.

I peeked through a knothole in the side of the barn. The woman stood still as a corpse in Marshall's chokehold, begging for mercy. He pointed a gun to her head, just like in the ballad. That was what she got for her kindness.

A couple of sawhorses blocked my path to the barn. I eased past them, careful not to trip over them and make a racket. I held my breath and peered round the barn door. Just then a hawk shrieked, loud and lonesome. Both Marshall and the woman looked my way. Seeing me standing there startled Marshall; he let her go and fired his gun.

I felt something whiz past my head. I'd turned away just enough for it to miss me. I pulled those sawhorses over to block the doorway and ran. And ran. I heard Marshall stumble and curse as he followed me, but I was faster. My legs were longer, and I was in better shape. He'd spent too much time sitting, playing his banjo.

Eventually, I began to drag, my heart hammering so hard it scared me. I caught a break when the trail split up ahead and a rhododendron thicket just beyond the left fork offered a place to lay low. I tried to slow my rasping breath; Marshall surely would've heard it. I pulled out the cell phone, but again, no service.

After half an hour like that, I crawled outta the thicket. I got the feeling Marshall had taken the other trail or maybe turned round. I started running again when it dawned on me he'd likely gone back to kill the peddler and his wife.

Chapter 61: Abit

As I made my way back to the barn, it'd grown dark and harder to see if Marshall was hiding behind bushes or trees, waiting to kill me. I felt woozy a time or two, oncet when I realized the top of my ear had been shot off. I touched it, which started it howling with pain.

When I crested a hill, I could see two cop cars below parked under the security light, a white van plus three black SUVs parked at crazy angles nearby. No ambulance, which I hoped meant the wife was okay. As I hurried past the barn, I didn't want to look inside and yet I couldn't stop myself. It was empty except for a team, clad all in white, scouring the scene of the crime under bright work lights.

I stepped up on the long wraparound porch. Through the dining room windows I could see a cluster of FBI agents, sheriffs, and other coppers. When I walked inside, Curtis ran over.

"Hey, everyone! Abit's here. He's okay," he said, throwing his arms round me. "I'm so sorry, Abit. A coal truck overturned on a narrow road. We were stuck for almost an hour." Well, that answered one question. Then I asked how the wife was. "She's badly shaken, but yes, she's fine physically. She said you saved her life—and her husband's."

I'd been feeling like a coward for running away, but I reckon my running off did give her and her husband a break.

For now. "But Marshall's still on the loose. I couldn't catch him." (I didn't mention that would've been hard to do since I was running *ahead* of him.)

"Not your job, son. We've got a team searching the area." That was Stoltz, who'd just walked over. He paused and patted me on the back, apparently his only gesture of comfort. "Thanks for stepping in."

"I thought you'd be after me for stepping in *it*. But I couldn't sit back while she was screaming."

"Like Agent Maynard said, she credits you with her life.

I believe that was when I fainted.

Chapter 62: Della

I always felt a burst of energy when I returned to D.C. Creative power radiated in that town like a second sun. It wasn't always the good kind, but fortunately we had elections to deal with that.

Earlier that week, I was packing for my trip to D.C. to see Alex when Aggie Metzger, Stoltz's ex-wife, finally returned my call, though a telegram would have had more words: *Ezra explained your call. The Yard Hotel, Monday, seven o'clock. Come alone.* Very cloak and dagger; I felt like a character in a David Baldacci novel.

When I hung up, my cell phone rang again. I expected to hear Metzger's voice telling me something she'd forgotten, but it was Sheriff Horne breaking the news that Abit was missing in Kentucky. He promised to let me know as soon as he heard anything.

I wasn't budging until I knew Abit was safe. I paced around my apartment, loaded the Jeep, walked Rascal, and killed time in the store with Mary Lou.

It was already dark when Horne reported that Abit was okay. I had a good cry, grabbed Rascal, and took off for D.C. in spite of the late hour; I knew the route better than my GPS.

Rascal was the perfect passenger, curling up on the backseat and sleeping most of the way. He'd wanted to ride shotgun, and I'd wanted him there, but I knew if I'd had to slam on the brakes, the little guy wouldn't have stood a chance. When I parked in front of Alex's home in Georgetown, Rascal hopped out and marked the big oak tree in the front yard, expanding his territory four hundred and fifty miles.

We'd gotten in so late I didn't even want to know what time it was; I just crashed. The next day Alex relaunched our homecoming with a midday meal he'd planned for the evening before: grilled lamb chops marinated in lemon juice, olive oil, and rosemary and a bottle of 1989 Bourgogne Pinot Noir. We ate slowly and caught up on our news. I told him what little I knew about Abit's latest adventure, and once I assured him Abit wasn't hurt badly, I could see how proud he was of "our boy," a term he'd started using back when Abit *was* a boy.

Eventually we got around to my rendezvous with the FBI. When I explained to Alex what little I knew about the meetup with Agent Metzger, he insisted on coming along. "To hell with her demand to come alone," he said, genuine concern darkening his face. I knew he expected me to object, but to be honest, I was relieved. I'd been away from D.C. long enough to lose my bravado, especially in the District's shadier areas.

On Monday, Alex drove us to the address—a small old hotel near the Navy Yard. I saw a woman sitting in the lobby who had to be Metzger. It felt as though I should utter a code word, but the meeting turned out to be nothing like that.

She stood as we approached and smiled. "Hello, I'm Agent Metzger. I know you must be Della Kincaid. I used to enjoy reading your articles." She looked over at Alex and frowned. "I said to come alone."

Alex stuck out his hand. "Alex Covington. And I play racquet ball with your boss, if that helps."

"Oh, yeah? Anyone could say that."

"Okay, he has a Semper Fi tattoo on his ass." She looked at him strangely, and he added, "Which I noticed in the changing room after racquet ball."

Metzger laughed. "I suppose that doesn't narrow it down much, given how many Always-a-Marines roam the Earth, but I believe you. And I recognize your byline. Great job on the Social Security series."

Now that both our egos had been burnished, we relaxed. As I looked around the slipping-toward-seedy hotel, it hit me that Metzger hadn't been worried so much about me bringing someone from *my* side as being seen by anyone from *hers*.

The meeting didn't last long. I placed a box of reports, lists, research, and a detailed summary of my findings on the table in front of her; she put the box in a duffle bag without looking inside.

"Thanks for your kind words, Agent Metzger, about my reporter days," I said. "I was a good enough reporter to know how valuable this information will be in the right hands, and I've compiled some good intel for your review.

But I'm also a good enough reporter to know I don't have enough. And I don't have the ability to get more."

"That's where I come in." She went back to all business and let us know we were done when she stood and hoisted the duffle. "Be sure to thank Ezra for me. If this material is what I think it is, I plan to thank him myself. Without his recommendation, I doubt I would have taken you seriously. I wish I could keep you informed, but with any luck, you'll see the results in a 40-point headline." We shook hands and started to walk away.

"Oh, one other thing," Metzger said. "Do you have any idea who this whistleblower is?"

I shook my head. "Just that he's a hero."

(It seems only fair to mention that a couple of years later Westonia Bank was fined and sold off, ensuring most of its transgressions would be hidden in capitalism's dark basement until its name was forgotten. Or until, with any luck, some future dogged journalist starts digging.)

Chapter 63: Abit

Fiona and Conor came home!

When I saw them walk through the security gate in Asheville, it felt as though my heart started beating again. I could've sworn Conor had grown. He seemed bigger and older, even though it had been only a few weeks. I guess that's what world travel does for you. I hoped to give it a try.

But Conor wasn't too big to pick up and squeeze. As I held him close, all the tensions of the past weeks just left me. Usually when I put him down, he'd run off, but this time he stayed close and took my hand. I didn't pick up Fiona and squeeze her (though I wanted to), but I did give her a big kiss—and got one back.

We talked and talked on the drive home. Her father was going to be fine after some treatments Fiona helped with. Their weather hadn't been as rainy as ours, so they'd traveled a good bit round Clifden, and Conor got to meet all kinds of relatives.

My shot-off ear was on the left side, so she couldn't see the wound. I could tell Fiona was too give out to hear about all that, so I just gave her the basics and promised to tell her more over breakfast in bed.

It was late when we pulled up the drive toward home. I'd put Mollie inside with an early dinner since it would be dark when we got back. When our headlights hit the house, we could see her fuzzy face parting the curtains in the upstairs window as she stood on our bed. By the time we came inside, she'd gotten all settled looking on the oval rug in the living room, certain she'd fooled us into thinking she'd been there all evening.

After their long time away, Mollie musta thought it was just me coming home. Dogs were like that, content, after a time, to settle in with whoever would feed them. But when she saw Fiona and Conor, she went over to the boy, put her head against him, and made the most pitiful crying sounds. Before long, though, those two were romping round on the rug like the old friends they were. As they played, I bent over to touch my boy's head, and Fiona saw my ear.

"Jaysus, Joseph, and Mary! What in the world happened to ye, Rabbit?"

Her hand reached for my ear, like she was gonna soothe the wound, but I took hold of it just in time. "Nothing that won't heal in a week or two. Let's not talk about it now." Normally that wouldn't be enough to calm her, but she was too weary to argue.

The next morning, she was up before me, what with the big time difference and her body clock off, so I didn't get to make her breakfast in bed. When I heard her up, I found a piece of paper and wrote a note, promising it another time, no expiration date.

I went downstairs and hugged her while she stood at the stove. After a while, she told me to take a seat. She'd made me something I'd had at Nigel's oncet: a fine English breakfast with sunny-side up eggs and bacon and fried bread and tomatoes and mushrooms. And tea and toast and marmalade.

"Wonderful," I said between bites. "A full English!"

"Make that a full Irish," she said, but she was just kidding. Even after a trip back home, she didn't harbor bad feelings against the Brits.

I'd set the note at her place, and when she read it, she leaned over and kissed me. Her eyes were kinda puffy, but she looked happy to be home.

Around ten o'clock, I made a pot of coffee, and we sat together while Conor played outside with Mollie. We could hear him laughing, which was a sharp contrast to what I had to tell Fiona. I fumbled round for the right words until she said, "Rabbit, just come out with it. Don't sugar-coat it. That ear of yours frightened me last night, but as long as you're standing safe and sound in front of me, I know I can take it."

So I told her about "The Peddler and His Wife" and Kentucky and the overturned coal truck and the noisy hawk and, well, everything. Her hand flew to her mouth when I told her about Marshall White. He'd even fooled Fiona, queen of the Irish gypsies.

"That bastard took half your ear off. Let me look closer," she said. When I bent my head over, she just kissed it and added, "Whoever tended to you did a fine job." I heard her voice tremble, and next thing I knew, she threw her arms round me and cried 'til my shirt was wet.

After that she asked lots of questions about Marshall and what happened next; I filled her in best I could. "He's on the run, honey. But the FBI figures he's headed for Winston-Salem." I explained about the fancy hotel and "Poor Ellen Smith."

"Well, he's taken murder ballads to a new low. I don't *ever* want to play one again—I don't care how pretty Polly is or how wise Omie is!" She did that little foot-stamping thing. I was trying to comfort her when she jerked away. "What happened to Vern?"

"He's with family services here in the county. His babysitter was looking after him while Marshall was terrorizing Kentucky, but then the authorities took him somewhere. That's all I know."

"Oh Rabbit, he should come here and be with Conor. They are more than friends; they're closer than some brothers." She got up to make some calls, and I knew nothing would stop her 'til that lad was sitting on our front porch.

Chapter 64: Abit

Marshall was still on the loose, but I wasn't worried about the seventy-three-day ticking clock anymore. He'd blown that the week before when he'd left the peddler and his wife alive.

The FBI was crawling all over the hotel in Winston-Salem, and a couple of agents stayed round Harlan County. But I figured Marshall woulda been crazier than we already knew if he were hanging out there.

I called Wallis to bring him up to date on Marshall. He hollered into the phone something about that SON OF A BISCUIT, stopping his rant long enough to tell me how much he liked my made-up swearword and hoped I didn't mind him borrowing it. I laughed and said I was proud it was up to his standards. Then I told him what I'd really called about: without his know-how, the FBI would still have their heads up their BLUNDERBUSS. His turn to laugh before telling me to come see him soon.

Life for us had started up again. I was working on some orders, finishing up one I'd needed an extension on. When I told the customer I'd had my ear shot off chasing a dangerous criminal, the woman told me she'd read about that in the *Mountain Weekly* and for me to take all the time

I needed. She added something about how the table was worth even more now that it was by someone famous. That sounded kinda silly to me, but I reckon it was her nerves talking.

Fiona was back working at the hospital after a coupla extra days off getting used to Eastern Time again. And Vern had, indeed, come to stay with us, for now. He didn't ask much about what had happened to his father, but you could tell he was confused. We all felt sorry for the little guy and were doing everything we could to make things seem normal. When Conor and Vern asked after Marshall, I just told them he was away on a gig. A gig from hell.

It was my turn to make supper that evening, so round four o'clock I headed to the kitchen. Conor ran in and asked if he and Vern could go down to the creek and play. "Okay, but don't get your shoes wet. Take them off before going in the water." He laughed at me—I guess that was obvious, even to an 8-year-old—and ran off with Vern.

When Fiona got home just after five o'clock, she asked after the boys. I was in the throes of cooking, so I told her to take a beer down to the creek where she'd find them. A nice way to leave work behind—a creek, a beer, two boys.

A few minutes later, she came running home, hollering at me through the open kitchen window. "The boys aren't there, Abit." I looked out where she was standing, holding two little pairs of shoes.

Sheriff Horne drove over right after we called. When he came into the house, he gave me a nod, a gesture I took as an apology for making fun of Wallis' and my theories. But that didn't matter to me anymore; I just wanted to find our boys. Besides, I'd heard about Mary Lou and Duane getting back together, and while I was happy for my old friend, the dark circles under Airhorn's eyes reminded me of the heartache he was suffering.

Fiona came downstairs after I called up to her. We sat together in the living room and Airhorn said soothing things like *we'll get those boys back* and *they likely just wandered off*. Then we told him everything we could think of. We wanted to make sure he knew, like we did, that it was Marshall who had our boys. No question about it. I'd seen the emptiness in his eyes, just from that quick look I got before he shot at me.

One good thing: Fiona and I hadn't started snapping at one anothern with blame. Who could've known it wasn't safe for two little boys to play on their own farm?

That night we couldn't sleep not knowing where our boys were. The next morning, Fiona called in sick again—sick at heart was as real as a cold or cough. We didn't bother making any breakfast; neither one of us could have eaten a bite. I did perk some coffee, and when I brought a couple cups into the living room, I noticed an envelope stuck under our front door.

Chapter 65: Abit

Fiona tore open the envelope.

Marshall musta sneaked up during the night and stuffed the ransom note under our door. During all that time I'd stared at the ceiling, wide awake, why couldn't I have heard him and caught him on our porch? And why for oncet in her life couldn't Mollie have barked? I usually liked her being so quiet, but not that time.

Fiona let out a howl when she read what he wanted: $20,000. "… enough money to get away and start over," he wrote. Like we were friends, and he was just asking for a small loan to tide him over. "Where would we ever get that kind of money, Rabbit?"

"We could mortgage the farm—again." I'd sunk all my inheritance, small as it was, into the farm, but I'd sell everything I owned to get those boys back.

Stoltz took over from Airhorn oncet it was an official kidnapping. He arrived little more than an hour after the sheriff's call. I don't know how he made that trip so fast, but I was grateful he cared enough to risk his own neck on those windy roads. I asked after Curtis; he was due back from Charlotte that afternoon.

I introduced Stoltz to Fiona, and she left to go make tea. We talked some but it wasn't 'til she came back and served us that we got down to the real business at hand.

The plan was to meet up with Marshall, who'd given us the deadline of nine o'clock that evening. He also included instructions on how to find him and the boys. Sounded like Marshall planned to leave Vern behind when he "started over."

A coupla FBI folks showed us a small suitcase with $20,000 in it and explained how the handover would go. I thought it must be play money, but they assured me it was the real thing. They didn't plan on Marshall getting his hands on it before some ninja FBI men and women hiding in the woods grabbed him.

It all felt too unreal for both me and Fiona, like a bad TV movie. But we paid attention and were grateful for the support. Of course this time there was no question that I'd come along—I had to be the frontman who delivered the money. Fiona said she didn't know if her legs would carry her. Stoltz kindly suggested she come along, but remain in the truck; he seemed to understand she could never stay at home alone, either.

For the rest of the day, neither one of us had anything to occupy our minds. I couldn't work in my shop. For sure I would've cut off a finger. Shiloh was out there working hard to help us keep our deadlines. And I knew he was visualizing a good outcome for us.

I scrambled us some eggs and made toast from a whole wheat loaf a neighbor'd brought over. That was all we could keep down, that plus more tea.

When Curtis arrived, he said all the right things and explained he'd be heading up the FBI team that would be going out to the site well before nine o'clock. He promised they knew how to do this so Marshall wouldn't see them.

Fiona and I prayed. I didn't know what to say other than how much I loved both the boys, and I asked Jesus to help them have the opportunity to live full lives. I offered mine in exchange, but I knew he didn't work thataway.

Like a coupla robots, we walked out to the truck about eight-thirty, carrying that suitcase that meant life to our boys. I drove, though to this day, I don't remember a thing about getting there. Fiona was good about reading the directions while holding a flashlight. When we pulled up just before nine o'clock, no one was in sight. I was glad about the FBI not sticking out.

After a warm day for that late in the fall, the evening had turned cold. I wanted to have the truck going so we could have some heat, but I was afraid we wouldn't hear the boys.

Fiona's teeth were chattering when she spoke. "This wait is killing me, Rabbit. I know we can't hurry things up, but I'm fixing to start screaming like a banshee."

I knew she meant it, but what could I say to soothe her? I wanted to start hollering too.

After that, we didn't say anything for the longest time. I jumped in my seat when she spoke again. "Those boys mean the world to me. And to you, I know." She squeezed my hand, and something passed between us like I hadn't felt before. "I swear if they come home to us, I will never again waste a precious moment wishing for more. Two fine boys are more love than most people get to have, and I'll be grateful for what I have."

I hugged her hard and fought back my own fears. I tried to picture our life together, happy on the farm with two young'uns running round making noise and mess and everything wonderful about being that young.

I looked at my watch; it was only ten after nine. It felt like we'd been waiting an hour.

"Do you think he's playing a trick on us, Rabbit?" Fiona said, sounding like the life was draining outta her. I felt about the same, but I was trying to hold it inside for her sake. I wrapped my arms round her while she let out another wave of misery.

When my watch read twenty-five after nine, I said, "Shug, I can't sit here and wait. I don't want to screw anything up, but I've got to get outta this truck." We were in this together, and I couldn't just go running off without her agreeing.

"Go out there and find that bastard," she said, still crying her eyes out. "I'll stay in the truck with the suitcase."

The truck door made an awful cry in the silent night. Then I shouted, "Marshall! Marshall White! We're here for the boys."

Just an old hoot owl answered my plea. I walked round in circles, straining my eyes to see in the dark. Nothing. That bastard had played a trick on us. Was there no end to his evil?

I feared the worst for our boys and started crying. Then out of nowhere came the unmistakable sound of a harmonica blasting a string of off-key notes. A song of desperation.

In a flash, FBI agents rushed forward and called out to one anothern in an area off to the left. I ran toward them, and in the dark I almost tripped over a root. The near-fall hurtled me forward in a low crouch, my arms out to regain my balance, so when Conor and Vern came running outta the woods, they thought I was opening my arms to them, down at their level, in order to grab them and love them and take them to safety. And I was.

Fiona was right behind me, and next thing I knew we were all in a huddle, hugging and crying and carrying on. We heard the FBI shouting, and for oncet, I was happy *not* to be in the middle of things. Though I wasn't happy to learn Marshall had slipped away again.

Chapter 66: Abit

The next day, I saw our neighbor walking up the drive leading a big German shepherd. He'd heard about what we were going through, and since it was well-known Mollie wasn't much of a watchdog, he wondered if we'd like to keep Layla until Marshall was caught. I was about to come to Mollie's defense, but then I knew he was right.

Fiona and I were both grateful for the kindness, though I wasn't sure how Mollie would take to a new dog in her house. I should've known. She gave Layla a play bow, and that was all it took for her to have a new friend. They slept together in the living room, keeping watch over us for three nights. I slept better than I had in weeks, knowing Layla would light into Marshall if he came near us.

The FBI finally caught him. Not in Winston-Salem, but sneaking round Fort Thomas, Kentucky, just below Cincinnati. Come to find out he'd had enough sense to skip "Poor Ellen Smith" since he knew we were on to him. He'd moved on to "Pearl Bryan," the next murder ballad on the list in *Traditional Tales of True Crime Ballads in the Southern Appalachians*. Wallis and I were both proud of our detective work. We knew the FBI had to have referred to that same list in order to widen their search.

Not surprisingly, in the end Stoltz took most of the credit, giving a nod to Curtis and the FBI team. Wallis didn't care, and after I got a mess of stove wood split the day I'd heard about Stoltz's preening, I didn't care either. I chose to see it as payback for all the help they'd given us in getting our boys back.

Curtis stopped by before heading home (even though our farm was in the other direction). He wanted to thank me for my help in getting him a promotion. My heart sank; I figured I was losing my friend. But it turned out he'd still be working outta Charlotte. We talked about a dinner at the house sometime soon, this time with Fiona and the boys.

Oncet Marshall was behind bars, we asked the boys more about what had happened. (Fiona'd been too superstitious to talk about it while Marshall was on the run.) Marshall had found them playing in the creek and said they were going on a camping trip together. They lived in a tent for a few days, and both boys said they thought it was fun. At first. We didn't want to upset Vern any more than he already was, so we left it at that.

Later, Conor came into our bedroom while Vern was in the bathroom and told us he'd felt scared and sad, having just come home from Ireland and already missing me and Mollie. I wanted to know where he'd gotten a pair of shoes to wear, and he showed me the blisters from wearing a spare pair of Vern's.

While we were talking, I could tell reliving those days was upsetting Conor all over again. His mama soothed him as we talked more and came up with a plan to go back to Lake Meacham. He settled down and even laughed at one of my stupid jokes. Then he pulled out his harmonica and played a funny little tune he'd taught himself.

Chapter 67: Della

I got a call from Abit while I was up in D.C. He filled me in on the kidnapping and the eventual capture of Marshall White. I couldn't even imagine the terror they'd been living through.

Alex and I both wanted to be with them, so we packed up in record time (though Rascal liked Alex's backyard so much, I had a little trouble getting him into the Jeep). We drove down together; Alex planned to take the train back to D.C. in a week or two.

We were almost down to Roanoke when I looked over at Alex as he drove. The way the sun hit the side of his face, I could see how lined it had become, especially around his eyes and mouth. And how the skin now sagged under his neck. I watched him a while longer, and it felt as though I came to know each of the sorrows that had etched the wrinkles and creases—and I knew I was the cause of many of them. He looked so very vulnerable, as we all ultimately are.

I felt something come over me, like a soft blanket pulled up on a cold night. In that moment, I knew I wanted to spend every minute I could with him and stop wasting time on old grudges and lies.

He caught me looking. "What?"

"Oh, nothing. Just thinking about our lives together."

"And that's *nothing*?" I punched his shoulder in that way that means *cut it out*. "Okay, but I've been thinking about our lives together too," he said. "You know when I went off while staying at your apartment?" I nodded. "I was checking out a job offer in Chapel Hill. I didn't want to tell you about it in case I wasn't offered the job. But I was. For a new magazine."

"Tough time for magazine start-ups."

"Yeah, but this one seems different. And there's good backing. A couple of rich guys from the tech world want to make their mark in a different way. They're tired of too much distilled, dumbed-down crap that masquerades as news. I have high hopes for it."

"What will you write about?"

"I'll be managing editor. I'm bone weary of running all over the place to get the story. That's a younger person's game. And Chapel Hill cuts our commute from seven hours to three. I don't even have to work there all the time—just go over for editorial meetings and the like."

I was quiet, thinking about the wonder of coincidence.

"I thought you'd be more excited," he said.

"I am."

"You don't sound it."

"I'm just stunned that I was thinking about wanting to spend more time together, and then you tell me you've made that possible."

We rode for miles without saying more. He was first to break the silence. "Have you ever thought of getting married again?

"I've said this before, but to refresh your memory, I've never felt *not* married to you, even after the divorce."

"That doesn't answer my question."

"Do *you* think about getting married again?"

"Every day."

"What do you mean?"

"I mean *every day*," he said. "You have no idea how much shame I carry for that time in my life."

"Well, don't. I've put all that behind me. Us. I realized I've been carrying a lot of baggage too. Do you think it's time to stop that?"

"Yes, I do." He paused, taking a sip of what had to be cold coffee. "But you still haven't answered my question."

"I think we should spend as much time together as we can, but not rush into anything—for now—other than getting rid of the baggage. Is that good?"

"Yeah, that's good."

"Good."

Once we were back in town, I checked on the store, Abit, and Jessie, in that order. The store first only because it was there when we drove into Laurel Falls. I wasn't surprised Mary Lou had done her usual terrific job.

Then we headed out to see Abit and his family. I had to witness with my own eyes that all was well. They seemed to be returning to something close to normal. Conor even played an original tune for us on his harmonica. When I told Abit his ear looked like one of Rascal's, he laughed. That's when I knew he'd be okay.

On the way back, I dropped Alex and Rascal at home before stopping by the *Mountain Weakly*. Jessie was busy finishing up the Marshall White series, but she made time for a coffee at a café next door. The responsibility of writing the series seemed to have awakened a journalistic spark in her. I couldn't imagine her going back to school board meetings, and I told her so. I was surprised when she agreed.

"Okay, then I'll ask one more time. Would you like to cover the real estate scandal? I've got excellent contacts for you and the promise of an exclusive, at least from the local angle."

This time Jessie jumped at the opportunity. *Now that the hard work is done, she wants it*, I thought to myself. But that was okay. Time to pass the baton.

"Don't you want to share the byline?" Jessie asked as she tucked into the apple cobbler we were sharing.

"No, I don't. But I'll tell you what I do want?"

"Anything."

"Next time I'm in D.C., I want you to take me to lunch, somewhere *very* fancy."

"When and how's that going to happen?"

"Oh, you know, when the *Washington Post* snags the hottest new reporter covering an explosive bank-fraud story."

Chapter 68: Abit

Jessie Walsh at the newspaper wrote some articles about Marshall and the murders. I couldn't imagine how she stood being in the jail with him, but I guess the guards helped her feel safe enough.

She started with where he'd grown up. I wasn't surprised to read that was Chattanooga, where at 15 he'd already turned into a troublemaker. More than likely he was born not quite right in the head, but I knew something else was at play. I never doubted he was also a victim of that passed-down rage Curtis mentioned, from generations of hardship and heartache and just plain meanness.

When his family threw him out, he moved round for a while. Then eight year ago, he settled back near them, about the same time he took up with Vern's mama. When he started acting crazy again, the courts made him get medical help, but Marshall hated the pills they put him on. He said they made his music suffer, and he went offa them. That's when he first felt what he called "an itch that needed scratching," a wicked understatement if there ever was one.

He told Jessie something just came over him when the first girl told him she was a "Knoxville girl." A few months later, when the second girl said her name was Barbara Allen, he heard a voice saying she needed to live up to her name and die. While they didn't catch him for those murders back then, he did get arrested for a robbery and spent four year in prison.

After he got out, he settled down again with Vern's mother. But like the last time, the drugs that kept him halfway sane messed with his music, so he stopped. That's when Vern's mama ran off—and the itch came back.

When I finished reading the last article, I just sat in my chair a while, thinking how many forks in the road life throws your way—and how easy it was to choose the wrong one. And yet, somehow, Marshall had tapped into enough goodness not to abandon Vern when his mama ran off.

In the interviews, Marshall mentioned his music a lot, talking about how important it was, which reminded me how pissed off I got when Fiona kept saying how much Marshall put into his music. Now I could see that for the truth. But it wasn't until Airhorn came by our place to bring us up to date that I understood why Marshall'd latched on to the murder ballads so hard—and why he didn't want our band to play them.

"He's crazy as a June bug now," Airhorn told us, "performing in his cell to what he thinks is a big audience. The shrinks think Marshall is compelled to kill because he's actually living *inside* those stories. He *has* to kill because it's in the script he's living." He shook his head and added, "He's writing his own murder ballad, calling it 'Murder Ballad Blues.' The guards told me he hasn't finished it yet, just keeps singing a few lines over and over, driving them crazy."

"Have you heard Marshall singing it?" I asked. When he nodded, I asked if he could sing it for us. I'd heard Airhorn sing and play guitar in the copper band, The Rolling Stops, and I knew he had a good voice. He rifled through a file he'd brought and found a report that included the lyrics. After pausing for a moment, likely to get the tune right in his head, he cleared his throat and sang in a strong tenor:

Please don't let me linger in a place nobody comes to.
There's no one left to visit or lay flowers on my grave.
I've done a lot of bad things that kept true love away.
I doubt even Jesus thinks my life is worth a save.

Each girl I knew was special, pretty as you please.
They sashayed and pranced and flirted with such ease.
The man was full of bluster, quick temper and booze.
We lived and died together in the murder ballad blues.

When he finished singing, Airhorn looked a little sick. Then he brought up something else. "You know that numerology thing? He's really into it. I don't know much about it, but he's thrilled his cell number is eleven because according to him that's his master number. Something to do with faith. I hate to think what he has faith in."

I knew what: killing. That's what Jessie Walsh wrote, that he had a killer mindset. Not just that he saw his victims as characters in the ballads, but that the more recent ones deserved to die because they'd judged him. He'd told her his victim over in Randolph County criticized his music playing. That was a stupid thing to do. Not only was she wrong, but if she hadn't said that, she might've still been alive.

But I knew it wasn't fair to lay 20/20 hindsight on that poor dead girl. If we got killed for saying stupid things, I'd never have seen my tenth birthday.

Chapter 69: Abit

The house seemed awful quiet. Della and Alex had taken Conor and Vern off to Mystery Mountain, the way Alex had done with me all those year ago. Fiona, Mollie, and Rascal were upstairs, getting ready for our big day.

When the boys came home, all happy and wore out, they fell asleep on the porch swing I'd just put up—something Conor had been asking for, and I couldn't recall why I hadn't done it sooner. Alex and Della sat on the porch watching over the boys, taking it easy in a coupla rockers I'd made.

Fiona and I'd been busy all morning pulling together a special dinner to celebrate everyone being home, safe and sound—and Conor's ninth birthday coming up in a day or two. The day before, I'd made Mama's apple cake, the one I always wanted for my birthdays when I was a kid. (It tasted better the second day.) That morning I fixed my squash-and-tomato dish. Fiona made the rest.

While we were finishing up making dinner, the phone rang. My hands were free, so I answered. I was on so long, not saying a word, Fiona came over, asking me what was wrong.

"Thank you. Yes. I will tell her." I put the receiver down and turned to Fiona, but when I opened my mouth, the words wouldn't come. It took a minute or two before I could tell her the news.

We went out on the porch, where Della and Alex were still sitting; the boys had gone off to play out back. I looked round to make sure they were outta earshot.

"What?" Della asked. "You're acting all funny."

"Well, it seems Airhorn and the family services folks have completed their check into Vern. One of the things they needed to know was whether Vern was Marshall's boy. Turns out …"

I wasn't trying to hold back, but I was still having trouble finding my words. Finally, Fiona blurted out, "His mam got pregnant by somebody else while Marshall was in the nick the first time. That plus some blood tests mean we now know Vern's blood isn't tainted by Marshall's."

I let out a big sigh and managed to add: "We'd've loved him no matter what, but now we don't have to wonder about Conor's new brother."

I saw Della's face change. I thought she was fixing to cry, but then she smiled.

"That's not everything," Fiona said. "As you know, after Vern's mother left him, Marshall didn't abandon him. That seems to count for something in his favor. His public defender told the courts that Marshall, during one of his saner moments, asked that we care for Vern. We don't know how much weight the wishes of a serial killer have on the courts, especially now that we know Marshall has no claim as a blood relative, but we can hope."

"The only thing we do know is that it will take months of waiting," I said. "In the meantime, it's back to one day at a time, like you're always saying, Della."

I called the boys in from play, and we all sat round our curly maple dining table. Fiona was grinning from ear to ear when she brought in a cottage pie, only this one looked different. Instead of just taters on top, she'd made three sections—a fat stripe of creamed spinach, then a stripe of mashed taters, then one of mashed carrots. The Irish flag. I knew she'd been homesick since she got back, but I didn't realize how much.

As we tucked in, she stood up. "I hope you boys like this meal because you'll get a lot of this in Ireland." Then she laughed. "My da is paying for the four of us to come stay with him in Ireland next year. It will be good having a summer Rabbit won't be getting into trouble."

We'd see about that.

GLOSSARY

Blighter: Unlikeable, contemptible person

Blighty: Affectionate term for England, originally used by soldiers from World War I and World War II

Bloke: Man

Bottle and stopper: Cockney rhyming slang for *copper, police*

Break: Musical term for a solo within a song

Christmas crackers: Table decorations that usually have a tissue paper crown, corny jokes, and a trinket tucked inside. When the two ends are pulled apart, they make a snapping/cracking sound.

Cottage pie: Savory dish of ground beef and vegetables topped by mashed potatoes

Dicky bird: Cockney rhyming slang for *word*

Eejit: Idiot (Irish)

Elevenses: A break for refreshments around eleven o'clock in the morning

Git: Someone who is silly, annoying, or incompetent.

Guts for garters: Slang for being in big trouble

Hit and miss: Cockney rhyming slang for *kiss*

Mum and dad: Cockney rhyming slang for *mad*

Nick: Prison or jail, especially at a police station

Nipper: A child, especially a small boy

Pears: Shortened from "apples and pears," which is Cockney rhyming slang for *stairs*

Peelers: Irish and later English police officers, originally from Sir Robert Peel, who started the first peacekeeping force in Ireland in 1814

Pillock: Stupid person

Plonker: Fool

Porkie: Shortened from "pork pie," which is Cockney rhyming slang for *lie*

Raindrops: Charming plinky sounds a banjo player makes to back up a vocal

RICO: The Racketeer Influenced and Corrupt Organizations Act, a U.S. law fighting organized crime

Rosie: Shortened from Rosie Lee, which is Cockney rhyming slang for *tea*

Smalls: Underpants

The Troubles: The violent sectarian conflict in Northern Ireland spanning four decades in the mid- to late 20th century

Your free book is "Waiting for You."

Want to spend more time with Abit Bradshaw and Della Kincaid? Get your free copy of my novelette, *Waiting for You.*

I've pulled back the curtain on their lives before they met in Laurel Falls—between 1981 and 1984. You'll discover how Abit lost hope of ever having a meaningful life and why Della had to leave Washington, D.C.

Haven't started the series yet? *Waiting for You* will get you started in style.

Get your free copy of *Waiting for You* here:
www.lyndamcdanielbooks.com/free

Dear Readers ...

I hope you've enjoyed Book 4 in my Appalachian Mountain Mysteries series. I sure enjoy writing them!

I've been a professional writer for several decades now, and it still thrills me when readers write to me. Sometimes they have questions about the stories and the characters. Other times they leave reviews and, well, make my day!

> "Reminds me of *To Kill a Mockingbird* ... finding your books is like finding a rare jewel." — J.M. Grayson

Before I started writing fiction 10 years ago, I wrote more than 1,200 articles for major magazines and newspapers and 15 nonfiction books, including several books on the craft of writing. I'm now working on my fifth Appalachian Mountain Mysteries novel.

Book Reviews ...

I'm touched whenever people post reviews on Amazon, Goodreads, book blogs, etc.

> "FIVE STARS! Lynda McDaniel has that wonderfully appealing way of weaving a story ..."
> — Deb, Amazon Hall of Fame Top 100 Reviewer

I'd really appreciate it if you'd take a minute or two to leave a review. (It's easy—just a sentence or two is enough.) Often readers don't realize how much these reviews mean to the success of an author. In today's online world, reviews can make a huge difference—so thanks in advance for posting a few sentences.

And Free Book Club Talks …

I'd love to drop by your book club and answer your questions—whether about my books, what inspired them, or even how to write your own books. We can easily meet through **Zoom**. To keep things lively, I've created an all-in-one ***Book Club Discussion Guides*** to download **free.** Check it out on my website: https://www.lyndamcdanielbooks.com/book-clubs

I get a kick out of hearing from readers, so don't be a stranger! You can contact me directly at LyndaMcDanielBooks@gmail.com or through my website www.LyndaMcDanielBooks.com.

Lynda McDaniel

P.S. I thought you might enjoy an excerpt from the first book in the series (following the book club questions.)

Murder Ballad Blues
Book Discussion Guide

1. What do you think the book's title is referring to? How does it relate to the book's theme?

2. What was the author's purpose in writing this book? What ideas was she trying to get across?

3. What was unique about the setting of the book and how did it enhance or take away from the story? How did the setting impact the story?

4. What did you already know about the Southern Appalachians? What did you learn? Did you have any misperceptions?

5. Did the characters seem believable to you? Did they remind you of anyone you know—even if they're from a different part of the country?

6. Abit Bradshaw has come into his own through music and woodworking. What skills in your life helped you feel creative and productive?

7. Why was Della Kincaid so determined to respond to the whistleblower's mailings? What in her personality and professional life motivated her?

8. What are the major conflicts in the story?

9. What feelings did this book evoke for you?

10. At the end of Chapter 26, Della Kincaid says:

"When it finally sank in that Nigel was safe, I sat on the bench and cried in front of God and everyone. My customers were well acquainted with life's troubles, so anyone passing by took it in stride. Two women gently laid their hands on my downturned head before walking on."

Have you ever been comforted by strangers? Helped by people you didn't know?

11. Were you surprised by any cultural differences you read about? Have you been to any of the places mentioned in the story?

12. In Chapter 53, Abit Bradshaw says: *"I walked to the store (Coburn's), opened the front door, and for the first time ever, felt I might not be welcome.*

"Okay if I come in?"

"Of course it is, Abit." Della frowned at me. *"Why are you asking permission? Don't tell me you're sorry about speaking up. That negates what you accomplished."*

How do you feel after you've been angry at someone or spoken out about what you believe in?

13. Can you relate to the characters' predicaments? Have you experienced anything similar?

14. What did you think when Della Kincaid was attracted to FBI Agent Stoltz? Have you ever had feelings for someone you knew could never advance? What were those reasons?

15. How do characters change, grow, or evolve throughout the course of the story? What events trigger these changes?

16. Are there any characters you'd like to deliver a message to? If so, who? What would you say?

Excerpt from Book 1
Appalachian Mountain Mysteries Series

"A Life for a Life"

Prologue: Abit
September 2004

My life was saved by a murder. At the time, of course, I didn't understand that. I just knew I was having the best year of my life. Given all the terrible things that happened, I should be ashamed to say it, but that year was a blessing for me.

I'd just turned 15 when Della Kincaid bought Daddy's store. At first nothing much changed. Daddy was still round a lot, getting odd jobs as a handyman and farming enough to sell what Mama couldn't put by. And we still lived in the house next door, though Mama banned me from going inside the store. She said she didn't want me to be a nuisance, but I think she was jealous of "that woman from Washington, D.C."

So I just sat out front like I always did when Daddy owned it, killing time, chatting with a few friendly customers or other bench-sitters like me. I never wanted to go inside while Daddy had the store, not because he might have asked me to help, but because he thought I *couldn't* help. Oh sure, I'd go in for a Coca-Cola or Dr. Pepper, but for the most part, I just sat there, reared back with my chair resting against the outside wall, my legs dangling. Just like my life.

I've never forgotten how crazy it all played out. I *had* forgotten about the two diaries I'd kept that year. I discovered them while cleaning out our home after Mama died in April. (Daddy had passed two years earlier, to the day.) They weren't like a girl's diary (at least that's what I told myself, when I worried about such things). They were notes I'd imagined a reporter like Della or her ex-husband would make, capturing the times.

I'd already cleaned out most of the house, saving my room for last. I boxed up my hubcaps, picking out my favorites from the ones still hanging on my bedroom walls. (We'd long ago sold the collection in the barn.) I tackled the shelves with all my odd keepsakes: a deer jaw, two dusty geodes, other rocks I'd found that caught my eye, like the heart-shaped reddish one—too good not to keep. When I gathered a shelf full of books in my arms, I saw the battered shoebox where I'd stashed those diaries behind the books. I sat on my old bed, the plaid spread dusty and faded, and started to read. The pages had yellowed, but they stirred up fresh memories, all the same. That's when I called Della (I still looked for any excuse to talk with her), and we arranged a couple of afternoons to go over the diaries together.

We sat at her kitchen table and talked. And talked. After a time or two recollecting over the diaries, I told Della I wanted to write a book about that year. She agreed. We were both a little surprised that, even after all these years, we didn't have any trouble recalling that spring.

Chapter 1: Della
April 1985

I heard my dog, Jake, whimpering as I sank into the couch. I'd closed him in the bedroom while the sheriff and his gang of four were in my apartment. Jake kept bringing toys over for them to throw, and I could see how irritated they were getting. I didn't want to give them reason to be even more unpleasant about what had happened earlier in the day.

"Hi there, boy," I said as I opened the door. "Sorry about that, buddy." He sprang from the room and grabbed his stuffed rabbit. I scratched his ears and threw the toy, then reclaimed the couch. "Why didn't we stay in today, like I wanted?"

That morning, I'd thought about skipping our usual hike. It was my only day off, and I wanted to read last Sunday's *Washington Post*. (I was always a week behind since I had to have the papers mailed to me.) But Jake sat by the door and whined softly, and I sensed how cooped up he'd been with all the early spring rains.

Besides, those walks did me more good than Jake. When I first moved to Laurel Falls, the natural world frightened me. Growing up in Washington, D.C. hadn't prepared me for that kind of wild. But gradually, I got more comfortable and started to recognize some of the birds and trees. And wildflowers. Something about their delicate beauty made the woods more welcoming. Trilliums, pink lady's slippers, and fringed phacelia beckoned, encouraging me to venture deeper.

Of course, it didn't help that my neighbors and customers carried on about the perils of taking long hikes by myself. "You could be murdered," they cried. "At the very least you could be raped," warned Mildred Bradshaw, normally a quiet, prim woman. "And what about perverts?" she'd add, exasperated that I wasn't listening to her.

Sometimes Mildred's chant "You're so alone out there" nagged at me in a reactive loop as Jake and I walked in the woods. But that was one of the reasons I moved to North Carolina. I *wanted* to be alone. I longed to get away from deadlines and noise and people. And memories. Besides, I'd argue with myself, hadn't I lived safely in D.C. for years? I'd walked dark streets, sat face-to-face with felons, been robbed at gunpoint, but I still went out whenever I wanted, at least before midnight. You couldn't live there and worry too much about crime, be it violent, white-collar, or political; that city would grind to a halt if people thought that way.

As Jake and I wound our way, the bright green tree buds and wildflowers soothed my dark thoughts. I breathed in that intoxicating smell of spring: not one thing in particular, but a mix of fragrances floating on soft breezes, signaling winter's retreat. The birds were louder too, chittering and chattering in the warmer temperatures. I was lost in my reverie when Jake stopped so fast I almost tripped over him. He stood still, ears alert.

"What is it, boy?" He looked up at me, then resumed his exploration of rotten squirrels and decaying stumps.

I didn't just love that dog, I admired him. He was unafraid of his surroundings, plowing through tall fields of hay or dense forests without any idea where he was headed, not the least bit perturbed by bugs flying into his eyes or seeds up his nose. He'd just sneeze and keep going.

We walked a while longer and came to a favorite lunch spot. I nestled against a broad beech tree, its smooth bark gentler against my back than the alligator bark of red oak or locust. Jake fixated on a line of ants carrying off remnants from a picnic earlier that day, rooting under leaves and exploring new smells since his last visit. But mostly he slept. He found a sunspot and made a nest thick with leaves, turning round and round until everything was just right.

Jake came to live with me a year and a half ago when a neighbor committed suicide, a few months before I moved south. We both struggled at first, but when we settled here, the past for him seemed forgotten. Sure, he still ran in circles when I brushed against his old leash hanging in the coat closet, but otherwise, he was officially a mountain dog. I was the one still working on leaving the past behind.

I'd bought the store on a whim after a week's stay in a log cabin in the Black Mountains. To prolong the trip, I took backroads home. As I drove through Laurel Falls, I spotted the boarded-up store sporting a For Sale sign. I stopped, jotted down the listed phone number, and called. Within a week, I owned it. The store was in shambles, both physically and financially, but something about its bones had appealed to me. And I could afford the extensive remodeling it needed because the asking price was so low.

Back in my D.C. condo, I realized how much I wanted a change in my life. I had no family to miss. I was an only child, and my parents had died in an alcoholic daze, their car wrapped around a tree, not long after I left for college. And all those editors and deadlines, big city hassles, and a failed marriage? I was eager to trade them in for a tiny town and a dilapidated store called Coburn's General Store. (Nobody knew who Coburn was—that was just what it had always been called, though most of the time it was simply Coburn's. Even if I'd renamed it, no one would've used that name.)

In addition to the store, the deal included an apartment upstairs that, during its ninety-year history, had likely housed more critters than humans. Plus a vintage 1950 Chevy pickup truck with wraparound rear windows that still ran just fine. And a bonus I didn't know about when I signed the papers: a living, breathing griffon to guard me and the store—Abit Bradshaw, Mildred's teenage son.

I'd lived there almost a year, and I treasured my days away from the store, especially once it was spring again. Some folks complained that I wasn't open Sundays (blue laws a distant memory, even though they were repealed only a few years earlier), but I couldn't work every day, and I couldn't afford to hire help, except now and again.

While Jake and I sat under that tree, the sun broke through the canopy and warmed my face and shoulders. I watched Jake's muzzle twitch (he was already lost in a dream), and chuckled when he sprang to life at the first crinkle of wax paper. I shooed him away as I unwrapped my lunch. On his way back to his nest, he stopped and stared down the dell, his back hairs spiking into a Mohawk.

"Get over it, boy. I don't need you scaring me as bad as Mildred. Settle down now," I gently scolded as I laid out a chunk of Gruyere I'd whittled the hard edges off, an almost-out-of-date salami, and a sourdough roll I'd rescued from the store. I'd been called a food snob, but these sad leftovers from a struggling store sure couldn't support that claim. Besides, out here the food didn't matter so much. It was all about the pileated woodpecker trumpeting its jungle call or the tiny golden-crowned kinglet flitting from branch to branch. And the waterfall in the distance, playing its soothing continuo, day and night. These walks kept me sane. The giant trees reminded me I was just a player in a much bigger game, a willing refugee from a crowded, over-planned life.

I crumpled the lunch wrappings, threw Jake a piece of roll, and found a sunnier spot. I hadn't closed my eyes for a minute when Jake gave another low growl. He was sitting upright, nose twitching, looking at me for advice. "Sorry, pal. You started it. I don't hear anything," I told him. He gave another face-saving low growl and put his head back down.

"You crazy old hound." I patted his warm, golden fur. Early on, I wondered what kind of mix he was—maybe some retriever and beagle, bringing his size down to medium. I'd asked the vet to hazard a guess. He wouldn't. Or couldn't. It didn't matter.

I poured myself a cup of hot coffee, white with steamed milk, appreciating the magic of a thermos, even if the contents always tasted vaguely of vegetable soup. That aroma took me back to the woods of my childhood, just two vacant lots really, a few blocks from my home in D.C.'s Cleveland Park. I played there for hours, stocked with sandwiches and a thermos of hot chocolate. I guess that's where I first thought of becoming a reporter; I sat in the cold and wrote up everything that passed by—from birds and salamanders to postmen taking a shortcut and high schoolers sneaking out for a smoke.

A deeper growl from Jake pulled me back. As I turned to share his view, I saw a man running toward us. "Dammit, Mildred," I swore, as though the intruder were her fault. The man looked angry, pushing branches out of his way as he charged toward us. Jake barked furiously as I grabbed his collar and held tight. Even though the scene was unfolding just as my neighbor had warned, I wasn't afraid. Maybe it was the Madras sport shirt, so out of place on a man with a bushy beard and long ponytail. *For God's sake*, I thought, *how could anyone set out in the morning dressed like that and plan to do harm?* A hint of a tattoo—a Celtic cross?—peeked below his shirt sleeve, adding to his unlikely appearance.

As he neared, I could see his face wasn't so much angry as pained, drained of color.

"There's some … one," his voice cracked. He put his hands on his thighs and tried to catch his breath. As he did, his graying ponytail fell across his chest.

"What? Who?"

"A body. Somebody over there," he said, pointing toward the creek. "Not far, it's …" he stopped again to breathe.

"Where?"

"I don't know. Cross … creek." He started to run.

"Wait! Don't go!" I shouted, but all I could see was the back of his stupid shirt as he ran. "Hey! At least call for help. There's an emergency call box down that road, at the car park. Call Gregg O'Donnell at the Forest Service. I'll go see if there's anything I can do."

He shouted, "There's nothing you can do," and kept running.

Jake led the way as we crashed through the forest, branches whipping our faces. I felt the creek's icy chill, in defiance of the day's warmth, as I missed the smaller stepping stones and soaked my feet. Why didn't I ask the stranger more details, or have him show me where to find the person? And what did "across the creek" mean in an eleven-thousand-acre wilderness area? When I stopped to get my bearings, I began to shiver, my feet numb. Jake stopped with me, sensing the seriousness of our romp in the woods; he even ignored a squirrel.

We were a pack of two, running together, the forest silent except for our heavy breathing and the rustle we made crossing the decaying carpet beneath our feet. Jake barked at something, startling me, but it was just the crack of a branch I'd broken to clear the way. We were both spooked.

I stopped to rest on a fallen tree as Jake ran ahead, then back and to the right. Confused, he stopped and looked at me. "I don't know which way either, boy." We were just responding to a deep, instinctual urge to help. "You go on, Jake. You'll find it before I will."

And he did.

Chapter 2: Abit

Four cop cars blocked our driveway.

I thought I might've dreamed it, since I'd fallen asleep on the couch, watching TV. But after I rubbed my eyes, all four cars was still there. Seeing four black-and-whites in a town with only one could throw you.

All I could think was *what did I do wrong*? I ran through my day real quick-like, and I couldn't come up with anything that would get me more than a backhand from Daddy.

I watched a cop walking in front of the store next door, which we shared a driveway with. As long as I could remember, that store hadn't never had four cars out front at the same time, let alone four *cop* cars. I stepped outside, quietly closing our front door. The sun was getting low, and I hoped Mama wudn't about to call me in to supper.

I headed down our stone steps to see for myself. Our house sat on a hill above the store, which made it close enough that Daddy, when he still owned the store, could run down the steps (twenty of 'em, mossy and slick after a rain) if, say, a customer drove up while he was home having his midday dinner. But of an evening, those same steps seemed to keep people from pestering him to open up, as Daddy put it, "to sell some fool thing they could live without 'til the next morning."

I was just about halfway down when the cop looked my way. "Don't trouble yourself over this, Abit. Nothing to see here." That was Lonnie Parker, the county's deputy sheriff.

"What do you mean nothin' to see here? I ain't seen four cop cars all in one place in my whole life."

"You don't need to worry about this."

"I'm not worried," I said. "I'm curious."

"You're curious all right." He turned and spat something dark on to the dirt drive, a mix of tobacco and hate.

That's how it always went. People talked to me like I was an idiot. Okay, I knew I wudn't as smart as others. Something happened when Mama had me (she was pretty old by then), and I had trouble making my words just right sometimes. But inside, I worked better than most people thought. I used to go to school, but I had trouble keeping up, and that made Daddy feel bad. I wudn't sure if he felt bad for me or him. Anyways, they took me out of school when I was 12 , which meant I spent my days watching TV and hanging out. And being bored. I could read, but it took me a while. The bookmobile swung by every few weeks, and I'd get a new book each time. And I watched the news and stuff like that to try to learn.

I was named after Daddy – Vester Bradshaw Jr. – but everyone called me Abit. I heard the name Abbott mentioned on the TV and asked Mama if that was the same as mine. She said it were different but pronounced about the same. She wouldn't call me that, but Daddy were fine with it. A few year ago, I overheard him explaining how I came by it.

"I didn't want him called the same as me," Daddy told a group of men killing time outside the store. He was a good storyteller, and he was enjoying the attention. "He's a retard. When he come home from the hospital, and people asked how he was doin', I'd tell 'em, 'he's a bit slow.' I wanted to just say it outright to cut out all the gossip. I told that story enough that someone started calling him Abit, and it stuck."

Some jerk then asked if my middle name were "Slow," and everybody laughed. That hurt me at the time, but with the choice between Abit and Vester, I reckoned my name wudn't so bad, after all. Daddy could have his stupid name.

Anyways, I wudn't going to have Lonnie Parker run me off my own property (or nearabout my property), so I folded my arms and leaned against the rock wall.

I grabbed a long blade of grass and chewed. While I waited, I checked out the hubcaps on the cars—nothing exciting, just the routine sort of government caps. Too bad, 'cause a black-and-white would've looked really cool with Mercury chrome hubcaps. I had one in my collection in the barn back of the house, so I knew what I was talkin' about.

I heard some loud voices coming from upstairs, the apartment above the store, where Della lived with Jake, some kind of mixed hound that came to live with her when she lived in Washington, D.C. I couldn't imagine what Della'd done wrong. She was about the nicest person I'd ever met. I loved Mama, but Della was easier to be round. She just let me be.

Ever since Daddy sold the store, Mama wouldn't let me go inside it anymore. I knew she was jealous of Della. To be honest, I thought a lot of people were jealous a lot of the time and that was why they did so many stupid things. I saw it all the time. Sitting out front of the store most days, I'd hear them gossiping or even making stuff up about people. I bet they said things about me, too, when I wudn't there, off having my dinner or taking a nap.

But lately, something else was going on with Mama. Oncet I turned 15 year old, she started snooping and worrying. I'd seen something about that on TV, so I knew it were true: People thought that any guy who was kinda slow was a sex maniac. They figured since we weren't one-hundred percent "normal," we walked round with boners all the time and couldn't control ourselves. I couldn't speak for others, but that just weren't true for me. I remembered the first one I got, and it sure surprised me. But I'd done my experimenting, and I knew it wouldn't lead to no harm. Mama had nothin' to worry about, but still, she kept a close eye on me.

Of course, it was true that Della was real nice looking—tall and thin, but not skinny. She had a way about her—smart, but not stuck up. And her hair was real pretty—kinda curly and reddish gold, cut just below her ears. But she coulda been my mother, for heaven's sake.

After a while, Gregg from the Forest Service and the sheriff, along with some other cops, started making their way down Della's steps to their cars.

"Abit, you get on home, son," Sheriff Brower said. "Don't go bothering Ms. Kincaid right now."

"Go to hell, Brower. I don't need your stupid advice."

Okay, that was just what I *wanted* to say. What I really said was, "I don't plan on bothering Della." I used her first name to piss him off; kids were supposed to use grownups' last names. Then I added, "And I don't bother her. She likes me."

But he was already churning dust in the driveway, speeding on to the road.

That evening, all I could think about was Della and what them cops had been doing up in her apartment. Four cars and six men. I wudn't even hungry for supper. Mama looked at me funny; she knew I usually didn't have no trouble putting away four of her biscuits covered in gravy.

"Eat your supper, son. What's wrong with you?" she scolded, like I were 8 year old. Well, what did she think? Like we'd ever had a day like that before. I asked to be excused, and Daddy nodded at her. I couldn't figure out why they weren't more curious about everything.

"Do you know what's going on?" I asked.

Daddy just told me to run along. Okay, fine. That was my idea in the first place.

Even though the store were closed, I headed to my chair. A coupla year ago, I'd found a butt-sprung caned chair thrown behind the store. I fixed it with woven strips of inner tube, which made it real comfortable-like, especially when I'd lean against the wall. I worried when Daddy sold the store that the new owner would gussy everything up and get rid of my chair. But Della told me I was welcome to lean on her wall any day, any time. Then she smiled at me and asked me to stop calling her Mrs. Kincaid; I was welcome to call her Della.

I liked sitting there 'cause I could visit with folks, and not everyone talked down to me like Lonnie and the sheriff. Take Della's best friend, Cleva Hall, who came by at least oncet a week. She insisted on calling me Vester, which was kind of weird since I wudn't used to it. At first, I reckoned she was talking about Daddy. But then I figured she had trouble calling me Abit, which was pretty nice when I thought about it.

I'd been on my own most of my life. Mama and Daddy kinda ignored me, when they weren't worried I was getting up to no good. And I didn't fit in with other folks. Della didn't neither, but she seemed okay with that. She chatted with customers and acted polite, but I could tell she weren't worried about being accepted. Which was good, since folks *hadn't* accepted her. Sure, they bought her food and beer, but that was mostly 'cause the big grocery store was a good ten or more mile away out on the highway. They'd act okay to her face, but they didn't really like her 'cause "she wudn't from here." Truth be told, I liked her extra 'cause she wudn't from here.

I couldn't understand why Della *chose* to live in our town. It weren't much, though I hadn't never been out of the county, so how would I have known whether it was good or not? I had to admit that the falls were pretty to look at, and even Daddy said we was lucky to live near them. And we did have a bank, a real estate and law office combined, a dry goods store, Adam's Rib and few other restaurants (though we never ate out as a family). And some kinda new art store. But there wudn't a library or gas station or grocery store—except for Della's store, which sat two mile outside of town on the road to the falls.

After supper, I felt kinda stupid sitting out front with the store closed and all, but I hoped Della would hear me tapping the chair against the wall and come down to talk with me. Mama didn't like me to be out of an evenin', though I told her I was getting too old for that. It was funny—Mama was a Bible-readin' Christian, but she always thought the worst things. Especially at night. She never told me this, but I figured she thought demons came out then. (Not that she weren't worried about demons during the day, too.) I hated to think of the things that went through her head. Maybe I was slow, but so be it if that meant I didn't have to wrestle with all that.

I looked up at Della's big window but couldn't see nothin'. I wanted to know if she was all right—and, sure, I wanted to find out what was going on, too. Then a light went on in Della's kitchen. "Oh, please, please come downstairs," I said out loud. But just as fast, the light went out.

Chapter 3: Della

I switched off the kitchen light and limped back to the couch. No aspirin in the bedside table or in the bathroom or kitchen cabinets. Good thing I lived above a store.

Earlier in the woods, I'd twisted my ankle as I scrambled over a mass of tangled limbs trying to get to the open space where Jake waited, barking. Under the towering canopy of giant oaks, little grew, creating a hushed, cathedral-like space. Usually. Jake finally quit barking when he saw me, but he began a strange primal dance, crouching from side to side as he bared his teeth and emitted ugly guttural sounds. I closed my eyes, trying to will away what I knew lay ahead.

A young woman leaned against a fallen tree trunk blanketed in moss. Her head flopped to one side, long black hair covering half her face, though not enough to hide the vomit that pooled on her left shoulder and down her sleeve. She looked vaguely familiar; I'd probably seen her at the store.

I edged closer and reached out to feel her neck. Cold and silent. She looked up at me with the penetrating stare of the dead; I resisted the urge to close her eyes.

The woman, her skin smooth and clear, seemed no older than twenty or so, but her face was locked in a terrible grimace. Pain would do that, possibly the last sensation she'd felt. Just below her left hand lay an empty syringe. I thought about drug overdose or possible suicide. I'd seen both before.

I knew it wouldn't be long before the sun slipped behind the mountains and took the day's warmth with it. We needed help, soon. I held out little hope that Madras Man would call Gregg. And yet, for some reason, I didn't want to leave the young woman alone.

For the first time in what felt like hours, I thought about the store, which really wasn't that far away, as the crow flies. And Abit, who was usually around, even on a day the store was closed. I looked at Jake and recalled how he somehow knew the command, "Go home." I had no idea how he'd learned it, but he'd built an impressive reputation on it. Not long after we moved to Laurel Falls, Vester ordered Jake off his porch. (Leave it to Jake to find the sunniest spot to lie in.) He told him, "Go home, Jake." And he did. He stood up, combed his hair (that all-over body shaking dogs do), and trotted down to the store, scratching on the door for me to let him in. The men hanging out on the benches started laughing and calling him Rin Tin Tin, admiring his smarts.

I searched through my pack for something to write on, but it offered only keys, wallet, and remnants of lunch. I looked at the woman's backpack. *No, I couldn't*, I told myself. But as long shadows blanketed the mountains, I opened a side compartment and rifled through it. I found a small, blank notebook with an attached pen, tore out a sheet, and wrote a note describing the location, best I could. I wiped my prints off the pen and notebook, and put them back in the pack. The note went inside the bread bag I'd stashed in my pocket after lunch; I tied it to Jake's collar.

"Go home, Jake. Go home!" It was a longshot, but worth a try. His brown eyes looked sad, but then they always did. "Go home, Jake. Be a good boy."

The third time I said it, he turned and ran, though not down the path we'd taken. *God, I hope he knows where he's going*, I thought, as he raced up the creek bank. And I prayed Mildred hadn't called Abit inside.

I watched Jake climb the steep trail and head over the ridge. When the last of his golden fur disappeared below the horizon, I laid back against the red oak, avoiding the stare of the dead woman. It would be at least an hour before anyone could get there.

A Life for a Life and all books in the
Appalachian Mountain Mysteries series
are available at book retailers.

Books by Lynda McDaniel

FICTION
Waiting for You (free prequel)
A Life for a Life
The Roads to Damascus
Welcome the Little Children
Murder Ballad Blues

NONFICTION
Words at Work
How Not to Sound Stupid When You Write
How to Write Stories that Sell
Write Your Book Now!
(with Virginia McCullough)
Highroad Guide to the North Carolina Mountains
North Carolina's Mountains
Asheville: A View from the Top

Made in the USA
Coppell, TX
18 November 2020